Granit Jones was born in London but grew up on the south coast of England. Having graduated from Portsmouth Polytechnic with a mechanical engineering degree, he spent most of his career working for a Dutch offshore construction company. He retired in 2016 and now lives near Portsmouth with his Finnish-born wife. They have two daughters who have flown the nest to start their own independent lives.

To my wife, Kirsi, who continues to put up with me.

Granit Jones

The Caratacus Reincarnation

AUSTIN MACAULEY PUBLISHERS™

LONDON * CAMBRIDGE * NEW YORK * SHARJAH

Copyright © Granit Jones (2021)

The right of Granit Jones to be identified as author of this work has been asserted by the author in accordance with section 77 and 78 of the Copyright, Designs and Patents Act 1988.

All rights reserved. No part of this publication may be reproduced, stored in a retrieval system, or transmitted in any form or by any means, electronic, mechanical, photocopying, recording, or otherwise, without the prior permission of the publishers.

Any person who commits any unauthorised act in relation to this publication may be liable to criminal prosecution and civil claims for damages.

This is a work of fiction. Names, characters, businesses, places, events, locales, and incidents are either the products of the author's imagination or used in a fictitious manner. Any resemblance to actual persons, living or dead, or actual events is purely coincidental.

A CIP catalogue record for this title is available from the British Library.

ISBN 9781786935519 (Paperback)
ISBN 9781786935595 (ePub e-book)

www.austinmacauley.com

First Published (2021)
Austin Macauley Publishers Ltd
25 Canada Square
Canary Wharf
London
E14 5LQ

Whilst this story is a work of fiction, I have called upon my experiences working for Heerema Marine Contractors when describing places. Heerema very kindly allowed me to use an image of one of their installation vessels on the cover of this book. For this, and for all the good times, they have my thanks.

Prologue
February 1998

Moscow, Russia

30 seconds was all it took. 30 seconds to go from a happy family to a lifetime of sadness. 30 seconds of mayhem and screams. 30 seconds that would change the young girl's life for ever.

Not that she understood any of this. For her it was like the times she had been allowed to use the roller coaster in the fair ground that regularly visited Moscow's Gorky Park. Or the time when her father would be in a good mood, perhaps having been praised by his superior at work, and would spin her around and around until she would squeal with fake fear that very soon led to happy chuckles and a cry for more. And when both father and daughter had exhausted themselves there was always laughter and ice cream from the little kiosk not far from the family's small apartment.

But this time was different. The laughter was missing and had been replaced by the terrifying scream of a dying engine. For the four-year-old girl the play had yet to become the reality and the joyful chuckles had yet to become the tears of tomorrow.

The engine carried on screaming; a dead foot firmly placed on its life support system. It was like a diabetic gorging on chocolate. In truth it was amazing that the engine continued to work at all. The crash had sheared the main drive shaft that would normally have transmitted power to the rear wheels of the ancient Lada Nova. The engine carried on screaming as the wheels on the overturned car slowly stopped turning.

30 seconds is not a long time but for the young girl trapped between the back and front seats of the car it was just the beginning. Although the car no longer twisted and turned the engine continued to scream its torturous cry of agony as if it was desperate to escape the wreckage. The joy had turned to fear and with

the fear came the tears. The young girl started crying. Why didn't her daddy comfort her as he always did when she cried? She hadn't been naughty but even when she was, the tears would always bring an instant forgiveness. Her mother would perhaps be a little less forgiving but the girl had always found the tears were a way for instant attention from her father. Why then did her father not comfort her now and make the screaming stop? She knew her father was close because she could see the back of his head over the top of the driver's seat. She could even have reached out and touched him if she could have moved her arms but they were trapped between the seats.

And the little girl cried. For five minutes she cried and the engine died. For five minutes the snow continued to fall onto the distressed car and the up rooted tree. And when the life eventually went out of the tortured arrangement of pistons, crank shaft and oil the cold started to creep in.

Amazingly not only had the engine managed to retain life long after it should have died, so too had the front windscreen, so the cold did not have it all its own way. It had to fight its way into the warm, crushed citadel of the misshapen Lada but with the engine no longer able to provide the heater with energy the cold slowly penetrated the car's interior. And so, the cold, which had first laid the trap of the black ice that had caused the Lada to skid and hit the tree, now moved in to finish the task of destroying the young girl's family. As the cold penetrated the car it found only a single person still alive, a frightened young girl who couldn't move and who cried for her daddy who would never come.

Chapter 1
February 2026

Ulsan, South Korea

The man departing from the 08:20 hr shuttle flight from Seoul looked just like all the other businessmen who made the hour-long journey from the nation's capital to the industrial city of Ulsan. With his dark brown, short cut hair, brown eyes, designer stubble and wearing a pin stripe suit with a grey tie, white shirt and black shoes he blended in well with the other western business men making their way through the small but modern airport. Like a large percentage of the Boeing 737 passengers he had come to visit the industrial giant that was Hyundai Heavy Industries or HHI for short.

HHI dominated the city of Ulsan employing many thousands of workers in its shipbuilding and offshore fabrication facilities. Within the city the main hotel was owned by HHI, as were the biggest department store, many restaurants and a large number of the high-rise accommodation units – each given a unique number to make it easier for the many workers who came from all over Korea and beyond to identify their allocated living space. When someone worked for HHI they not only became an employee but also became one of the family being looked after from cradle to grave. In a highly hierarchal society like the Korean society the concept of one employer for life was nothing unusual. The company looked after the employee and the employee worked hard for the company and took pride in producing a quality product. This is one of the reasons that South Korea has been able to become such an industrial power house and the 'go-to place' for heavy fabrication and shipbuilding.

As the flight from Seoul was a domestic flight there was no need to clear customs and go through the time-consuming tedium that is immigration. This had all been endured the day before when the man had arrived at Seoul's Incheon International Airport on a flight direct from London's Heathrow airport. Not that

Incheon was any worse than any other airport, in fact it was a lot better than many he had passed through over the many years that he had been travelling the world, plying his rather unique trade. It was just that after a 11-hour flight, even sitting in the front of the plane, all that he wanted on arrival in South Korea's capital was to get as quickly as possible to his hotel to have a shower and to get some sleep. As a frequent flyer he was always amused to see the heroes of modern movies jumping from one time zone to another and disembark the plane as if they had just been on a half hour bus ride. Perhaps it was something to do with age but long-haul flights took their toll these days. Life would be a little easier if he could join the airline's frequent flyer program which would have allowed the use of dedicated lounges and priority at check in and arrival services, but as he very seldom travelled under the same name this was not an option.

Today his passport showed him as being Mr James Cartridge from London, Great Britain. His business card identified him as a Senior Surveyor for an offshore survey company and if anyone were to ask, he was in South Korea to facilitate the installation of survey equipment on one of the offshore modules being fabricated by the HHI facilities in Ulsan. Whilst his trip was to do with the HHI facilities his real purpose was far removed from his cover story.

As he departed the airport with his single piece of carry-on luggage and boarded a local taxi his thoughts turned to his present assignment. As usual he had no idea who his ultimate client was, only that the money was good and the task not particularly onerous. The biggest problems were logistics and the procurement of the tools needed to perform the task. It wasn't as if the HHI store would stock the specific brand of high explosive and remote detonator that he needed but then he was being paid as much as anything for his contacts and ability to obtain deadly items as for his ability to perform the allocated task. Contacted via an intermediary and after a small amount of haggling over the price, the package that had been delivered to his Paris PO box was concise and exact as to the task. He liked this about this intermediary. Very professional to deal with, good information and most importantly a good payer. But then being a good payer was also a form of protection for the intermediary. The man who was using the name James Cartridge was not one to forgive anyone that betrayed him and particularly anyone that betrayed him over money. In the past, at least two people who now occupied plots in their local grave yard had made that mistake. The message had been sent and received many years before and now the money was delivered at the time and place agreed. In this case a numbered

Swiss bank account, half, non-refundable, before he left Europe and half when the job was done.

After half an hour drive the taxi dropped him outside the Lotte Ulsan Hotel in the centre of Ulsan. After paying the 6000 Won fare he walked up the road to the Lotte City Hotel and booked in for four nights. Whilst he did not suspect anyone knew of his existence in South Korea, he intuitively tended to break any trail that could subsequently be followed. If anyone should question the taxi driver and find he had been dropped outside the Lotte Ulsan Hotel, a quick check of the register would end the trail.

He fully expected to complete his task within two days but experience told him that heading straight to an airport after an assignment was not always the sensible thing to do. If all went well the incident would be reported as an accident but in case not, the first thing the police would be looking for would be someone that suddenly left a hotel and made for the airport. So, let the dust settle, literally, take it easy and relax for a couple of days after the assignment and then return to Europe. Such small attention to detail meant that he had remained under the radar for all the years he had been plying his trade and avoided the attention of the authorities. He had never been to this part of Korea before so he may even hire a car and take in the sights. But before that he had a job to do.

Chapter 2
February 2026

London

Richard Green surveyed the 16 other people sitting around the table and wondered who would be his friend and who his enemy. For Richard there was no in-between. You were either for him or against him. Time would tell but Richard had no doubt that before the end of his term as Prime Minister there was a high likelihood that the make-up of his cabinet would change dramatically.

At 63 years old Richard was still an impressive looking man. 6ft 3 inches tall with brown hair and eyes, of slim but muscular build he was wearing his trademark blue and white striped shirt, a red tie and a blue suit. He preferred to get his clothes from Crew Clothing Company but also had Jaeger and Marks and Spenser's clothes in his wardrobe. Not really a follower of fashion he just wore what he felt comfortable in, or to be more specific what his wife, someone for who getting the right colour match was important, bought for him.

Today and looking around the table a lesser man would have been thinking 'what have a got myself into?' but all Richard was thinking was how do I deliver on my promises and who around the table can I trust.

Three years before Richard had been just another retired manager who wondered why he had quit work. Still feeling he had much to give and not getting much satisfaction out of gardening and playing golf he found himself spending most mornings reading the paper from cover to cover before attempting the crossword. Always one who had an opinion on most subjects he realised that something was going seriously wrong with the way the country was being run. Traditionally a Conservative voter, Richard, like many others, had turned his back on the party after the fiasco that was Britain's decision to leave the European Union often referred to as Brexit. A lack of leadership allied to the protectionism of the vested interest groups had allowed the dream of the UK returning to being an independent nation to be dashed. The compromise position adopted by the Conservative party in their negotiations with the European Community had watered down the intent of those hell bent on leaving the control of the European union to such an extent that whilst Britain had formally left the European Community they were still well and truly bound by its rules and edicts. Even those people who had voted to stay in the European Community saw this for what it was, a betrayal of what the majority of the British electorate had voted for when the referendum on Britain's membership of the European Union had been held. The establishment had succeeded in putting their own interests ahead of that of the decision of the majority of the British people. And people weren't happy. The Conservatives had gambled that the socialist opposition, whilst led by a charismatic elder statesman, was so extreme that the traditional Conservative electorate would have no option but to vote for the Conservatives if only to prevent the socialists from taking power. They had seriously underestimated the anger in the country; so whilst most Conservative voters could not bring themselves to actually vote for the socialist, they did abstain in vast numbers. The socialists won the subsequent election with a landslide victory albeit with a very low turnout.

Once in government the real powers behind the scene of the socialist party wasted very little time in consolidating their position. Within four weeks the charismatic but ineffectual idealist that had led the party into the election had been replaced on the grounds of ill health by his considerably more radical deputy. The subsequent ousting of moderate members of the socialist party by 'active encouragement' to retire or by trumped up charges leading to de-selection by the local party membership, long ago taken over by the extreme left, transformed a middle of the road socialist party into one dominated by the Marxist ideals. For the first time in its history Great Britain had a communist government. At the same time the Conservative opposition party had imploded leaving very little opposition to the idealists now entrenched in the palace of Westminster.

Within three years the country was effectively bankrupt. Borrowing heavily to enact its communist ideals the state took control of the railways, utilities, banks and many areas of the media. Theoretically the terms of the Brexit deal should have allowed The European Community to block such actions on the grounds of unfair state aid, but the reality was that the Marxists just ignored any attempt by the EU to interfere.

The state broadcasting service, always sympathetic to a mild form of socialism, found itself in the hands of a communist committee that fed the nation its news, heavily censored to hide the truth. Those members of the public who did not understand the interaction between the financial markets and the money in their pocket didn't see the risks of the government's policies and accepted the good news stories being peddled by the controlled national broadcasting media. But stock markets and the value of the pound fell whilst inflation rose to levels only previously seen in third world economies or economies decimated by war. To try and control the situation the communists imposed further controls and restrictions including attempts to nationalise land and property. Wages had long ago been dictated by the state and rent and capital controls were imposed. But the one thing the communists were unable to control was the external financial markets which had determined that lending good money after bad to a country clearly in decline was not a good thing. Those brave enough to take the risk extracted a high price in the form of interest payments that just increased the countries debts.

As more and more money was needed to repay debt and as the tax take reduced due to the inefficiencies of state-run concerns, the money available for public services dried up. One of the strange misunderstanding of the public is that somehow the government can conjure up a pot of money out of nowhere, whereas the reality is that any money the government has to use for public services has to come out of the pocket of either a hard-working individual in the form of taxes or from a profitable company. Destroy a company's profits and remove the incentive to work and government revenues dry up. Cut off access to the borrowing or reach the limit of what others are willing to lend and so the money available to public services also dries up. The resulting price inflation and rise in the unemployment levels became visible to all and whilst the government tried to blame external factors such as immigration and unsympathetic external bodies, the voting public slowly began to realise the mistake they had made.

Unfortunately, even after it became clear that the Marxist policies were leading the country into an economic disaster there was no way of removing those responsible for the mess. Individuals so convinced of their own virtuosity even managed to convince themselves that their policies were not to blame and so just promoted more of the same – like feeding heroin to an addict in the hope that it would cure them.

In Great Britain general elections are held every five years and as the date of the next election loomed those in charge tried very hard to enact a change of law to abolish elections on the grounds of national security. With no opposition worth talking about they very nearly got away with it but there is a good reason why Great Britain has been a democracy for so long. As parliament attempted to change the law to allow the formation of a dictatorship the judiciary supported by the armed forces with the leadership of the monarchy blocked the attempt and so five years after the communists had taken power a new general election took place.

Richard Green like many of his compatriots had followed the decline in the countries fortunes with firstly concern but then more and more with dread. As someone that had worked and saved all his life such that he would be able to enjoy his final years in some comfort, he soon realised that the policies of the socialist party would eventually lead to his own destitution along with large numbers of like-minded persons. One term of the Marxist administration had been a disaster for the country but a second term would be a disaster for anyone with savings or property to their name.

It was clear that the conservative opposition party was still weak and by attempting to woo the country with policies that were socialist in nature but less extreme than the socialist's own policies just added to the despair of the middle classes.

Richard Green decided that the only solution was for a dramatic change in the normal two-party politics of the United Kingdom. He also realised the difficulties of breaking the mould. Many attempts had been made in the past to change the political landscape. The rise and fall of the popularity of the Liberal Party and latterly the UKIP party, showed how the electoral system with its 'first past the post' philosophy made it very difficult for any new party to gain a foothold that would challenge the entrenched position of the incumbents. People were worried that if they shifted their vote to a new party it would result in the opposition party candidate winning as a result of the split vote. Nevertheless, Richard also sensed that there was a real desire for change in the country. He didn't get this from the state controlled national broadcaster but from reading the still independent newspapers and particularly the leaders and letters page where more and more desperation was being conveyed.

The difficulty was how to even start a new party and then how to convince the electorate that said new party would deliver a better future. He also had to find a way to convince sufficient numbers of people that their vote would not result in the election of the opposition candidate as a result of a split vote. With only twelve weeks to go until the election the task was daunting but Richard was nothing but tenacious. By using the internet and social media he quickly advertised his intention. At that time, he had no party, no candidates, no backers and very little in the way of firm policies except the desire to stop the Marxists that had led the country to the brink of bankruptcy, both financially and morally.

Within a week his web site was inundated with offers of help. From financial backing, often from people with a lot more to lose than Richard if things didn't change, to assistance with spreading the message and offers to stand as candidates under the banner of Richard's new party, The Progressive Conservatives. Of particular importance was the offer from established politicians that had become disillusioned with the two-party system or had fallen foul of the Marxists regimes purges.

Amazingly within eight weeks of his first deciding to challenge the established order Richard's new party had published its manifesto, established a political structure within nearly all the constituencies of the country, received enough financial backing to fight the election on an equal footing with the other parties and had selected a candidate to fight every one of the 650 electoral places available. The final four weeks before the election were the most hectic of Richard's life but come the date of the election, polls had Richard's party in the lead to such an extent that if the polls were correct, Richard would have an overall majority.

Last minute attempts by the socialists to have Richard's party declared illegal failed in the courts and on the morning after the election it was clear that not only had Richard won the election but he had won by a landslide. Ex-supporters of both the conservative party and the socialist party had turned their back on the established order and voted for change. Now it was down to Richard and his political colleagues to give the electorate what they had promised.

After the celebrations had died down Richard's first task was to form his cabinet. Effectively to organise the management team that would run the country. It soon became clear that politics was considerably different from running a project or even managing a company. Whereas in the world that Richard was used to everyone within the project team broadly had the same aims and goals. The project manager would be responsible for reviewing the contract and translating that into a project plan. This would be conveyed to the project team who would be allocated individual responsibility for whatever specific area of the project that was their speciality. Most importantly everyone would be a unit working to ensure the project was a success in terms of safety, quality, cost and performance. The ultimate target was always the successful completion of the project with individuals taking pride in that success.

Theoretically running a country should have been the same as running a project but as Richard was soon to find out not all team members had the same agenda. As an added complication, because of the speed of setting up the party, Richard did not personally know many of the team that he would have to work with so he had had to rely on his skill at character assessment along with whatever knowledge he could gain on an individual from past history. There was also the expectation from many members of the party to be rewarded for their part in the recent election win. Whilst Richard was very aware that the skills needed to sell the parties message to the electorate were different from the skills needed to manage the country, not all his new colleagues had the same judgement.

It had taken five days but Richard at least had chosen the personnel that would form his management team. Now it was time to start the hard work.

Chapter 3
February 2026

South Korea

Carrying a black work bag and wearing steel toe capped boots, an orange pair of overalls over a checked shirt and jeans, the man known as James Cartridge boarded one of the many shuttle buses that transported the thousands of fabrication workers from various parts of the city of Ulsan to their work place in the massive HHI fabrication yard. The bored bus driver had made this trip a thousand times over the past 20 years and only gave a cursory glance at the pass that James showed as he boarded the bus, although even a detailed inspection of the pass would have elicited no different reaction. The pass was identical to the real passes issued by the fabrication yard, the only difference was that James's pass had not come from the efficient security office in the main administration building of the yard but from a small back street private enterprise in Seoul. Costing $250 it had been prepared in the 24 hours between landing in Seoul and departing to Ulsan. Not only had this got James a pass but also got his name on the list of expected visitors issued daily to the yard's gate security personnel. As James took his seat at the back of the bus, he felt comfortable in the knowledge that his entrance to the fabrication yard would not be a problem.

Half an hour later he stepped down from the bus at the first stop, just outside the city of portacabins that most western contractors used as their office and logistic bases. As expected, the bus had not even been stopped at the yard entrance and any concerns James may have had if his bag was to be searched were groundless. Not that there was anything too conspicuous in the bag. Anyone that wasn't looking for specific items would not have been able to ascertain the ultimate intentions of the items in the bag.

Consulting his map, he identified where in the yard was the item of interest to him. His client had been very specific regarding the target and where to find the new build vessel known in HHI as hull 3,226 but known to the vessel owners as Kalevala. With an area of over 1750 acres and stretching nearly 2.5 miles along the coast, the Hyundai Heavy Industries Shipyard and fabrication complex was one of the biggest in the world. Capable of building a medium sized bulk carrier every six weeks the yard was incredibly efficient when it came to repetitive work. With ten large dry docks and nearly 400 acres of enclosed fabrication facilities it was able to operate a conveyor belt system, manufacturing various sections of the ships in different parts of the yard before bringing them together in the dry dock where they would be lifted in place by one of the 1000 tonne gantry cranes. Once in place the individual sections would be welded together to form a complete hull. After the water tight hull had been completed and painted the dry dock would be flooded and the hull would move to one of the many outfitting quays where the outfitting would be completed leaving the dry dock available for the next vessel. In the nearly 50 years since the yard was first opened over 3000 ships had been completed, an average of 60 ships a year.

The Kalevala, named after the Finnish epic that recounts how the northern heroes overcame the powers of darkness whilst taming the land was different from the other vessels under construction in that it was a one-off vessel. Unique in fact. A tripled hull semi-submersible vessel at 250 metres long, 110 metres wide and 52 metres from the keel to the main deck she was bigger than any battleship ever built. Mounted on her stern were two 20,000t capacity cranes, by far the world's largest, which enabled the Kalevala to lift a single offshore platform topside of up to 35,000 tonnes. With accommodation for over 800 personnel and a power plant capable of producing 112 megawatts she had a top speed of 14 knots and cost over $2.5 billion to build.

Because of her size and unique construction, the Kalevala could not be built in the same manner as the production line vessels. HHI's largest dry dock had to be utilised which meant it wasn't available for other vessels, something that had to be built into the vessels price and one of the reasons for the high price tag. But with a high price tag came a good profit margin for HHI so they were willing to take on the project despite the effect on their normal ship building activities.

It didn't take Cartridge long to find the Kalevala. Even in a yard the size of HHI the Kalevala towered above the shipyard cranes and other vessels. Nearing completion, she was moored alongside the southernmost jetty and accessed by two stairways, one to the stern and the second to the bow. To get onto either stairway meant passing a guard booth where each individual had to obtain a vessel specific pass. Cartridge was prepared for this and understood that this was more a safety procedure than for security. In case of a fire or other emergency on the vessel the abandon ship siren would sound and as personnel left the ship they would hand in the passes. This way it would be easy to determine if anyone was missing or left on the ship. Cartridge was interested in getting into the vessel bow so took the forward stairway. As suspected, he was issued with a pass without a second glance from the official looking, but not very bright, guard on duty.

Climbing the nearly 100 steps to the Kalevala main deck was no hardship for Cartridge. As a fitness fanatic he enjoyed road cycling, swimming and running and was a veteran of the iron man triathlon which required the competitor to swim 2.4 miles, cycle 112 miles before running a full 26-mile marathon all in under 17 hours. Cartridge was not even out of breath by the time he reached the top deck and took his bearings. Having studied the blue prints of the Kalevala he knew that to get to the very bow of the vessel he would need to first go down three decks to the equipment deck and then take an elevator through a deck support column to one of the three hulls. Making his way through the temporary spaghetti of cables and pipes being used by the myriad of electricians, fitters, pipe fitters, welders, platers and all the other trades that were busy in their endeavours to complete the great ship in time for the handover ceremony due in 14 weeks' time, he soon found the elevator he was looking for and took it to the bottom of the middle of the three hulls.

Making his way along the corridor that stretched the full length of the ship he opened the last water tight door and entered the forward compartment. Pushing the button to close the water tight door behind him, as expected, he found himself alone. This part of the ship had been completed months before and there was no reason for anyone to be working here at this stage. Placing his bag on the floor Cartridge extracted a small block of RDX explosive disguised to look like a lunch box, a small detonator in the form of a ball point pen and an electronic timer that looked like an electrician's multi meter. Using duct tape, Cartridge taped the RDX behind the flange of one of the frames that formed the shape of the hull and against the hull plating. Turning on the timer he set a time that coincided with the next shift change, about six hours ahead, and carefully connected the timer to the detonator. Using the same duct tape, he taped the timer next to the RDX and inserted the detonator. To a man like Cartridge this was a simple task and one he had performed many times in the past. What was a little unusual about this assignment was that the client had been clear that fatalities were to be avoided if at all possible whereas most of his clients considered the more casualties the better. Whatever, he was being paid to do a job and whoever paid the piper called the tune.

Exiting the apartment, he made sure the water tight door was closed and made his way back to the main deck. Making himself look busy he waited until the lunch hooter sounded and then made his way off the vessel along with the other 300 workers on the ship. Unlike them he did not go to the company canteen but instead went back to the bus stop to await the first shuttle bus to leave the yard. He only had a few minutes wait and within half an hour was back outside his hotel.

By the time the timer had finished its countdown Cartridge was already sitting in the bar of the Lotte City Hotel drinking a glass of Hite extra cold beer. The explosion in the forward compartment of the middle hull was small but sufficient to breach the hull and allow the waters of the Sea of Japan to flood in. As the explosion took place during the shift change there were very few people on the vessel at the time of the explosion and it may even have gone unnoticed had it not been for a cleaner that happened to have been working on the main deck above the site of the explosion. He felt a slight tremor through the deck plating and had the sense to report this to his supervisor who in turn reported to the ship construction manager. Meanwhile a couple of welders had been sitting on the dock wall eating their tea when they noticed a disturbance of the water like a water spout around the bow of the middle hull. This also got reported up the command chain to the ship construction manager who took both reports very seriously and instigated an investigation. Being a conscientious type and having once before experienced an accident that resulted in a hull breach, the ship construction manager organised a search of the ship. Coming to the water tight door in the middle hull, instead of just opening the door he first opened the small tell-tale, a tap that opened a small pipe that went through the door and if the compartment was flooded would allow a trickle of water to flow. Fortunately, the tell-tale was not blocked and clearly showed that the forward compartment was full of water. There had been times in the past when enthusiastic painters have painted over tell tales so even though the compartment is flooded no water comes through the small pipe. In one tragic case a British submarine was lost as a result of such an occurrence leading to the loss of many lives. But in this case the tell-tale did its job and the water tight door remained shut until divers could be sent down on the outside to assess the damage.

Within a week a cofferdam had been built around the damaged compartment, water had been pumped out and repair work had started. The man known as James Cartridge meanwhile had left South Korea and returned to Europe where he ceased to exist. Having reverted to his real name of Jason Chadwell he was pleased to see that the remaining payment for the work had been transferred to his Swiss bank account via the normal convoluted route to prevent any risk of the security services tracing either the originator or the benefactor. He waited for his next assignment.

Chapter 4
February 2026

London

The headquarters of the Oceanic Energy Company Plc was an imposing building. Set in the heart of London just a few minutes away from the Tower of London, that ancient symbol of the Norman conquest of Great Britain dating from the eleventh century, the Oceanic building could not be more different from its more famous neighbour. Towering a little over 200 metres above pavement level it consisted of 42 stories and had a total of 81,000 square metres of office space. At a construction cost of nearly £250 million it was one of the most expensive buildings in the City of London. Started just before the socialist government had been elected it had been completed within three years, one of the last such major projects completed before the construction industry effectively imploded as a result of the economic collapse.

The building itself set new standards in comfort and efficiencies. With an exterior made totally of a new type of glass that contained solar energy panels whilst retaining the transparency expected of glass, the building was energy self-sufficient on a sunny day. Even when the London weather showed its less than benevolent side, not an unusual occurrence, the solar panels were still able to provide over 50% of the needs of the building. The use of the latest energy efficient lighting, insulating materials and even energy capture from the heat generated by the occupancy of the building all led to the building having one of the lowest carbon footprints in the city. It was therefore something of an irony that the building's occupancy was an oil company more often associated with feeding the world's pollution rather than reducing it.

The Oceanic Energy Company Plc had been formed only eight years ago. Taking advantage of the low interest rates in place at the time a group of rich entrepreneurs had seen an opportunity to acquire the tail-end production facilities of a number of oil fields in the North Sea. In the boom days of the North Sea, The United Kingdom had provided nearly 5% of the world's oil production but those days were long since passed. The infrastructure installed in one of the most inhospitable seas in the world had nearly finished its purpose after, in many cases, over 40 years of hard work. But the riches found beneath the sea was now almost depleted. The vast sums of money invested by the major oil companies to develop the oil and gas fields had been repaid many times over but now the quantity of oil and gas being produced only just covered the cost of keeping the infrastructure in place. When the price of oil was at $120 per barrel it was worth keeping the deep-water platforms producing, particularly as the alternative was that the major oil companies would have to pay to make safe the abandoned oil wells and then remove all the infrastructure, a process that could cost almost as much as putting the structures in place in the first instance. Eight years ago, the oil price had dropped as a result of the discovery of shale oil in America and environmental policies being enacted world-wide to such an extent that it was no longer viable for the majors to keep the platforms producing. As big multi-national companies they had large overheads in addition to the costs of the production facilities which meant that for every barrel of oil sold at the new lower price they lost five dollars. Not a very good business model.

Enter the Oceanic Energy Company Plc. With considerably smaller overheads and with the sole intension of running the existing facilities literally into the sea, they saw the opportunity to buy the production rights and infrastructure from the majors. Whereas at the new, lower price of oil the major oil companies lost money for every barrel produced, the Oceanic Energy Company had estimated they could actually make money. Not a great deal as the quantity of oil being produced was relatively low but enough to make the gamble worthwhile. Because the real goal was to use the existing facilities as a platform to find new pockets of oil and gas that had perhaps been missed by the majors. And in this they had been successful beyond their wildest dreams.

The general opinion was that the North Sea was in terminal decline. It had been explored for over 50 years and in that time the theory was that any large hydrocarbon deposits would have been found years ago. But Oceanic Energy Company had an innovative young geologist on their team that had identified a specific geological formation that in his not very humble opinion would contain considerable quantities of oil not seen in the UK sector since the days of Brent and Forties.

The young geologist was called Ted Simpson and he had the advantage over other mortals in that his father was one of the richest men in the country. Having made his money in property Jim Simpson was very proud of his two sons of which Ted was the eldest. Having paid for Ted to go to the best private school, the anticipation was that Ted would go on to Oxford and take a degree in politics or economics before following his father into the property business. But young Ted surprised everyone when he announced that he didn't want to go to Oxford or Cambridge but instead wanted to take a geology course at Portsmouth University. Despite Jim's attempts to dissuade the younger Simpson, Ted was adamant in his wishes and Ted had inherited his father's stubbornness. What Ted didn't tell his father was that one of the reasons he wanted to attend Portsmouth University was to do with a certain young lady who had captured his heart. The infatuations would dwindle and eventually die but by this time Ted had begun to find he really liked the subject of geology and was actually very good at it. In particular he was fascinated by the pre-salt deposits found in parts of Africa and South America where large oil reserves had been discovered under the traditional oil fields at depths of 4000 metres below seabed. The problem with the finds in South America and Africa was that often the seabed was itself 2000 metres below the sea surface making drilling and eventual production very expensive. A breakeven cost of $80 per barrel was required to allow companies to make a profit. But the fields were huge. Whereas in the North Sea a good discovery in the past 20 years could be 100 million barrels of oil in place with most considerably smaller, the pre-salt fields were in the billions of barrels. Enough to make the considerable initial investment a viable proposition with the knowledge that any infrastructure would be producing half a million barrels per day for over 40 years. Ted's theory was that similar geological features would be found under the North Sea and he managed to persuade his father that his theory was worth investing in.

Jim Simpson was one of the founders of Oceanic Energy Company Plc and from the outset his intent was to use the tail end production buy outs as the stepping off point to prove his son's theory. Jim never doubted his son would be proved correct and was willing to risk a large part of his fortune to find that proof. There was also the dream of riches beyond anything he had in the past to consider if Ted was proved correct.

Within two years of the formation of Oceanic Energy, drilling had commenced using a modern state of the art jack-up Drilling Unit. Unlike in South

America and Africa the water depth in the North Sea was only 120 metres. This reduced the drilling costs but even so at $150,000 per day the negative cash flow from the Company was considerable. The location identified for the first well was close to the Norwegian border but also crucially close to the existing Brent offshore platforms. The concessionary area had been acquired as part of the tail end production deal which made the task of getting the various licenses in place considerably easier and, as important, considerably faster. The location had been chosen by Ted Simpson based on his analysis of sub surface seismic surveys that had the ability to penetrate the 4–5,000 metres of various rock types to 'see' what lay below the existing oil-bearing structures.

Four weeks after commencing drilling and against all the odds the Jack-up drilling unit proved Ted's theory correct and in the most dramatic fashion. Oil and gas trapped below 4000 metres of rock is under enormous pressure and very hot. Fortunately, this had been considered when preparing the drill hole. Lessons had been learnt from the disaster suffered in the Gulf of Mexico a few years before when the Deepwater Horizon drilling unit had struck oil under similar conditions. Inadequate blow out prevention measures had led to a massive blow out that had killed 11 people and released an estimated 200 million gallons of oil into the Gulf of Mexico. Aside from the tragic loss of life and the destruction of the drilling unit the subsequent oil spill caused an environmental disaster in certain parts of the Gulf of Mexico. Oil major BP accepted their responsibility for the disaster and paid a heavy price, close to $60 billion, a figure that had severe consequences for the Company in its ability to carry on trading. A lesser company would have gone bankrupt under such a heavy liability. Certainly, Oceanic Energy could not countenance such a tragedy and along with considerably stricter regulations to prevent such an incident from ever happening again, they had a blow-out prevention system capable of handling the expected temperatures and pressures; or at least that was the theory.

When the oil-bearing reservoir was eventually breeched by the drilling unit the temperature was an expected 175 degree Celsius but the pressure exceeded 12,000 psi, considerably higher than expected but still within the safety margins of the blow out preventers. They did their job and prevented another disaster but with little margin for error. Subsequent investigations of the oil reservoir identified at least 15 billion barrels of oil in place. Now all Jim and Ted Simpson had to do was get the oil out of the ground and into the refineries.

Six years later the board of Oceanic Energy Company Plc, now more normally referred to as OEC Plc, were meeting to discuss the on-going progress in developing the Caratacus Oil Field as the formation had been named. Delays in getting the necessary licences in place due in part to the challenges from the Norwegian authorities who postulated that the field stretched across the border between the United Kingdom and Norway, since disproved, and the inefficiency of the UK authorities in processing the necessary paperwork meant the development of the field was nearly two years behind schedule. Strikes and a belligerent attitude by certain unions and government departments had also contributed to the delays but at last there was light at the end of the tunnel. New production facilities were under construction in Norwegian, Swedish, Korean and British fabrication yards. Further drilling had been carried out to maximise the flow from the Caratacus Field and the necessary pipeline had been laid to a newly expanded oil refinery on the Shetland Islands. But despite the apparent progress being made, all was not well with OEC Plc.

Chapter 5
February 2026

Hartlepool England

Something was wrong. The two headed bison, gently grazing on the fresh green pasture by the side of the milk river Dong was normal enough. The sun's rays shining out of the chocolate coloured sky and reflecting on the golden spear of the completely naked Amazonian warrior was as it should be. Even the little man, perfectly formed but only three feet tall who walked alongside the Amazonian warrior was not out of place in this strange land. But still something was wrong. The little man sensed it first but decided it was the rustling of the wind through the hard, metallic fruit of the Yang tree which formed the staple diet of the Amazonian. Only on occasional days did the tall blond and incredibly attractive warrior race of females catch a Tring bison (as the two headed animal was called) to supplement the Yang fruit diet. Having discounted the sound, the little man continued alongside the warrior ready to serve her whenever she asked, a task he had been born for.

The next to hear the sound was the warrior herself who immediately froze. She didn't want to lose the prey she had followed so patiently. A Yang fruit diet could be very boring. It might be all right for the little man but the woman occasionally needed meat. The warrior hoped that by keeping perfectly still and quiet the sound would go away but instead it continued to penetrate the land until even the Tring bison was alerted to its monotonous tones. The bison lifted its heads to try and locate the source of the noise but it seemed to be all around and getting louder. The warrior woman sensing that she was losing her prey attempted to spring forward but the sound seemed to have paralysed her body. The little man and the Tring bison were also paralysed as the sound broke into the very fabric of the land causing it to fade into a dark mist.

The phone ringing by the side of David Saunders persisted until finally he was forced to abandon the strange land with its race of beautiful warriors. The girl waiting on Leeds Station for the 07:45 hrs train to London may have been flattered or offended had she known that she had been used as the model for an entire race of female warriors. But then even Saunders's conscious self did not realise that the brief glimpse of the beautiful woman with the long legs had so registered with his subconscious that an entire dream scenario would be formed around her. Not that Saunders could recall any details of the dream on awakening, such was the way with dreams. Probably just as well. Even before Saunders's conscious self regained complete control over a protesting sub conscious, his hand was flapping about in the general direction of the phone in a frantic effort to stop the noise that had invaded his private fantasy. As he turned over to reach for the phone, his still sleeping wife stirred alongside in their king-size bed. The Amazonian warrior certainly looked nothing like his wife.

The small green icon on the iPhone was pressed at the same time as complete consciousness returned accompanied by a glorious silence as the ringing stopped. Not for the first time did Saunders think about changing the ring tone to something less harsh but as a heavy sleeper, his experience was that a lighter ring tone would not penetrate his sleep and as Chief Executive Officer for one of the world's most successful offshore construction companies, there were times when he needed to be available at all times of the day and night.

'Yes' Saunders slurred into the mouthpiece, the sleep still not fully dissipated as he pulled himself up into a sitting position careful not to wake his wife who still retained whatever fantasy world her subconscious self had decided to generate.

'David?'

Saunders realised his brief answering of the phone had not been sufficient for the early morning caller to identify him. However, the questioning use of his first name had been sufficient for Saunders to identify the caller and all vestiges of the fantasy world were soon forgotten.

'David Saunders speaking. This had better be good, Ron. It's half past two in the morning.'

The man at the other end of the line inwardly steeled himself.

'I'm afraid good cannot be considered the right word, David.'

Ron Thompson, SMS's residential engineer in the Korean fabrication yard of Hyundai Heavy Industries, had known David Saunders for 15 years and in that time had earned the right to use his bosses first name, a practise which Saunders generally did not encourage amongst his employees.

Early morning phone calls never seemed to bring good news thought Saunders by now totally alert.

'Go on.'

'I'm afraid we've had a serious incident on the Kalevala. Earlier this morning there was an explosion in one of the bow sections leading to considerable damage. The particular section is effectively a right off and will need to be re-fabricated. Fortunately, the explosion occurred at shift change time so it appears that there were no workers in the vicinity and the water tight doors prevented serious flooding of other parts of the ship. No casualties have been reported although that has still to be confirmed. The yard is carrying out a head count as we speak.'

Thompson stopped talking knowing his boss would need some time to assimilate the news. The silence stretched for ten seconds but Thompson knew better than to continue speaking. The message had been received and was been digested.

'Damn it. If it's not one thing it's another with that wretched boat. First let's be thankful that no one got hurt. Apart from the obvious human angle a fatality would have got everyone running around like headless chickens. But you know how critical the schedule is and the previous incidents have already put us behind. I assume it's too early to determine if this will affect the delivery date?'

'Too early to say just now. I've asked Daniel Lee, the HHI Project Manager, for his assessment and expect an initial response later today. Knowing the way that these guys can work miracles when they put their mind to it, I would expect little if any affect.'

'Let's hope that will be the case. I don't have to tell you the importance of getting the Kalevala to Europe before the middle of September. If we miss the installation season, we will be crucified by OEC. The Kalevala is the only vessels in the world that can install the Caratacus facilities and if we miss the installation season any delay comes down to us.'

'I'm fully aware of the consequences and have made it clear to HHI that a slippage to the sail away date as a result of this and other accidents that have beset this project is unacceptable. I don't really know what else I can do. The contract has considerable penalty clauses for late delivery. HHI are fully aware of this and will do everything they can to avoid a delay.'

'In all my time on projects I have to say I don't know one that has come close to this one for incidents and accidents. Only a couple of months ago we had the fire in the control room and before that there was the flooding of the bow thruster room during the commissioning process. If I were a superstitious type I would say this vessel is jinxed. In confidence I think that HHI have done a remarkable job in keeping things going despite all the setbacks but that doesn't mean it won't get nasty if we have to start imposing penalties for late delivery. You can bet the Koreans are already building a case for delays either being down to us or as a result of Force Majeure.'

'You can bet your pension on that. Look I have a meeting with Mr Lee in four hours' time. I'll let you know what comes out of it. Sorry to disturb your sleep but as a major incident I thought you'd want to know as soon as possible. What are you going to tell OEC?'

'I think I'll leave that until I hear back from you. No point in worrying them unnecessarily. But you did the right thing in letting me know. Hear from you later.'

David pushed the end call button on his phone and set it back on the bedside table. The possibility of going back to sleep didn't cross his mind so, not wishing to disturb his wife further, David got out of bed and wandered into his study. Sitting down in his favourite chair his mind drifted over the last few years and how Saunders Marine Solutions had ended up so dependent on the success of the Kalevala, the world's largest heavy lift crane vessel at present under construction in Korea.

Saunders Marine Solutions was founded by David Saunders 25 years before in an attempt to capitalise on the booming offshore construction industry. The collapse of the price of oil in the late 1990s had put many of the existing offshore construction companies out of business and forced those that remained to either dramatically reduce their fleet or consolidate with other companies. By the time that Saudi Arabia had finished demonstrating to the other members of OPEC, the oil cartel that controlled more than 50% of the world's oil supply, that they were in control, the price of a barrel of oil had collapsed to below $10. Nearly all offshore construction projects were cancelled or postponed and the work for the very expensive offshore construction vessels stopped overnight. Having made its point, discipline was reinstated and Saudi Arabia turned off the taps reducing the supply of oil to below the level of demand. Within a few months oil was back to $25 per barrel and the oil companies started dusting off the postponed and cancelled projects. At the same time the western governments realised how vulnerable they were to OPEC and were determined to find ways of breaking the dependency. The result was to encourage exploration and production from oil fields located in areas of the world not controlled by OPEC. Meanwhile new technology meant that fields in deeper and deeper water could be located and developed and what's more these deep fields were on the doorstep of some of the most industrialised areas. The Gulf of Mexico, West of Shetland, South America, West Africa, Australia and parts of the Far East became the focus points for new developments. In fact, nearly anywhere that wasn't the Middle East. The major difficulty was that the developments were very often in deep water necessitating very specialised and very expensive construction vessels. It was in this market that David saw his opportunity.

Having convinced a group of investors that Great Britain had the ability and talent to challenge the existing operators, mainly Dutch, Italian and American. and seeing a slight niche in the market, he designed and built a medium size crane vessel that was ideal for operations in the North Sea but could also be used in some of the deeper fields being developed in Africa.

Despite misgivings by some of his investors that nearly resulted in SMS going bankrupt and the newly completed vessel, called The Saga, operating at close to break-even point, David managed to win sufficient orders to keep paying the bills and put a bit aside for future investments. Eight years later and with oil prices drifting ever higher, David took an opportunity to order two more crane vessels but this time considerably bigger and able to operate worldwide. With oil companies budgeting up to $50 billion for a development and with offshore labour costs being ten times higher than onshore costs, anyone that could reduce the number of hours needed offshore to complete a development and at the same time reduce the project duration by up to a year could command a high price, commensurate to a percentage of the savings achieved. Whilst the cost of building the two new crane vessels was astronomical, with lump sum contracts that recognised the savings achieved by the use of such vessels, the cash flow into SMS became a torrent. Within ten years the two new vessels were paid for and still working hard. The Saga had been converted to a specialise pipelay vessel to enable greater flexibility of contracts and life was good. But other had seen the success of SMS and wanted a slice of the action.

In China a boom in the construction of new shipyards had led to a collapse in the ship building price which in turn led to an upsurge in the fabrication of new ships of every shape and size. This was equally true of new heavy lift vessels and before long the relatively tight supply market for suitable construction vessels changed with the arrival of new and more advanced vessels. At the same time and as a result of the new developments allied with concerns in the Middle East of the effect of high oil prices on the world economy, the price of oil started to slide. In America the growth of shale oil production contributed to an acceleration in the decline of the oil price and before long it was the 1990s again. Bankruptcy of those companies who had over extended to build the new vessels followed and whilst a few vessels were taken out of the market, many were bought by those companies with the deepest pockets at knock down prices often using money loaned from the banks at very low interest rates.

The inevitable consequence was a collapse in the market price for heavy lift construction vessels. David had seen it before and felt he had enough projects in hand to survive until the inevitable pick up as the supply/demand balance became restored. But he had not foreseen the effect of the American shale oil bonanza. Saudi Arabia once again stepped in to try and drive down the price of oil and put the shale oil operators out of business but it was too little too late. As the price of oil continued to fall so the deep-water developments that were the life blood of SMS dried up.

David responded in the only way he knew how and the only way he could. He would have to outperform his rivals in order to win the high value work that was still available. To do that he needed to have the biggest crane vessel ever built. Enter Kalevala. With two 20,000-ton capacity cranes it was twice as large as the next largest crane vessel and would mean large production facilities could be completed totally onshore. After completion the facilities would be transported to their offshore location where Kalevala would lift the single production unit as a single lift onto the previously installed substructure. The subsequent reduction in offshore hours that traditionally would have been needed to connect smaller units together offshore would cut hundreds of millions from the cost of development. In addition, oil would be produced at least two years earlier, a major advantage for the oil companies cash flow. This latter point was of particular interest for OEC when it came to developing the Caratacus field.

Chapter 6
February 2026

Moscow

Alexander Khurin sat with his long legs crossed on a wooden bench. He was totally naked except for a towel strategically placed across his lap. With a balding head and signs that his previously taut torso was developing a bit of a droop, it was clear to all that age was beginning to take its toll on the hard man of Russia. Not that anyone was going to voice such observations. Vanity was one of Khurin's weaknesses. A short temper was another. Combined with the capability to make people mysteriously suffer fatal accidents meant Khurin was not someone that one took lightly.

After being close to Khurin for more years than he cared to remember, Igor Antipov was not interested in Khurin's looks. Sitting side by side in the 100-degree heat of the sauna the two old friends had enjoyed the ritual hot and cold cleansing process every Saturday evening since they were at military college together. There were not many people that the President of Russia trusted completely but his friend and Russian Prime Minister was one such person. Theirs was not a trust based on shared values, although they had this in abundance, or kinship but rather a trust built up in the harsh world of reality, firstly in fighting for Mother Russia against the insurgents of Chechen and later in the vicious world of Russian dog eat dog politics.

After the break-up of the old Soviet Union Russia effectively became an anarchic state ruled by the mob. A weak but popular president had become a figure head but spent most of his time trying to see what was at the bottom of a bottle of Vodka. This left the way for the Russian equivalent of the Mafia to share the country's spoils often to the detriment of the Russian people. Not that the people weren't used to such treatment. Both under the Tsars and subsequently under the communists the people were seen as useful but expendable. This was their lot and by and large they accepted it. As long as they had food on the table and vodka to allow them to forget their poor existence, they left politics to the leaders be they royalty, communists or gangsters. Fiercely loyal to Mother Russia, partly as a result of the state propaganda machine but mainly because Russia was a nation of nationalists that believed in a strong state, if that meant they had to make sacrifices to achieve this goal then so be it. The people just accepted the situation and got on with their lives. All, that is, accept for a small group of ex GRU personnel who saw that by stripping the state assets for their own gains the gangsters were weakening the state. Not only were they taking control of the oil fields, gold mines, aluminium smelters and steel mills the money they made, in the billions of dollars, was exported out of the country and out of the reach of the authorities. They knew that one day the politicians would take control again and when that day came, they had no intension of being in Russia.

Khurin and his colleagues in the GRU looked on with despair at what was becoming of their beloved Russia. Once considered to be the second most powerful country on earth, a country which had the ability to control the destiny of other countries just by dint of its military might, Russia had become almost a laughing stock. Sure, they still had atomic weapons but they had no way of delivering the ordinance as their once powerful armed forces, navy and air force, failed to keep pace with western modernisation. Old client states that had contributed to Russian wealth had broken away and gained their independence taking their valuable mineral deposits with them. Even worse, those same states now looked to the west for their protection and security. Almost paranoid about western invasion, perhaps justified from a historical context, The Soviet Union consisted of a whole buffer belt between Russia and the west. If a western invader wanted to emulate Napoleon or Hitler it would first have to go through one of these buffer states giving Russia time to mobilise its army. Protected from a nuclear strike by its powerful nuclear deterrent it was protected from a more conventional invasion by its buffer states. Whilst the west feared a Soviet expansion, The Soviets feared a western invasion. With the breakup of the Union of Soviet Socialist Republics or USSR, and the loss of an effective nuclear deterrent Khurin and his compatriots felt very vulnerable to western aggression.

Ironically the solution to their concerns came in the form of changes to the Russian political system instigated as part of the breakup of the old USSR. The president was no longer nominated by the Communist party but had to be elected by the people with elections taking place every four years. What's more a maximum of two terms were allowed so when the second term of the incumbent president was finished a new president would be elected. Khurin made sure, first by gaining the confidence of the new breed of business leaders and secondly by appealing to the nationalism of the people, that he would become the next president. It helped that the opposition was not very well organised and unlike Khurin, did not have the support of the armed forces and secret police. It also helped that one of Khurin's main rivals fell gravely ill a few weeks before the election was due to take place and subsequently died. Khurin was duly elected with a landslide.

His initial term of four years was used to gradually play one business leader off against another. Divide and rule were old tactics but they worked for Khurin. Having isolated his most dangerous opponents he spent his second term stripping them of their wealth or arranging their death. Not that there was any evidence of Russian state involvement. Khurin was too clever to allow any indication of his involvement. Natural causes or suicide were the reason for the deaths and whilst it was clearly suspicious that so many of Khurin's enemies succumbed to such a death there was never any proof of Moscow involvement.

Meanwhile Khurin had also embarked on a charm offensive with his enemies in the west and with his supporters back home. It was a clever balancing act. At the same time as convincing the west that the old USSR was no more and that a new modern Russia was taking its place, one that embraced the west's values, he also managed to convince the people back home that he was a hard man that understood the concerns and wishes of the Russian people and would protect them from western aggression. He also convinced them that they needed him and so when his second term was complete, he used his friends within the administration to change the rules. There was to be no limit to the number of terms anyone could serve as president and elections would be every six years.

Now with effective dictatorial powers, Khurin had an iron grip on Russia and he intended to use that power to make Russia great again.

First, he cleared out the rest of the Russian businessmen that voiced anti-Khurin sentiments. Not all met with accidents or committed suicide. Some accepted the situation and gave their support to the new Russian leader. If that meant they had to hand over a portion of their wealth then so be it. They still had more than they could spend in a lifetime, a lifetime that would be considerably longer by supporting Khurin rather than by being against him. A few tried to fight Khurin and paid the ultimate price.

Secondly, he poured money into the armed forces and started rebuilding the nuclear umbrella. The west in the meanwhile was too occupied with social issues such as diversity and historical crimes based on modern sensibilities to spend any money on their armed forces which gradually deteriorated. Hadn't the cold war been won? Why did the west need a large armed force when the only threat was from a small group of terrorists that required a completely different approach to protect the people than a large and well-armed military?

Having quietly but effectively modernised the armed forces he set about rebuilding the buffer zone. His starting point was to regain an ice-free port on the Black Sea. Whilst Russia is the largest country on Earth it has very few outlets to the sea, a big drawback for a nation that wants to be seen as being a true world power. Having a navy means the Russian flag can be flown around the world. It also means that submarines carrying nuclear missiles, almost impossible to detect and hence a considerably stronger deterrent than land-based missiles, have access to the world's oceans. Unfortunately, the traditional Russian port on the Black Sea was now part of the Ukraine, a country that had turned away from its old Soviet master towards the west. Suspicious of Russian intent, Ukraine refused to allow Russia to use the Black Sea port. Russia took them anyway, by force, reasoning that the west was too weak and too preoccupied with its own issues to interfere. An excuse that the Black Sea port was occupied primarily by Russian speaking people and hence should really have been part of Russia when the old USSR was broken up was sufficient. An excuse right out of the Hitler school of diplomacy. The reality was that Russia had used its armed forces to annex part of another nations land. Like Hitler before him, the Russian President had judged the western response correctly. A lot of hot air and political waffle led precisely to nothing. Russia retained control of the Black sea port and now had access via the Dardanelle Straights to the open oceans.

Further inroads into Ukraine followed but this time the west started to see the danger. Having previously determined that any future risk would come from middle eastern terrorists, the risk from the old enemy in the east started to become clearer. Old buffer states such as the Baltic countries, Rumania and Bulgaria started to become concerned. The past protection offered by the NATO alliance which should have given assurances suddenly became less reassuring as The USA turned its attention towards new threats from the Far East and away from Europe. Countries that had milked the good will of American protection whilst at the same time failed to spend money on their own defence began to feel vulnerable and looked to increase their military spending. This was not easy in a west that had become accustomed to spending its wealth on social, politically correct projects and with administrations filled with idealists and elitists.

Khurin had anticipated this and had already instigated a propaganda blitz against the west. He used social media to spread false news and targeted the naive youth. He knew that eventually all western politicians had to stand up in front of the electorate and seek re-election. His manipulation of the masses via social media had a small but significant effect on the voting public. Particularly vulnerable was Great Britain with its first past the post form of electing the government and a population that was deeply unhappy with the handling of the Brexit negotiations. Khurin knew that he only needed to influence a very small part of the population in critical constituencies and he could swing the election. He used this ploy along with some underhand vote rigging tactics whereby some left-wing individuals were able to vote more than once, with incredible success and led the way to the election of the Socialist/Marxist party. Just how involved the Socialist party was in this process will never be known but it didn't matter because the policies of the socialists could not have been better for Khurin. At a stroke he had removed the threat of interference from one of the wests strongest and most principled countries. Without Great Britain the rest of Europe only had France to give a credible defence and with The USA turning its back on Europe Khurin's Russia was back in business.

Further inroads into Ukraine forced the Ukrainian government to cease all attempts to turn to the west and although remaining independent, Ukraine effectively once again became a vassal state to Russia. At the same time the Baltic states came under increasing threat with border skirmishes and clear Russian aggression leading the governments of Latvia, Lithuania and Estonia to become increasingly fearful for their independence. Khurin no longer needed to pretend and made clear his ambition to bring these states back into his sphere of influence. With America looking more and more towards the threat posed by China and Great Britain under the control of a sympathetic government, Khurin's ambition of putting Russia back on the world stage appeared to be a done deal. And then Great Britain voted the Marxists out of power and installed a new government. It was this development that occupied the discussion of the two old friends in the sauna located in an old Dacha on the outskirts of Moscow.

'So, Igor, it looks like we miscalculated the ability of the British socialists to hold on to power.'

Khurin threw some more water onto the heated coals to release a burst of hot steam into the small room. After the immediate effect of the steam dissipated, he continued,

'I have to admit to being surprised that our friends over there didn't manage to shut down the opposition. After all they had managed to gain control of most of the media and the electoral process so what went wrong?'

'As much as it pains me to admit it, I'm as surprised as you are, Alexi. All our efforts to influence the electorate through social media and to fund sympathetic commentators to the cause of the socialists seemed to be paying off. The British people are normally easily led by the empty promises of more money for social causes without seeming to understand where the money comes from. The British economy was basically wrecked and another term of so-called socialist rule would have removed Great Britain from the world stage for good. As you know this would remove a serious obstacle from our goals in the Baltic states, Rumania and Ukraine. Without Great Britain's military, the rest of Europe is too weak and divided to offer any real threat to our plans. Years of under investment in their armed forces and their considerable dependency on our gas supplies makes them impotent. America has already turned its back on Europe as a result of the threat from China and even if they did react our intelligence indicates there is no real enthusiasm for American personnel to be put at risk to solve what is seen in America as a European problem.'

Antipov shrugged his broad shoulders letting the small droplets of moisture run down his hairy back onto the towel under his substantial buttocks. At over 110 kilogrammes in weight Antipov was no longer the slim, muscular GRU officer that, as a younger man, had won the Hero of the Russian Federation for his exploits in the second Chechnya conflict. As a politician Antipov spent too much time sitting down and eating good food and not enough time exercising. In contrast Khurin carefully cultivated his iron man image and that involved a vigorous exercise regime. Worried about the unhealthy lifestyle of his closest friend, Khurin often pushed Antipov to take more care of himself but for Antipov life was too comfortable and so what if he was a little over weight. Antipov continued talking.

'We had successfully shut down the conservative opposition by the normal approach of leaking make-believe scandals and misinformation but we were too slow to react to the danger that Richard Green posed. In our defence the speed with which he managed to start a new party and then turn the electorate was nothing short of amazing. 12 weeks ago, there was no opposition to the socialists and today there is a new party in control of Great Britain.'

'An unfortunate situation to be sure but I suspect one that shouldn't stand in the way of our plans. The last five years have already had a devastating effect on the British economy. Military spending is non-existent and what weaponry they do have is obsolete and rotting away in storage. The promotion of personnel on the basis of diversity targets means that much of the management in the British civil service is more interested in meeting arbitrary targets rather than proactively preparing the country for external risks. Our own propaganda has helped a lot here. I was particularly pleased when we were able to manipulate the promotion of Joan Stapleford to head of MI5 and Rachel Stewart as The Commissioner of the Metropolitan Police. Both lightweights with a sense of their own importance, they supported the socialist government almost blindly. A great pity that we couldn't quite get Mahendra Khan to be head of the Joints Chief of Staff. That old war horse, General Jordan, was too popular when push came to a shove but without funds he at least was neutralised.'

Khurin paused for breath and wiped the sweat from his forehead before continuing.

'No, I don't think Richard Green's Progressive Conservatives will be able to do very much. They won the election on the back of many promises but they have very little experience of politics and more importantly no money with which to do anything. We should be ready to move within a couple of years and whilst a pity that the UK hasn't been completely neutralised, I can't see that in that time they will be able to regain their place on the world stage. The socialists have done their job too well. Thank goodness for useful idiots.'

'I tend to agree.' Antipov nodded. 'The only slight concern I have is that The European Union has started to wake up to the risks posed by no longer having the UK or America to assist them and are spending more on their military. I suspect though that they have become too comfortable and our charm offensive has had a beneficial effect. Whilst the Poles and the French are always suspicious, the Germans are too busy trying to prevent a rise in the fascist movement due to their earlier immigration policies to pay too much attention on what we are doing.'

'What about our efforts in Turkey? How close are we to getting them to withdraw from the NATO alliance? Whilst NATO is considerably weaker than it was, as long as it exists, we cannot do anything without risking American involvement. They may not want to assist Europe but existing treatise give them no alternative. Our sources in America have advised that they are looking for a way to walk away and as you know we have some influence at the highest level in the American Government, but this has to be handled in such a way that the breakdown of NATO is not seen as being instigated by the Americans.'

'Things are going well in Turkey. The failed coup we organised a few years ago to allow Erdogan to take control of the country worked beyond expectations. When Erdogan surprisingly stepped down in 2023, we were concerned that the country would revert to a western looking secular state but along with some election manipulation we were able to ensure Yusuf Demir was elected president. Whilst Erdogan was a charismatic leader who had fallen out with the west, Demir is an opportunist who is much easier to control, a characteristic which we have used to our advantage. Relationships between Turkey and America are rock bottom and it will only take a small shove for Turkey to break off diplomatic relations. When that happens NATO will be finished. Turkey will ally itself to Iran for security purposes and Europe will have to side with America and distance itself from Turkey. As you know most of the gas for southern Europe goes through the Black Sea pipeline via Turkey. At an opportune time, we will cut the gas and ensure that Turkey gets the blame leading to Greece and Bulgaria suffering power shortages. Whether armed conflict results is not clear but we can be quite sure that diplomatic relations will deteriorate considerably. At the same time by reducing gas supplies to Northern Europe we will effectively have Europe in a strait jacket. That will be when we make our move on the buffer states. Europe will be paralysed; America will stand by and watch and the UK will be too impoverished to do anything but make idle threats. By the time the dust has settled we will have moved our borders to the same location as the old Soviet Union and installed a missile defence system to prevent any counter attack. Puppet governments for each of the conquered states are being instigated and will be ready to take over the countries once the armed forces have finished cleaning out any opposition. Russia will again be able to take its place at the top table.'

'I'll certainly drink to that. Let's get out of this heat and find a nice cold beer.'

Chapter 7
September 2024

Naples

Over one million people call the city of Naples their home. It is the capital of the Italian region of Campania and the third largest city in Italy. Located approximately a third of the way up the leg of Italy on a bay of the same name, part of the Tyrrhenian Sea, it has a typical Mediterranean climate. Warm to hot in the summer months, pleasant during the autumn and spring with mild winters. The balmy climate and relatively close proximity to Rome made it one of the favourite places for the ancient Roman elite to escape from the suffocating summers of Rome. Many fine palaces were constructed along the water front and on the Island of Capri situated a few miles offshore from Naples. Along the coast in Sorrento the Emperor Tiberius constructed a massive palace from which he effectively ruled the Roman empire for the last years of his life. More recently the centre of Naples has been designated a UNESCO world heritage site and contains many beautiful buildings. Badly damaged during the second world war it has been sympathetically renovated in the years since the end of the war. The saying 'see Naples and die' can be attributed to an earlier age but the hidden meaning that nothing is more beautiful than Naples could still apply even though many other places would dispute this.

Dominated by Mount Vesuvius to the east it sits in a natural basin which only recently has been identified as the calderas of an active super volcano which is many times the size of Vesuvius. Fortunately for Naples, whilst Vesuvius is prone to regular eruptions of a magnitude that to date have not put Naples at risk, the super volcano, called Campi Flegrei, only erupts once every few thousand years. The last major eruption is thought to have occurred about 39,000 years ago when it would have been the largest eruption in Europe for hundreds of thousands of years. When the next eruption will be no one knows but when it comes Naples will cease to exist. The rediscovery of Pompeii and Herculaneum after being buried beneath the ashes of Vesuvius focused the mind of Neapolitans on the dangers that Vesuvius continues to exhibit reinforced by regular earthquakes that rattle the city. But it is the Campi Flegrei which holds the bigger threat particularly as recent seismic records indicate that the magma chamber beneath the bay of Naples is beginning to show signs of expanding. Perhaps that is why people from Naples tend to be very philosophical about life and have a 'live for the moment' sort of mentality.

One such Neapolitan was Marco Paglia. Born and raised in the city Marco was well aware of the twin threats that nature had placed on his doorstep but if it bothered him it certainly didn't show. At 1.7 metres tall and weighing 76 kilogrammes Marco was not a particularly imposing figure. Once the weight was primarily muscular but the passage of time had reduced the muscle and there were signs that a bit of flab was taking over. Each morning when Marco looked at himself in the mirror, he promised that he would join a gym to try and turn back the clock but then the day took over and all thoughts of exercise vanished. Besides, the well-tailored suits, hand made in Milan, were designed to hide any excess of the middle regions so Marco was able to convince himself that he didn't look too bad for someone of 67 years old.

Sitting in his tenth floor office on the Piazzale Molo Carlo Pisacane near the port region of the city, Marco let his eyes gaze out of the window. From his elevation he was able to see the lorries entering and leaving the port, a sight that he never tired of. As Chief Executive Officer for Rostella S.p.A, an offshore transportation and construction company, Marco was well aware of the importance of international trade. As a younger man he had spent a lot of times in the port region both as a driver and later as a custom official where his knowledge of the workings of the port were invaluable. Not just to the authorities but also to young Marco who soon found an entrepreneurial spirit working with some of the biggest and most respectable names in Naples. In Italy tax avoidance was a way of life and not really seen as a crime provided one wasn't caught. And so, by helping reduce the tax burden on seemingly honest importers Marco was just contributing to the free flow of trade and helping his fellow Neapolitans, something that also fortuitously contributed to improving the life style of Marco himself. In time Marco had built up quite a nice nest egg and having decided that the life of a customs official, whilst financially rewarding, was not very satisfying went about doing something about it.

He bided his time until one of the regular recessions hit the Italian economy. He had already built up a good picture of those companies that were not particularly well managed and who were most vulnerable to the down turn; and top of the list was Rostella S.p.A., a family run company that specialised in transporting goods from Spain and France into southern Italy via Naples. It had long been one of Marco's client companies.

By helping Rostella avoid customs duties Marco had seen the company flourish but he had also seen that the owners had not used the money wisely. Instead of building a nest egg for the inevitable down turn the owners had spent the windfall on good living and poor investments. Having borrowed against their assets they had nowhere to hide when the recession hit. This was the moment that Marco had been waiting for. Acting as an honest broker but in reality, acting on his own behalf, Marco bought up the company's debts through a series of shell companies.

Having acquired sufficient debt to make a difference Marco then secretly informed the authorities of the company's custom misdemeanours and supplied sufficient proof, being careful to ensure his name did not appear on the paperwork, such that even the lax Italian police could not ignore the fraudulent activities. The subsequent prosecution and fines pushed the company into bankruptcy and Marco as biggest debtor was able to buy up the rest of the company for considerably under market value. At the age of 43 Marco found himself sole owner of Rostella S.p.A.

He quickly went about transforming the company from a simple road haulage company to one that managed the total importation of goods. He set up joint ventures with shipping and freight forwarding companies which enabled him to undercut his competitors and start to win a bigger market share until eventually he was the dominant Neapolitan importer. He was helped by a sudden influx of European money intended to help the Italian economy to recover from the recession and also by his willingness to take calculated gambles that if they went wrong would put him on the wrong side of the law. Any profit he made he put back in the business and having seen the implications of too much debt, always made sure his debt levels were manageable. He also had the one important attribute needed when starting out in business, luck, although he would often be heard to say that he made his own luck, something that was at least partly true.

Eventually he was able to buy out his joint venture partners and soon found himself at the head of one of the biggest integrated transportation companies in

Italy and someone that had a reputation for getting things done. It was this latter quality that had been his introduction to the world of offshore construction. Already the owner of a number of offshore vessels that supplied the various oil fields in the Mediterranean and beginning to stretch further afield, his was one of the few companies in Italy that had any knowledge of the offshore construction market. Whilst Italy had a large state-owned oil company which was active in offshore exploration, Italy did not have a big offshore support infrastructure and so had to depend, like so many others, on foreign companies. One Italian company based in Venice tried to challenge the foreign construction companies by building a fleet of transportation barges and heavy lift vessels but was hit by the same market forces that led to the eventual creation of Saunders Marine Solutions and the company went bankrupt. Unlike the British government that left business to the businessmen, the Italian government was much more supportive of its industries and was not about to allow one of its strategic companies, one that supported the state oil company, be taken over by a foreign concern.

Initially a request was sent to the state oil company to take over the assets of the failed offshore construction company but when this was demonstrated to be not in the best interest of the oil company Marco Paglia was approached. A deal was soon put in place that saw Marco's company take over the assets of the failed construction company for a fraction of the assets value, the difference being written off by the Italian government. Whilst against EU rules and despite complaints to the European courts from existing companies who saw the deal with Rostella S.p.A. as being exactly what it was, a government subsidy through the back door, nothing was done and Marco found himself in charge of one of the biggest offshore construction companies in the world. He also had the luxury, courtesy of the Italian government, of a guaranteed income stream. Any offshore work needed by the Italian oil companies went to Rostella S.p.A. irrespective of the price charged.

Whilst a great benefit, the Italian oil company did not have enough work to cover all the capital and day-to-day costs of the business so it still needed to compete on the open market for other work. In this it came up against Saunders Marine Solutions and the two companies soon became fierce rivals in bidding for the lucrative heavy lift market. In the boom years there was plenty of work to go around and both companies flourished but when the market turned and the work dried up, just like Saunders Marine Solutions, Rostella S.p.A. found itself in difficulties and increasingly needing to support its offshore activities with its general shipping activities. Marco started to lose money. With a large workforce to pay and the capital depreciation of assets to consider Rostella needed nearly $350,000 a day just to cover costs. Unfortunately for Marco, at the same time as the work dried up the European Union started to take a much more serious look at unfair competition and would not countenance any further support by the Italian government. Meanwhile the Italian government had not forgotten the support already given to Rostella so when Marco proposed disposing of the offshore assets and reverting back to a pure shipping support company the Italian government made it very clear that should he do so then they would be looking very closely at some of his more dubious past dealings.

Marco had a problem. Looking away from the window he reached for the phone and dialled a number. After four rings the phone was answered by Martina Levi, Paglia's private secretary.

'Ciao, Marco, what can I do for you?'

Martina and Marco had worked together for 20 years and during that time had on occasions been lovers. In her early 50s Martina was still a classically beautiful Italian woman. With short cut dark hair, an intelligent face dominated by a smile that always seemed to be present and a figure that turned heads of men half her age she was fiercely loyal to Marco Paglia. Those times when friendship and loyalty had extended to becoming lovers were infrequent and just seemed to happen naturally with never any thought that they were putting happy marriages at risk or that the relationship would interfere with their work.

'Martina, please could you arrange a meeting of the board for 16:00 hrs this afternoon. I think that everyone is in the office today so whilst at short notice I would expect all to attend. The meeting will be informal and shouldn't take longer than an hour. If anyone asks it is to discuss recent events in the offshore market. Please ask everyone to confirm their attendance by midday.'

'No problem, Marco. I'll email everyone and reserve the board room. Do you want coffee and anything to eat?'

'Just coffee will be fine. Thanks.'

Marco put the phone down and started making notes in his note book. It was time to formulate a solution to the problems of the offshore division.

Chapter 8
February 2026

North Sea

Jim Stieger had just finished his shift as a control room operator on the Saebo Drilling rig and was making his way to the canteen for his evening meal when the alarm sounded. With all the sensitive equipment on the rig and the hostile environment in which it was always expected to work, alarms were not an infrequent event. Jim was tempted to just ignore it but years of training to respond and react to emergencies kicked in and he promptly did an abrupt turn and headed towards his muster station on the top deck.

The Saebo Drill rig was not a particularly new drilling unit but had been well maintained and recently modernised to the highest standards. Hired by OEC to expand the Caratacus field it had already completed and temporarily capped ten wells. To reduce the development time OEC had organised the well drilling programme to run in parallel with the construction of the processing facilities. Whilst the production facilities were being fabricated onshore the drilling of wells, the most expensive part of the development, continued offshore. Caratacus would eventually be served by 60 wells stretching out from the central drilling complex over a distance of eight kilometres. Included within the development facilities would be a permanent drilling unit which would in due course replace the Saebo unit but until then Saebo was contracted to prepare the first 12 wells. Obtaining a positive cash flow to offset the immense cost of bringing the field on stream was OEC's primary objective and the use of the Saebo unit was critical to that goal.

As Jim approached his muster station next to lifeboat three his subconscious for the first time identified the alarm as being that sounded to warn of a gas leak. Although Caratacus was primarily an oil field there was always some entrained gas present and the huge size of the reservoir meant that the amount of gas could be considerable. One of the biggest dangers when drilling a well was to encounter a gas pocket. This would be a totally unexpected source of gas and would allow a sudden release through the drill pipe to the drill deck. Even if no gas pocket is hit, entrained gas at a very high pressure can find its way from the main reservoir to the drill floor despite all the failsafe apparatus. If a source of ignition is also present the result could be catastrophic, one of the reasons that all sources of ignition are banned on oil rigs.

Having confirmed his attendance at the muster station to the lifeboats coxswain, Jim got on the phone to the rig control room to find out what was happening. He fully expected a quick answer and to be reassured that the alarm had been triggered by a faulty sensor or some such malfunction but instead the phone just rang with no response. This was very unusual and very worrying. Jim knew that the control room was manned around the clock so the fact that no one answered the phone could only be because they had their hands full. IE a real emergency. Putting the phone down Jim turned to the lifeboat coxswain, one of the rigs Marine Co-ordinators called Gary Taylor, to ask what he knew about the situation when an announcement was made via the tannoy system.

'Attention, all personnel. Attention, all personnel. This is not an exercise; I repeat this is not an exercise.'

Jim recognised the voice of the Offshore Installation Manager, the man in charge of the rig.

'We have detected a significant quantity of gas on the drill floor which appears to be leaking from one of the rig's blow out prevention valves. Whilst we are confident the leak has been isolated, as a precaution we have activated the subsea blow out prevention valves and would request all non-essential personnel remain at their muster stations until further notice. Fire crews are asked to stand by in a state of preparedness. Needless to say, all possible sources of ignition are to be stopped immediately and all hot work permits are suspended. That's all for now.'

The tannoy went dead.

This was certainly not what Jim had expected. In all his 22 years working offshore he had never actually experienced a genuine emergency. Sure, he attended the offshore survival course every four years and knew the basics of what to do in an emergency but had never expected that the training would be needed. It had always seemed like an excuse to have a few days in Aberdeen with his mates, getting paid by the company to drive around in lifeboats, jump in a warm swimming pool, get out of an upside-down simulated helicopter crash and play about with various firefighting equipment. Throw in a bit of first aid and some theoretical lessons and afterwards to the bar for a few beers and it was all rather 'boys-ownish'. Now as he stood next to lifeboat three on the lowest deck of the jack-up rig, still 25 metres above the waters of the North Sea, he tried to recall all he'd been taught. The prospect of ending up in the water, even in the relative calmness of that warm summer's afternoon, filled him with dread. The alternative was to get into the lifeboat. He dreaded the cramped and uncomfortable conditions but consoled himself that at least it was better than dying of hypothermia, drowning or being burnt alive.

Just as these thoughts flashed through his head, he suddenly felt the whole rig tremble. Like being caught in an earthquake. Anything hanging down started to sway and the deck plating beneath his feet vibrated. Along with the other 12 men standing at the muster station Jim grabbed onto a handrail to prevent himself from falling. Almost immediately afterward he heard the noise of an express train rushing through a tunnel. A sort of whooshing sound that seemed to be coming from the centre of the drill rig. Increasing in pitch the noise got louder until suddenly a massive column of flames erupted out of the rig until it was as high as the top of the drill derrick. Within seconds debris from the explosion started to drop back down onto the platform and on to the people waiting at the muster station.

Frozen to the spot Jim saw a two-metre length of pipe land on the head of one of the stewards and knock him over the side. Other smaller bits of debris caused cuts and bruises but fortunately the blast had sent most of the debris over the side of the rig where it landed in the sea. As if it was needed, through the cacophony of sound coming from the aftermaths of the gas explosion Jim heard the gas release alarm change to an abandon rig alarm punctuated by a tannoy announcement to 'abandon rig'.

Dazed and confused the training took over. Zipping up his survival suit and tightening his life jacket he made his way to the life boat which by now had been swung out over the sea. The coxswain quickly directed everyone to a seat in the 12-man lifeboat before climbing in himself and taking the driver's seat. Having started the engine, he ordered the door to be closed before pulling on the life boat release line. The life boat gently dropped to the water until it was floating alongside the stricken rig but still attached by the lifeboat falls. Opening the aft hatch, the coxswain released the rear line and at the same time directed one of the survivors to open the front hatch and release the front line. Fortunately, the waves were less than a metre high so the lifeboat was not moving up and down very much but releasing the two lines was a tricky operation with the risk that fingers could be trapped if adequate care wasn't taken.

At last the lifeboat was free and was able to motor away to join the other five boats that had been able to get away from the rig. The coxswain, in constant radio communication with the other lifeboats handed out seasick pills but in reality, they were too little too late and it was not long before the atmosphere in the little boat was very unpleasant. Used to the firm foundation of a fixed jack-up rig, the rig's crew were not mariners and the erratic motions of the little boat soon took its toll. The coxswain ordered the two hatches opened to try and get some fresh air into the interior but the scene in the boat was one of abject misery. But they were alive. Those that had a view out of the open hatches watched in horror at the burning rig. The orange-red flames still erupted from the centre of the rig, the heat from which could be felt by those in the little boats over half a mile from the flames. As they watched the apocalyptic scene, they could still see people moving about on the rig desperately trying to find an escape route. Some jumped into the water to escape the heat others could be seen hiding behind whatever cover they could find. Some just disappeared in the smoke.

Jim watched as one of the other lifeboats went back towards the rig to see if it could pick up anyone out of the water but as it approached the rig there was a sound that would haunt Jim for the rest of his life. A sound of screeching and tortured metal assaulted his ears as, to the shock of all that observed, the 30-metre-high drill derrick slowly toppled over towards the small lifeboat. The lifeboat saw the danger and tried to steer away from the falling mass of steel but gravity works faster than the small motor in the lifeboat. The outside edge of the tower hit the lifeboat on the port quarter which caused the lifeboat to turn on its side and disappear under the water being submerged beneath a thousand tonnes of steel.

One moment the little boat was there searching for survivors and the next it ceased to exist along with its compliment of 12 souls. Jim heard above the sound of the dying rig a human cry that chilled the blood. Taken aback he realise it had come from his own lifeboat and turning in his seat he saw a young girl looking at the enfolding scene over his shoulder. The cry was a precursor to deep sobs as the young girl lamented the loss of life and the human element of the tragedy. How many of the dead had been her personal friends? How many were work mates that only a few hours before had been sharing carefree banter with her and other work mates. The life of an offshore rig was an isolated one and deep bonds developed between colleagues who often saw more of their fellow workers than they did of their own families. As the remaining inhabitants of the life boats looked on, the platform safety vessel turned its high-pressure water hose onto the inferno and the flames started to die down. The actions of the OIM in closing the subsea blow out prevention valves cut off the supply of gas that was feeding the flames such that when the residual gas from the above water piping was consumed no further fuel was added. The water curtain from the safety vessel did the rest and when the first helicopters from the shore arrived to give assistance all they found was a burnt-out wreck but one that was still standing.

The final head count identified 19 people had lost their lives and a further 15 had suffered serious injuries mostly jumping from the burning rig. Strangely very few injuries were as a direct result of burns. As the lifeboat came alongside the platform rescue boat and Jim Steiner climbed the scrambling net to the deck of the safety boat, the one overriding thought was how, with all the safety measures incorporated in a modern drilling rig could such a tragedy have occurred? This would be a question asked time and time again.

Chapter 9
February 2026

London

Opening the meeting Richard Green addressed his full cabinet for the first time.

'Ladies and gentlemen, first let me pass on my thanks for you all for your contribution to the recent election victory. I think it is fair to say that we caused a bit of an upset in the supposedly orchestrated plan to re-elect our communist friends.'

A polite smile appeared on most lips as the understatement was recognised.

'But perhaps I shouldn't be saying congratulations but rather commiserations. The task in front of us is formidable. Even before the disaster of the previous regime, past governments were spending the future with gay abandon on whatever vanity project they could invent in order to buy off the voters. Amazingly as it seems to me the electorate couldn't or didn't want to see that they were being bribed with their own money extracted in the form of taxation. Whether they couldn't see or didn't want to see is irrelevant, what is relevant is that it took the extremes of the communist regime to expose the total folly of living constantly beyond one's means.'

Richard was fully aware that the previous government had labelled itself socialist but preferred to call it communist for a stronger effect.

'Our task is going to be to somehow keep the country moving forward, prevent a breakdown in law and order, cut spending on everything but the most important activities; all whilst not pushing the country into a deeper recession than it is already in. Simple, really.'

Green looked around the room at the smiling faces. His attempt at brevity was a deliberate ploy to help relax the people around the table but he knew that this would not last long. Difficult decisions were going to have to be made and Green suspected that by the end of the year he would be the most hated man in the country. The only medicine for the illness that had caused the implosion of the British economy was deep austerity in an attempt to reduce the debt burden. The folly of spending tomorrow's earnings today and living beyond the collective means of the country had to stop but as with an alcoholic trying to stop drinking the country had to be weaned off the spending binge to prevent serious cold turkey from kicking in. Green was also fully aware that the supporters of the previous regime would declare every attempt to cut back on spending as an attack on the so-called working classes to the benefit of the rich. Not a very original story and one that generally doesn't stand up to too much scrutiny but nevertheless still a story that much of the electorate would believe.

'However. I suspect that we do not yet all know one another so before we go any further, perhaps we can go around the table and introduce ourselves.' Looking to his right Green continued, 'Alastair, perhaps you'd start the ball rolling.'

Alastair Frank looked up from his note pad and addressed the meeting.

'Alastair Franks. I think most of you will know me. Shadow Chancellor under the conservative administration of ten years ago, I've been in politics most of my life although did spend the first ten years doing proper work for Lehman Brothers – before they went into administration I hasten to add. Richard has offered me the post of Chancellor so he clearly has a grudge against me.'

This latter said with a broad smile before turning to the lady on his right,

'Cynthia Graeme. Not a lot of political experience. Most of my working life has been spent in the building trade. Having recently sold my property development company I was one of the first to answer the call from Richard to start a new party. Whether as a reward or because no one else wanted it I have been asked to take the position of Home secretary. As a political novice I would appreciate any help that may be going on how to deal with the establishment.'

Cynthia was a formidable looking lady with grey hair and glasses. What she hadn't mentioned was that she had made many millions from her property company and had been one of the major funders for the Progressive Conservative Party. As she turned to her right it was clear that she had an inner strength and no one around the table doubted that she was the sort of person that did not suffer fools gladly. Some secretly pitied the 'establishment' as she called the civil servants and public services.

Gary Davies was next to speak.

'Gary Davies, 55 years old and previously a senior member of her majesty's customs and excise. Richard has offered me the job of Foreign Secretary which I have accepted. I'm not sure what qualifications I have for the role except a pretty good understanding of how foreign trade works. I'm looking forward to getting to know my department members and particularly to talking to our diplomats around the world. After the Brexit fiasco we have a lot of work in rebuilding old relationships and starting new ones. Unfortunately, from what I can see the previous government was more interested in pushing their internal agenda just at the time when we needed to be outward looking; so, we have some catching up to do.'

An unassuming looking man with a receding hair line and a beard, both showing the first signs of going grey, he was wearing a blue suit and matching tie.

Next to Gary was a much more dapper looking individual.

'Jason Bhatia. Degree in Physics from UCL followed by a 21-year career in the British navy rising to the rank of captain before deciding to try my luck in civvy street with the Royal Dutch Shell Oil Company. I've known Richard many years and when he asked me to pitch in with the PCP, I was only too pleased to help out. Now I find myself the Secretary of State for Defence. Some of my old colleagues are going to have a bit of a shock when they find out.'

And so, each person in turn took the opportunity to introduce themselves, some being more verbose than others but all full of a self confidence that only comes from people that have been successful in whatever life they have chosen.

'Thank you, everyone. I've arranged a little shindig for next Tuesday at 10 Downing Street which I hope you will all be able to attend. Spouses are included. As we will all be working closely together, I think it is important that we get to know each other better. I think it fair to say that with a few exceptions most of us are new to politics and will need to learn fast. Sometime in the not too distant future all of us will come against a problem that will seem insurmountable. It is then that knowing you have colleagues who you can turn to for support is so important.'

Green paused and looked around the room briefly letting his gaze settle on each and every one around the table.

'Now I'd like to ask Alastair to fill us in on what he has been able to find out about the country's finances. You all had an input to the manifest so you know what is expected from each of your departments but until you know what money is available, I can't ask you to prepare the department budget. Alastair, over to you.'

Alastair Frank remained seated and turned his gaze towards the room.

'Thank you, Richard. I will try and lay out the present situation. I have to say it is not a very pretty picture and considerably worse than I initially thought. Forgive me if I am teaching my granny to suck eggs as the saying goes but I would first like to give a very brief summary on how a country is financed.

'As you will all be aware the government doesn't have any money of its own. Any money that it spends comes from taxes, i.e. it comes from the pockets of the work force of the country. Every time you buy something which is VAT registered the government takes its cut. When you buy fuel for your car the government takes a cut. When you earn money or when you buy a house or buy shares or get interest on savings the government takes its cut. In fact, even when you die the government takes its cut. Sometimes the tax is called national insurance but this is a historical fudge by a previous government to try and disguise a tax rise. In addition, there are local taxes which are set by local authorities such as rates and occasionally a specific tax such as the TV licence used to fund the BBC. I think you get the picture. So practically everything the public does helps to fund the government. Let's look at this like the wages that you bring home but in the case of government the wages are legally extracted from someone else's pocket rather than from the profits of a company.'

Frank took a sip from the glass of water on the table in front of him before continuing.

'On the other side of the coin is the government liabilities. This is the money that all of us around this table will make available to our departments to spend. Whether it is on policing, the NHS, education, the armed forces, social security, care for the elderly, infrastructure spending, state pensions or refuge collection… the money has to be found out of the taxes collected. So, going back to my previous analogy, if the money coming in can be equated to an individual's wages the money going out can be equated to the household spending such as food, mortgage, heating, transport costs, capital expenses, holidays and all the other bills that households have. And just like with a household if the money coming in is less than the money being spent then the gap has to be made up by borrowing which brings me in a rather convoluted way to the crunch of the matter.

'If a country wants to borrow money it issues something called a government bond or in the case of the UK this is called a gilt. This is effectively an IOU to a financial institution for an amount of money. Of course, the financial institution will require to be paid interest on the loan. The amount of interest is generally dependant on the length of the loan but also critically on how comfortable the lender is that the money will be paid back. The more risk there is that a country will default on its commitment to repay a loan the higher the interest rate. It is something of an irony that the more difficulty a country has in paying back a loan the more interest it has to pay so there is less money to pay back the capital instigating a critical spiral of debt. Which is where we are today.'

Pausing again for effect, after a few seconds Frank continued.

'There are a number of rating agencies in the world that assess the ability of a country, or a business for that matter but let's keep to the country level, to repay their debts. Just before the election was called the UK's rating was reduced to a BB-rating which is into junk bond territory. I've had the chance since the election to look a bit closer at the level of debt that the last government managed to build up and I have to say I can understand the concerns of the rating agencies. There is no easy way of saying this but the United Kingdom is very close to bankruptcy. By that I mean we have a level of debt that is so high we are in the downward debt spiral.'

Cynthia Graeme interrupted. 'How can a country go bankrupt? All we need to do is increase taxes and reduce spending until we get more money in than we are paying out. Then we pay off the debt.'

'Ah, the old austerity fix. I agree in theory it should be as simple as you mention but the problem is that each gilt has an end date, i.e. the date when it has to be repaid. If there is insufficient money to repay the loan or the money that is available is potentially needed elsewhere then what normally happens is that as one gilt finishes another is taken out, so effectively the debt is rolled over. With a low credit rating the only way new financial institutions are willing to lend more money is if the interest rates are higher. At present the total debt that this country owes is close to 220% of the country's gross domestic product. Basically, we owe more than twice the total amount that the UK earns in a year. We've been there before. After the Napoleonic war for instance but then we had a growing economy and a high credit rating so we had time to grow the economy which increased the tax take and gradually the debt was reduced. And with time I'm convinced that with the right policies we can again get the finances back on track. The problem is we are very short of time. Within the next two years we have to refinance nearly £900 billion of debt which is nearly half the total GDP. We are already taking close to 50% of GDP in taxes so if we didn't spend any money for a year, we could solve the problem. But I suspect the public would get a bit upset if they suddenly found their pension or social security money stopped to say nothing of rubbish rotting in the streets or no health service.'

'What about re-privatising the railways or banks? That would generate a considerable sum.' This was from Jason Bhatia.

'There are also the overseas aid payments or the amount we still have to pay to Europe after the botched Brexit. If that isn't enough, we could reintroduce student loans and look very closely at the ridiculous salaries paid to some public bosses.

'Let's not forget the armed forces. We still pay almost 1% of GDP on our armed forces even after the last government took the axe to Trident replacement and the new fighters.'

Cynthia Graeme shot an accusing look at Jason Bhatia.

Richard Green interceded. 'Ladies and gentlemen. All cost saving measures will have to be considered. It is clear from what you have heard from Alastair that things are worse than we expected. What Alastair didn't tell you is that in addition to the financial deficit our foreign reserves have also nearly been completely exhausted. We still need to keep the country running and we need to make long term plans for improving the economy but in the short term we desperately need to find another source of revenue. Alastair and I will be giving this our priority in the coming months, basically taking the begging bowl around our gilt holders, but you all have the task to set your department budgets in such a way that makes previous austerity policies look like a walk in the park.'

Green continued, 'Sorry to put a damper on the election celebrations but the reality is that as we stand, we are looking at the UK defaulting on its commitments for the time in its history. The IMF were asked to assist in the 1970s after the then government had to go cap in hand to them for a mere £2.3 billion otherwise it is likely the UK would have defaulted then but we are a far cry away from that now. We need more than the IMF to save our bacon this time.'

'Perhaps we should just accept the situation and tell our creditors that we can't pay and force them to accept a rescheduling of the loans. If they don't like it, we declare a default. After all other countries default on a seemingly regular basis. Take Argentina for example.'

Gary Davies looked nervously around the table seemingly for support.

'At what cost?' Green shot back. 'Argentina has been a pariah on the world stage for the past 50 plus years. Its effectively been frozen out of the world capital markets and so has no way of controlling its economy. High inflation and even higher interest rates are the norm. They have had to link the Peso to the dollar to protect the currency otherwise it would be worthless. Basically, it is a basket case. Is that what you want for the UK?'

Frank looked directly at Gary Davies in an accusatory way.

'No of course not but from what I am hearing we may have no alternative.' Davies countered.

Richard Green continued, 'It is up to us to find an alternative. We have been elected because we promised a brighter future for Great Britain. And that is what I am determined to do. I am convinced that given time the policies set out in our manifesto will bring that brighter future. We just need to buy ourselves some time. Now I suggest we finish the meeting unless anyone else would like to make any suggestions and go back to your departments and start working on your budgets. Alastair will present the first budget of this administration in six weeks' time and by then all budgets will need to be presented, reviewed and accepted by myself and Alastair.

'And if anyone does have any ideas of how to pay back £900 billion by the end of next year, I'd love to hear from you. Meanwhile see you all at Number 10 on Tuesday when there will be, at least for that evening, no talk of budgets.'

With a smile and a nod around the table Richard Green stood up and left the room.

Chapter 10
February 2026

OEC Headquarters

Having just returned from a shareholders meeting Jim Simpson, the CEO of Oceanic Energy Company, threw off his jacket and reached for the bottle of a 12-year-old Glen Morangie single malt. Not normally one to have a drink before six o'clock in the evening, this day was not normal. Simpson always knew that it would be difficult to finance the development of the Caratacus field without support from the major oil companies but he naively thought that the promise of future riches would oil the wheels and keep the cash flowing. Perhaps if things had gone smoother. Multiple strikes and various development failures along the way to say nothing of the increase in interest rates on the company loans meant the project was considerably over budget and behind schedule. The financial reserves for the project were long since used up and OEC were eating into their overdraft facilities, something that had not gone unnoticed by OEC's investors. The special general meeting that Simpson had just finished chairing had not gone well and the pressure was now on Simpson to find further funds. It was looking increasingly like OEC would have to sell out at least some of the field to one of the oil majors after all.

As Simpson mulled over his next move whilst savouring the calming effects of the single malt his phone rang.

'Hello. Simpson, here.'

'Dad, have you seen the news?'

Something about the tone of his eldest son's voice rang warning bells in Simpson's mind.

'Not yet. I've just got back home after being the main course at a vulture feeding frenzy. Why, what's happened?'

'I really think you need to look at the news and then get yourself back to the office. Something of a disaster is taking place at Caratacus.' Ted Simpson's voice quivered. 'People have died, Dad.'

'What the hell do you mean, people have died.'

'Just look at the news.'

The phone went dead. With mounting alarm Simpson reached for the remote control and turned to the news channel. It was all there. The graphic pictures of the burnt-out drill rig, the lifeboats in the water, the standby vessel spraying water over the rig, helicopters flying around the rig presumably with other camera crews and the incessant commentary from the news anchor woman telling the world that the disaster had cost the lives of 15 people with more seriously injured. From what Simpson could hear the anchor woman was only mentioning the name of the drill rig and the rigs owners but hadn't picked up on the name Oceanic Energy. Simpson knew it would only be a matter of time before that changed and the spotlight would shift. After a few minutes Simpson had heard enough and after hitting the mute button on the television he reached for his phone and hit the speed dial for Clive Ridley, Oceanic's operations director. The phone was engaged but after the fourth attempt Ridley was on the phone.

'Jim, I've just been trying to get through to you. I assume you've heard the news?'

'Yes. Ted rang and I've just been watching the news. It looks like a bloody disaster out there. What do you know?'

'To be honest not much more than they are saying on the news. I have managed to talk to David Grant, the CEO of Saebo Drilling. They've set up an Emergency Control room in Aberdeen and am in touch with the Coastguards, police, medical facilities and pollution control. In addition, they've arranged media and relative response teams. It would appear from initial reports that the rig experienced a massive gas explosion but as yet no indications of cause. There is still confusion as to the number of dead and injured but the latest figure is 15 dead and many more injured. The death toll is expected to increase.'

'What's our involvement to date?'

'I'm at Heathrow as we speak on my way to Aberdeen. I'm due to arrive in three hours. In the meanwhile, we've mobilised our own media response team and prepared a holding statement which we will issue when the press latches on to our involvement. I would suggest you make your way to the office to be available when needed.'

As Ridley was talking Simpson could hear the loud speaker in the back ground calling the Aberdeen flight.

'I'm on my way. Who have we got in charge of the media response? You won't be aware yet but today we had a session with our investors and they were not happy. This is really going to upset them and how we handle the media could be critical to the next few months.'

'They've just called the flight so I have to go but in answer to your question, it's Jean Robertson.'

'That's a bit of a relief. If anyone can handle the pressure its Jean. I'll touch base with her when I arrive at the office. Meanwhile have a safe flight and give me a call when you get to the ER. Oh, and make sure that Saebo are told to keep to the script until we have had time to correlate our responses. What a mess.'

Simpson rang off. Taking a longing look at the amber liquid in the glass on the side board, still hardly touched, he reached for his jacket and car keys.

Chapter 11
February 2026

London OEC headquarters

'It is with deep regret that Oceanic Energy Company has to report that a large gas explosion occurred this afternoon on the Saebo Drilling Company's Jack up rig Triton. At the time of the incident the Triton was involved with operations on the Oceanic operated Caratacus oil Field. Early indications are that 17 people have lost their lives as a result of this tragedy and a further 17 people are seriously injured. Whilst all personnel have now been accounted for the death toll is expected to grow due to the serious nature of some of the injured. Our thoughts and sympathies go out to the families of the dead and injured. That is all for the time being. Further press statements will be made when we have additional information.'

Jean Robertson looked over the top of the rostrum in the hastily arranged press briefing room at the gathered ranks of Journalists. Even though she had made it clear at the start of the statement that she would not at this stage be answering questions, the room still erupted into a cacophony of sound as it seems every journalist present shouted out to her. Not someone that was easily intimidated Robertson gathered her prepared script and left the rostrum heading for an exit door to her left. She almost made it but a large bearded man was just that bit quicker and jumping up from his seat stood between Robertson and the door. Thrusting a microphone into her face he announced himself as being from the BBC and hastily asked if Oceanic knew what had caused the explosion. Before Robertson could respond or by pass the man, he continued by asking was it a terrorist act. Robertson brushed past him and went through the exit door but other journalists had picked up on the question and assuming that the BBC reporter knew something they didn't, before long were reporting the incident as a terrorist incident.

The next day at least three of the tabloid newspapers had headlines along the lines of "Terrorism on the high seas. 17 Dead". Reading the headlines Simpson turned to Jean Robertson who was sitting opposite him in his fifth floor office.

'How the hell did we go from an unfortunate accident to terrorism? No one said anything about terrorists and it's far too early to speculate on the cause of the accident. The HSE are only just mobilising to the remains of the rig to start their investigations and until they are finished anything else is speculation. Has Saebo got any further in their own investigations?'

'They've had the chance to talk to some of the survivors. The most senior survivor was a guy called Jim Stieger who had the good fortune to have been off shift at the time of the incident. The OIM and Jim's opposite number were in the control room when the explosion happened and their bodies were picked up out of the water late yesterday.

'According to Jim, the gas release came for a valve on the drill deck. The OIM had managed to shut the subsea safety valve so although still a massive fireball when the gas ignited the quantity of gas was limited. This saved the rig from collapse and protected the well. We still don't know what ignited the gas or how it came to be released in the first place but hopefully the HSE investigation will get closer to the facts. Jim also witnesses the sinking of the lifeboat three which had turned back to pick up survivors. The lifeboat was hit by the falling derrick but amazingly, although it was dragged below the surface and suffered flooding due to the open hatches, it had sufficient buoyancy to re surface. Had that boat sank or been trapped by the derrick the loss of life would have been even worse than reported.'

'With a death toll now of 17 and more expected it is bad enough as it is. I can't imagine what the families of the victims are going through. When things have settled down, we need to make sure they are looked after.'

Simpson looked tired having not slept in 36 hours. His shirt top button was undone and his tie missing. Jean had never seen him look anything but well presented. She realised how hard the incident and particularly the loss of life had hit him.

'A word of caution, Jim, if I may.' Jean looked into the tired eyes. 'This is going to end up in the courts and depending on what the HSE find, OEC could be looking at some serious allegations. Potentially criminal proceedings could be brought against you and other senior OEC personnel for neglect or worse. So, whilst I understand you want to do what's right for the families of the deceased you have to be very careful that you don't expose yourself. I would definitely make sure you discuss any action with legal before doing anything.'

'Yes of course. Thanks for the sound advice. It looks like we'll be condemned either way. If we open up to the families it could be used against us in the courts and if we don't, we will be portrayed by the press as heartless. Meanwhile our financial position is precarious. I had hoped to get one of the majors to help us out but I can't see anyone touching us with a barge pole until this has been settled. Any idea on what our insurance position is?'

'We've got people looking at it. We have full cover for accidents but if it is shown to be a terrorist action then we will not be covered. Also of course we will not be covered for consequential losses so the cost of delays will not be covered. From that perspective though we have been lucky. Before the accident took place, the Triton had completed ten wells and the 11th well was shut in before the explosion. We only need ten wells to meet our early oil delivery commitments so the incident shouldn't affect the first oil date assuming that we are able to clear the wreckage off the rig without damaging any of the subsea completions.'

'I think thankful for small mercies comes to mind on that.' Simpson smiled for the first time since receiving the phone call from Ted, what seemed like a lifetime ago. 'Assuming then that we don't have any further fabrication delays we could still be pumping oil by this time next year. All we have to do until then is somehow keep the wolves from the door. Without any further injection of cash from the financiers and without the oil majors we need to find another source of cash and soon. I think it's time that our austere finance director earned his crust. Time, I think to talk to Sidney. Thanks, Jean, for all your help. Best get back to the press room to see if anything new has come in and to formulate another press bulletin. As we have seen, if we don't keep feeding the beast it just makes it up, not always to our advantage.'

Jean stood up and taking her coffee cup with her left the room. Simpson rang his secretary and asked her to arrange a meeting with Sidney Bach, OEC's finance director. Ten minutes later Bach was sitting in the chair recently vacated by Jean Robertson.

'Right, Sidney, time for some blue sky thinking. All we need to do is to work out how to get hold of two hundred and fifty million dollars within the next eight weeks. For someone of your calibre that ought to be straight forward.'

Simpson looked over the top of his coffee cup and smiled to ease the tension he felt emanating from his finance director. Sidney Bach had worked with Jim

Simpson from before the time he'd taken on the role of CEO of OEC; when all they had to worry about was how much profit they were going to make out of their latest property investments. A pessimistic person by nature Bach didn't have the personality to handle the sort of risk-taking that was the hall mark of Simpson. Bach always seemed nervous when Simpson laid a financial quandary at his door, almost as if he thought that Simpson was somehow testing him. Simpson for his part had long ago realised that he needed someone that could counter balance his sometimes-impulsive actions and Bach was the ideal candidate.

'Ah, only two hundred and fifty million. After Monday's meeting with the backers and yesterday's explosion I figured we'd need considerably more than that. As you know it is still a year before we can realistically see a positive cash flow and, in that time, we have some pretty big bills to pay. If, on top of what we know about, the company gets sued over the Saebo incident then I would think two hundred and fifty won't be sufficient.'

Bach adjusted his Armani bi focal glasses before reaching for his own coffee cup.

'I'm happy to go over the figures again but I'm working on the assumption that despite the reaction we got on Monday at least three of the backers, when push comes to the shove, will be persuaded to increase their lending threshold. I'm also going to have a chat with our Norwegian and Korean fabrication friends to basically tell them that we will be revising the payment schedule such that we can delay the biggest part of their costs until after the oil starts to flow. They won't like it and it will probably cost us more in the long run but I have it on good authority that they have good lines of credit they can access if needed. The British will be more difficult to arm twist. I'm not convinced that their finances are any better than ours. I'm particularly worried about Saunders Marine who seem to be having their own problems. Without the Kalevala all we have is a pile of very expensive infrastructure rusting away on the quay side rather than sitting on Caratacus pumping oil. So, whilst there are some suppliers, we can arm twist, others have to be paid in accordance with the terms of the contract if we don't want the whole project to go tits up.'

'I heard something about Saunders Marine. We always knew we were taking a big risk to put all our eggs in one basket. Just how bad are things with Kalevala' Bach refrained from mentioning that he had strongly advised against relying on only one offshore contractor that could install the Caratacus infrastructure?'

'I truly don't know. They issue their monthly reports from which you would think that everything is hunky dory but then I hear from our Korean site team that there was an explosion on the Kalevala only last week. On its own that would be bad enough but they seem to be having the same difficulties with strikes and unexplained mechanical failures that we've been having. Apart from running out of money and now this recent Saebo disaster, the Kalevala is my biggest worry. I know you didn't want to be tied to a single contractor but the reality is that by using Kalevala we save something like one hundred million dollars in offshore fabrication costs even after we pay Saunders's exorbitant price. But if it puts your mind to rest, I didn't just ignore your concerns. I do have a backup plan if needed albeit not one I really want to utilise unless there really is no option. I'm afraid I'm not at liberty right now to say any more but in light of your previous concerns you have a right to know there is a backup.'

'I'll sleep a lot easier when I know that ship has sailed and is on its way to Europe I have to say. But going back to your original request and assuming you can limit the capital shortfall to two hundred and fifty million then I think I can re-negotiate with the banks our overdraft limits. At present we are not allowed to go above six hundred million without breaching the banking covenant. Had we managed to get the investors to stump up more capital we would come in just below the six hundred mark sometime next year. Thereafter the positive cash flow would reduce the deficit until in four years' time, apart from ongoing maintenance and operational costs which is equivalent to about eighteen dollars per barrel of oil pumped, everything else is profit. Without the extra capital I had estimated we would peak out at nine hundred and fifty million dollars and have already been in discussions with the banks. They are not stupid and see the potential future cash flow but are also not going to let us just increase our banking limit without some pain. They are talking for the full nine hundred and fifty million of increasing the interest rate by 0.75%. That puts about one hundred and forty million on the project cost. If we only need to go up to eight hundred and fifty million, I think I can get them down to 0.5% which saves about fifty million dollars. This is still ninety million more than our present cost projections but at least we can keep going and remain independent.'

'Thanks, Sidney. Not nice but needs must. Please go back to the banks with a proposal and let me know when you have something positive on the table. Meanwhile I'll get to work on renegotiating with the Norwegians and Koreans.'

Simpson got up to indicate the meeting was over. Finishing his now cold coffee Bach left the office leaving Simpson to muse over his next move. Picking up the phone Simpson asked his secretary to put him through to Rostella S.p.A in Italy.

Chapter 12
March 2026

The Kremlin

At 7:30 in the evening it was already getting dark in the Odintsovsky District of Moscow. President Khurin was sitting in a comfortable leather arm chair in front of a blazing log fire with a small glass of beer in his hand. Once a heavy drinker Khurin now limited his consumption of alcohol to a few beers. Too many times as an aspiring politician he had been lured into over consumption leading to some indiscretions which he went on to regret. As Russian president he was also very aware of other occupants of his chair who let alcohol be their down fall. So, a couple of beers and then onto water or orange juice even when, as today, he was amongst old friends.

Sitting to Khurin's right was Igor Antipov also with a beer in his right hand. Wearing an open necked blue shirt, light tan slacks and light brown leather shoes all hand made in Jermaine Street, London, Antipov gazed into the fire enjoying watching the flames dance around the apple tree wood that Khurin preferred to use. To Antipov's right sat Boris Romanov. More casually dress in jeans and a red polo shirt, Romanov was the Russian defence minister. At 60 years of age and with greying curly hair he had the appearance of someone's favourite uncle as he savoured a 15-year-old Belvedere Vodka; but when it came to Romanov looks were certainly deceptive. It would probably not be an exaggeration to say that Romanov was responsible for more deaths than any other single person alive in Russia. He would normally not be seen in public without wearing the full uniform of a Marshal of the Russian Federation but Khurin had made it clear that today's meeting was to be off the record and discreet.

The fourth person in the room was Vitali Nikolaev, a much younger man than the other three at only 45 years of age, Nikolaev was the Russian Foreign Minister. As he sat looking around the room at the other occupants, he wished he could light up one of his Moscow City cigars but as his father told him, to make one mistake was human, to repeat the mistake was stupid. Many years ago, he had made the mistake of lighting a cigar in the presence of Khurin and still had the emotional scars to show for it. Khurin loathed any form of tobacco be it a pipe, cigarette or cigar and woe betide anyone that smoked in his presence. The strength of loathing was probably irrational but having watched his father slowly die from emphysema after a lifetime of smoking cheap Russian black cigarettes, a lasting impression had been made on Khurin's psyche. So Nikolaev made do with sucking a nicotine substitute. At his own choice he was the only one in the room without a drink.

The house in which the four men had gathered was in Novo-Ogaryovo and was one of the official residences of President Khurin. The unofficial meeting had been instigated by Khurin at the beginning of his presidency and was intended to be a forum where the most sensitive topics could be discussed, off the record and away from any prying eyes and ears. As all four members of the Russian government lived in and around the Novo-Ogaryovo estate it was a convenient location to meet without arousing any suspicion from some members of the Duma that were not quite so like-minded as the four men in the room. It was easy to forget at times that Russia was still a democracy and that the Russian government was still accountable to the people, something that Khurin and his close band of friends found irritating but manageable. Not everyone in the Russian parliament, called the State Duma, supported Khurin believing he was leading the Russian Federation to disaster by his treatment of the west. They were not organised and impotent but Khurin knew that things could change very quickly if the people turned against him.

Carefully placing his glass on the table in front of the fire, Khurin reached for the file that he had been reading before being joined by the others.

'Gentlemen, I have just received a report from our friend in England,' he said without preamble.' It would appear that the country's finances are in a worse situation than we had hoped and it very much looks like the British government may have to default on its debts or at the very least go cap in hand to the international Monetary Fund for a bail out. Either way is good for us. Our people in the IMF will ensure that if Britain does seek help from them, they will pay a high price and if they default, they will be cut off from the credit markets for a long time. Either way they will be forced to make serious cuts in their spending plans. It is highly unlikely the people will accept any significant changes to their precious welfare state even if they can't afford it so at least initially savings will have to come from elsewhere. Our friend in Britain is already encouraging cuts to be made in the armed forces citing the low level of international tension that exists at present. On this latter point our use of social media to populate this latter message has been very successful particularly amongst the young whom I'm told believe everything that is published on Facebook and Google. However, the report does cite one area of concern that hasn't been considered to date.'

Pausing to take a sip of his beer, Khurin continued,

'Our friend in Britain has informed that Britain needs either to find nearly a trillion dollars by the end of next year or at least gain the confidence of the international money markets to allow the debts to be rolled over without a massive increase in interest rates. It is clear that finding that sort of money is not a viable option but if Britain can convince the markets that the money will be found in the foreseeable future, then debt roll over will be much more likely and even though we will use all our influence to encourage the markets to impose a high cost on such debt roll over, we don't control the whole market.'

From the looks on the faces of the other men in the room this was not new to them. The use of the financial markets as a means of control had first been practiced against Russia by the Americans to such an extent that some Russians still considered that this was the reason for the collapse of the old Soviet Union. That was not the view of the men around the room who were much better informed and knew that the old Soviet Union had collapsed because the ideology just didn't work, but it was in their interest to keep this from the public.

'The question that has been asked is how can Britain convince the financial markets that they are low risk. Clearly had the socialists remained in power this would not have been possible so the first potential problem was the Progressive Conservative Party winning the election. This on its own shouldn't have made any difference at least in the period that we are interested in. No matter who is in charge the economics are still awful and our experts have estimated that even with an aggressive austerity programme it will be at least five years before there is any sign of an improvement in the economy; and they don't have five years. There is however one major danger on the horizon that has been flagged up by our friend in Britain.'

Three faces changed from a look of relaxed contentment to one of interest. Khurin took another sip of his beer, replaced the glass and opened the file on his lap. As could have been predicted it was Antipov that broke the silence.

'Alexi, we've been over this many times and always we have come to the same conclusion. Great Britain is broke and is not going to be able to put up any resistance. Without Great Britain taking the lead the rest of Europeans will just capitulate and the Americans are too interested in China. Boris, tell Alexi what you told me as we walked here this evening.'

'Igor is right, Alexi. Yesterday we sent two Blackjack bombers to fly over the north of Scotland. This is something we have been doing quite frequently to test the state of preparedness of Great Britain's defences. Normally we get to about 12 miles of the coast and get turned back by one or two Typhoon fighters. This time we were only challenged by radio. No planes appeared. Of course, it could be a ploy to lull us into a false sense of security but with everything else we know it is much more likely that the RAF either don't have the planes or pilots to make the intercept. We know from our agents that the existing fleet of planes are sorely in need of maintenance and that defence cuts by the previous UK government mean funds for maintenance has not been available. I can't see how Britain will be a risk if they can't even put up planes to defend their own country.'

Khurin continued looking down in order to remind himself of what was contained within the report before responding,

'Igor, Boris, what you say is true but what would happen if Great Britain suddenly found a reliable and constant source of funds that would be sufficient to convince its creditors that they needn't worry about a default?'

'That would not be in our best interest. Our strategy regarding expanding our borders is based on not being challenged at least until we have consolidated the new territories. Our own armed forces are on the face of it formidable but we don't have the resources to sustain a military conflict if we are seriously challenged. Everything is dependent on the impotency of the west until we have the missile defence system in place.'

Romanov leant forward and placed another log on the fire.

'Surely, though, you are being hypothetical. We have been closely watching Great Britain for the last five years and nothing has indicated they have any cash left. If they had the socialists would have spent it by now. Besides we have sources within the British treasury that keeps us informed on the state of their finances and nothing to date has indicated they are anything but broke.'

Vitali Nikolaev leant forward. Until now he had remained silent. As the youngest member of the group he was also the most junior. As foreign secretary he theoretically had control of all the foreign policies of the Russian Federation but in reality, he just did as the other three in the room dictated.

'If I may intercede. It is true that Great Britain doesn't have any reserves to pay the debtors but it doesn't need to, provided it can demonstrate it will have the ability to pay? In that case the debtors will roll over the dept at similar interest rates which will allow the British time to correct the economy and slowly reduce the deficit. I assume President Khurin that you have received the same information that came into my possession last night regarding the oil discovery recently announced by Oceanic Energy?'

'You are correct, Vitali. According to the reports a small British company called Oceanic Energy Company has made a major oil discovery in the British sector of the North Sea. We of course knew about this but what wasn't clear until now was the scale of the discovery. How and why we missed this important information is something we will need to find out but it was only after a serious incident forced Oceanic to issue a number of clarification press statements that the size of the field became apparent. According to our information this discovery is bigger than all the other North Sea reserves combined and of similar size to some of the biggest fields in the middle east. Even if that is an exaggeration it is clearly a big find. What's more the field development programme is well under way and on target to start supplying oil by the middle of next year. Assuming this is the case then the UK treasury will be receiving a massive tax windfall in the form of petroleum revenue tax just at the time when the UK Gilts need to be repaid or rolled over. This tax windfall will continue for the foreseeable future and guarantee an income for the UK. Gilt holders will see this and fall over themselves to lend more money. What we will see is a government committed to reducing waste and spending on social services but also a government that has firmly stated that it wants to put Great Britain back onto the world stage, a government that will not have to worry about servicing its debt in the short term so in consequence a government that will find the resources to re vitalise its armed forces.'

Khurin paused to let the others absorb this new information.

'I understand your concerns, Alexi, but we are only a couple of years away from fulfilling our plan. Even if what you say is true the British will concentrate any extra money to reduce their debt unless they get wind of our intensions and we have been very careful to ensure that our ultimate goal is only known by a very small number of people. I would expect defence spending to be bottom of the list of priorities. The British would have to start spending the money now if they are to be in a place that they can challenge us in two years' time; and without any indication of our intent there is no reason for them to dramatically increase defence spending.'

Antipov sat back in his chair with a quizzical look on his face.

'In my experience we should never underestimate the British when it comes to military might. History is full of defeated countries that did just that. Whilst Igor is correct that the logical course of action would be for the British to pay down its debt before increasing defence spending, he perhaps is looking at this from a Russian perspective. To the British, being without a strong military is like you or I walking down the street without our trousers on. They feel exposed. The pacifists have been in charge for the last five years but with the recent election results the British have reverted to their norm and I can imagine one of the first things they will want to do is strengthen the military. If they have the means to do that, and this windfall could easily give them the means, then I would fully expect military spending to increase at least to a level where they feel secure. Whether that will be enough to thwart our plans I can't say but it could be enough to show leadership to the rest of Europe. I think we need to take this risk seriously.'

Nikolaev wondered if he had overstepped his position but the nods from the others in the room confirmed his analysis had been recognised.

'Thank you for your observations.' Khurin looked serious. 'I fully agree that this is a risk to our endeavours. Maybe not a fatal risk but if we can neutralise the risk then we should. It is clear that we can't undiscover the oil field so how else can we prevent the British from getting this windfall?'

Romanov looked thoughtful as he swirled the clear liquid around in the glass watching the partially melted ice cubes dance around the glass.

'Perhaps we don't need to undiscover the oil.' He looked up and directed his gaze towards Khurin. 'All we have to do is delay the flow of the oil to such an extent that confidence by the financiers is shaken. The British need that confidence if they are to start spending on the military in time to prevent us from putting our plans into operation. Without a clear timetable for the funds to start flowing the financiers will have to price in the added risk to their gilt roll-over by increased interest rates. Britain will then have to be more prudent in its spending. Whilst I am not so naïve as to think we can stop the flow of oil indefinitely we should be able to delay it. All we need is a clear run to recover the territories of the former Soviet Union and there after we don't need to worry about Great Britain.'

'You are probably right but how do you propose we can delay such a project?'

'Let me look into it in a bit more detail but I am sure there is an Achilles heel. There always is; it just needs to be found.'

'Then we will leave that problem in your capable hands, Boris, but don't leave it too long in finding a solution. There is too much effort already expended on our plan for it to be thwarted at this stage. We meet again in two weeks' time. Please have a proposal by then.'

Khurin sat back in his chair.

'Now onto other business.'

Chapter 13
March 2026

Scotland

The Tupolev TU-160 bomber named Petr Deinekin took off from its base in Murmansk and headed towards the Artic. The bomber was the newest to enter service in the Russian air force and was capable of supersonic flight. Known by the west as The Blackjack, it was designed as a stealth bomber and had the ability to deliver nuclear bombs nearly anywhere in the world. It had already been used in the Syrian conflict when its pay load was of a more conventional high explosive nature but it had also been used to launch cruise missiles. However, the present mission did not require a heavy ordinance and with no defensive capabilities the plane was no deadlier than a commercial passenger plane except for one thing. The Petr Deinekin was full of electronic surveillance equipment and its mission was to continue to probe the defensive capabilities of the western nations.

Flying north from Murmansk the Tupolev passed the northern most tip of Norway before turning to the west. Careful to stay to the north of the Norwegian air space the plane continued west until, approximately half way between the Norwegian mainland and Iceland, the plane changed course and headed south. Although able to achieve a top speed of twice the speed of sound the present cruising speed was a more sedate 530 miles per hour at a height of 30,000 metres intended to extend the flying time to 15 hours, more than enough to arrive at its destination, perform its task and return to Russia. Its crew of four were used to this long and tedious journey and spent most of the time monitoring instruments and using their air to air radar to detect other aircraft. In the days of the old Soviet Union the temptation to sit back and read a book or even have a glass or two of vodka would have been too great but this was the new Russian military and such a temptation never crossed the minds of the professionals that sat at the controls of the impressive aircraft. Such sloppiness would see them quickly at the back of the unemployment list with no hope of redundancy pay assuming they avoided being shipped straight to a military prison.

This was not the first time they had taken this flight path and despite the planes almost stealth capability the crew had no doubt that the various western air forces along the flight path would be on the alert for their passage. In fact, for most of the journey the plane had not made any attempt to hide its passage even reporting in to air traffic control in both Norway and Iceland. They had been joined briefly by an American F35A Lightning as they approached Iceland but after a brief exchange of pleasantries the F35 returned to base and the Tupolev continued on its journey southwards.

As it approached the north coast of Scotland its on board surveillance equipment picked up the tell-tale sign of a radar tracking beam. The radar frequency was recorded and compared to previous recordings confirming that this radar tracking station was the one based in the Shetland Islands. The information told the plane's crew that the radar station had not been upgraded for at least seven years, information that would be fed back to the Russian military intelligence to add to all the other information gathered on a weekly basis from these flights close to the UK airspace. The crew of the Tupolev were fully expecting that the British RAF would soon arrive on the scene and ensure they stayed outside the British 12-mile exclusive air space as had happened on previous occasions. The British had 12 F35 fighter aircraft permanently based at RAF Lossiemouth to defend the country from an airborne invasion from the north. The last time the Petr Deinekin had made this run they had been surprised when no planes had challenged them and they had penetrated the British airspace as far as the mainland when, detecting an anti-aircraft missile battery radar lock, they rapidly turned back out to sea. The reason for today's flight was to see if the previous non-arrival of the British air force was a one-off event or whether for whatever reason the British no longer had the capability to challenge the Russian bomber.

Continuing south towards Scotland the Tupolev entered the 12-mile zone. The Captain informed the rest of the crew who were now on full alert. They knew they were playing a game of cat and mouse that could turn nasty particularly as they had entered the 12-mile limit without seeking or receiving permission. By violating British airspace in such a way, they could be shot down without warning as a potential threat to the security of the country. Whilst it was highly unlikely this action would be taken without at least some form of warning by the British it would not have been the first time that such action had been taken. Only recently the Israeli air force had downed a Russian military jet that strayed too close to its boarders but the powers that be in Moscow had concluded it was highly unlikely Britain would want to risk a diplomatic incident that such action would incur.

Ignoring the radio requests from the British ground control to turn around the plane continued south, but about three miles from where the previous flight had picked up the anti-aircraft missile station radar the plane veered to the south east. Flying down the eastern coast of the Shetland Islands at a distance of five miles the Tupolev continued south. It wasn't until it got to within 15 miles of the Scottish mainland that its on board radar detection system picked up the first of two F35 fighter aircraft approaching at speed from the South. By this time the radio messages were getting increasingly aggressive and the crew on the Tupolev were getting increasingly nervous.

Having pushed his luck as far as he was willing the pilot opened the radio channel and informed air traffic control that his instruments had malfunctioned and he only now realised he was in British air space. It was neither original or believable but it was all part of the game. Turning the Tupolev to the east and then to the north east the Petr Deinekin increased speed to put as much space as possible between itself and the British fighters but within minutes the F35s were alongside. Looking across from the Tupolev's flight deck the pilot gave the British pilot of the lead F35 the thumbs up and continued to leave the 12-mile zone. The F35s stayed with the Russian bomber for a further 15 minutes until they were satisfied the threat was over before turning back to RAF Lossiemouth.

When the Tupolev had returned to its base in Murmansk its crew immediately reported their findings to military intelligence who passed the information up the chain of command until a report landed on the desk of Boris Romanov. Reading the report Romanov smiled. The mission had been a deliberate attempt to see if the previous report of a lack of action by the British air force was a one off or systematic. It was clear that the British could still put planes in the air but only as a last resort, an obvious sign of their weakness. If they couldn't afford to put planes in the air to protect their homeland, they would not be able to mount any opposition to any Russian operation. Now all he had to do was find a way to neutralise the threat from Oceanic energy.

Meanwhile three thousand miles away in a secret airfield on the Shetland islands, a unique and revolutionary new fighter plane was being pushed into its heavily camouflaged hanger. The plane code named 'Dragon' had been developed by BAE ltd, a British defence contractor, specifically for the British air force. Smarting after losing out to the Navy for funds as a result of the two new aircraft carriers that had come into service five years before, the air force high command had secretly entered into a contract with BAE to develop the new plane. Fully aware that the then government would never condone such an investment, the money for the development had to be filtered from other areas. The resultant prototype plane had now been handed over to the RAF for testing. To date only a single Dragon class plane existed and the savings from other areas of the RAF budget was insufficient to allow mass production, however the latest test had exceeded all expectations. Being a VTOL or vertical take-off and landing aircraft, it did not need a big runway to operate from and so could be based practically anywhere; but it was the planes manoeuvrability, speed and stealth capabilities that set it apart from other aircraft.

The prototype had deliberately been based in Scotland as the RAF was fully aware of the Russians use of the Blackjack to investigate British air defences so they decided to turn the tables on the Russians and use the Dragon to investigate the Blackjacks defences. The results were better than they could have anticipated. Unbeknown to the crew of the Blackjack, during the whole time the Russian plane was approaching the British Isles to the time the F35s arrived the Dragon had been on its tail.

Chapter 14
February 2026

Naples

As a major player in the offshore construction market Rostella S.p.A. had been one of the original bidders for the installation of the Caratacus offshore facilities. At that time the platform topsides which contained all the production facilities, accommodation for the crew members, the drilling equipment and all the utilities support equipment were separate modules of much smaller weight than the final design. The modules could all be installed by the Rostella operated Biglift1, a similar crane vessel in looks and design to the Kalevala but of smaller capacity. With two 10,000t cranes the size of modules was limited by the crane capacity. The drawback of smaller modules was that they required a support frame to be installed first and then all the other modules had to be installed on top of the support frame. Each module could not be any bigger than the crane vessel capacity and after installation would have to be connected together. Piping, electrics and access ways between modules all have to be installed offshore and at a cost of ten times onshore labour it increases the overall development cost and time.

    The Kalevala had been designed to avoid all this as the whole topsides could be lifted as a single unit. Rostella had bid a lower price for the installation of the smaller modules but when the cost savings for a single module versus multiple modules were considered, the Kalevala was considerably cheaper and hence the contract was awarded to Saunders Marine Solutions. Paglia had mentioned the risk associated with having a single supplier of the installation service but Simpson hadn't become a multi-millionaire by avoiding risk.

    The phone call from Jim Simpson had been half expected but had still caught Marco Paglia somewhat off guard. He knew the capacity of the Kalevala and had experienced first-hand, not only in the Caratacus contract but in a number of other contracts, that such a vessel, if proven, would be a game changer in the industry. This was one of the main reasons he had wanted to get out of offshore construction and concentrate on his transportation business but the Italian government had blocked such a move. His conundrum was what to do next. Consulting with his closest advisers and board members he realised that he had to invest to compete with Kalevala but he did not have the resources to build a similar vessel and besides there just wasn't the work for two such vessels. His solution came from an unusual source.

One day driving home from his office Paglia drove past a new road being built. The traffic was diverted around the construction site to allow access for two cranes to lift a prefabricated bridge into place. At each end of the bridge a crane was connected and slowly the bridge was lifted. When high enough to pass over its support structure the cranes edged sideways whilst holding the load until the bridge was over its supports. The bridge was then lowered onto its supports. Paglia stopped the car in the middle of the road and ignoring the angry reaction of the other Italian drivers expressed in the usual way by use of the horn, he stood and watched the cranes manoeuvring. He only observed the operation for a few minutes before getting back into the car and continuing his journey but the seed of an idea was already sprouting. By the time he had arrived home he was convinced that if a twin crane operation using two different cranes worked onshore then why not offshore. Why not use his two largest crane vessels, one at either end of the integrated Caratacus topside module? The combined capacity of Rostella's largest two crane vessels was thirty thousand tonnes compared to the Caratacus topside module weight of thirty-two thousand tonnes but for a small investment he could easily upgrade the two vessels to give the required capacity.

Convinced he had an answer to the challenge posed by Kalevala, Paglia went to his engineering department and asked them to analyse the proposal. The initial reaction was negative. Two floating objects moving at different rates and in different directions due to wave action but being attached to a single load would cause the whole system to become unstable with the risk of a catastrophic result. But Paglia was not one to accept a no without 100% evidence so he instructed his engineers to investigate fully, without any preconceptions, and report back. A few thousand manhours of analysis later and much to the surprise of the sceptical engineers they had been able to advise Paglia that theoretically a lift using two crane vessels was feasible albeit considerably more sensitive to inclement weather than a single crane vessel lift.

The next step was to demonstrate that the two crane vessels could be upgraded to increase their capacity. This proved to be easier than proving the two-crane vessel scenario and within a few weeks a fully engineered solution was available. Certainly, it would cost money but a fraction of the cost of building a new ship.

Wasting no time Paglia arranged a presentation to the industry. The solution for lifting larger modules was no longer in the hands of one company but Rostella could compete on equal terms with Saunders Marine. All very well but whilst Rostella was presenting a proposal that hadn't been proven and, just like the engineers employed by Paglia, the offshore construction business was full of risk averse engineers from the same stable, Saunders Marine was presenting a proven proposal albeit at a higher capacity. In addition, the market for super heavy modules was not that big and all Rostella had done by presenting an alternative proposal was give confidence for the oil companies to build bigger but still use Saunders with the knowledge that they now had a back stop. Until Rostella had proven the concept in anger so to speak the market would not trust him with a contract but without a contract Rostella couldn't prove the concept. It was a classic catch 22 situation.

The question that next faced Paglia was how did he get someone to trust him with a contract. He tried bidding on work at a lower and lower price but whenever the risk element was added on, he could never win against Saunders Marine single lift vessel concept. What he needed was to find a way to remove the Kalevala from the market so that the back stop had to be triggered.

Having been in the offshore industry for a long time he knew the way the oil companies costed their developments and also suspected that OEC Plc were in a difficult financial position. He sensed an opportunity. The offshore development had already been delayed by two years. How much more of a delay could OEC plc stand before they ran out of money? He suspected that they couldn't survive another year's delay and with the Kalevala due to arrive on location in August of 2026 he just had to facilitate a few months delay to the fabrication. Such a sensitive heavy lift couldn't be performed once the summer season in the North Sea had passed so if the Kalevala didn't arrive before the middle of September 2026 the installation of the Caratacus facilities would have to be delayed until the following year, a situation clearly unacceptable to OEC Plc.

Paglia took two decisions that would have long term consequences. The first was to arrange for his crane vessels to be upgraded at a cost of nearly fifty million dollars, money he had to borrow against his freight business assets; the second was to contact someone from the old days when he worked in the port area. Quietly putting the word out, he soon found someone that was willing to assist with his problem.

Most people when they think of organised crime in Italy automatically think of the Mafia but the Mafia is only one such criminal syndicate mainly based around Sicily. In Naples the Mafia equivalent is the Camorra. Unlike the Mafia which has a very hierarchal structure, the Camorra has a flat organisational structure meaning that there are many bosses of different families that sometime work together and often fight against each other. Paglia had kept close ties with one such family from his days in the port. Negotiations followed and a price was agreed. The unwritten but nevertheless enforceable contract called for everything to be done to delay the Kalevala but without injury or loss of life. Under no circumstances could Paglia's name be associated with any actions that may come as a result of the contract and payment for the work would be through multiple offshore companies. Paglia didn't want to know or care how the contract was fulfilled but whilst stage payments would be made full payment would only be forthcoming once the Kalevala arrival date in the North Sea slipped beyond 15 September 2026. The contract had been agreed in August 2025 and since then a series of incidents had caused delays to the Kalevala programme, the latest of which was the explosion in the forward hull section.

The Camorra family organising the disruptions had been very careful to ensure that they used a different person to perform each act of sabotage to prevent any pattern being detected by the authorities and so far, they had been successful in causing delay without putting lives at risk. Unfortunately for them they had underestimated the Korean's ability to find solutions to problems so were getting more and more desperate in the actions taken. Using explosions in the ship was a sign of their desperation. Any explosive leaves a signature which would soon be detected by the authorities if they chose to look for it. The hope and expectation were that the Koreans would blame the explosion on an accident and not carry out a full investigation. They almost got away with it.

The phone call from Jim Simpson was proof that the Camorra's actions were bearing fruit. OEC Plc were not yet ready to abandon Saunders Marine but the mere fact that Simpson had made contact to determine the availability of his crane vessels indicated to Paglia that his reading of the situation was correct. One more push should do it but he was running out of time. Having put the phone down after assuring Simpson he would revert with availability within the week, he picked up the phone again and dialled the number of his Camorra friend.

Chapter 15
March 2026

London Downing Street

The glass in the hand of Richard Green resembled one containing a sparkling wine but in reality, it contained coloured sparkling water. Whilst he enjoyed a drink, since becoming prime minister he considered it prudent to keep a sober head at all times. Alastair Frank had no such concerns and his glass, now half empty, had been filled with Denbies Greenfield sparkling wine. Produced on the south facing side of the North Downs it was an English sparkling wine of equal quality to those wines produced in that part of France which had a monopoly on the name Champagne. As well as being a British wine it was also cheaper than the French equivalent and although a few pounds here and there would make no difference to the bigger financial picture, Richard was very much aware how it was the little things, if leaked to the press, that could sway the public opinion.

'I saw on the news the tragedy that happened in the North Sea the other day. Just what you needed at this time. What's the latest death toll?'

Frank had a genuine expression of concern on his face.

'Probably the best person to talk to about that is Cynthia. As Home Secretary she is involved with the day-to-day operations but from my discussion with her earlier it appears that no one else has died in the last twenty-four hours so it appears that 19 will be the final figure. The drill rig owners, a company called Saebo Drilling, are Norwegian. I understand that there were three Brits amongst the dead and a couple of Danes but it appears that most of the fatalities were Norwegian citizens. Cynthia is in contact with the Norwegian and Danish authorities to make arrangement for the repatriation of the bodies of the dead and has instigated a full investigation by the Health and Safety Executive jointly with the Norwegians. As the rig was Norwegian registered but working in UK waters it was felt prudent to have a joint investigation.'

Green ran his hand through his short hair in an action that Frank had realised indicated that he found the subject difficult to talk about. In poker it would have been called a tell.

'I saw your press conference a couple of nights ago. It can't have been easy but for what it's worth I think you hit the right notes.'

Frank briefly put his hand on Green's shoulder;

'Do we have any ideas yet of what caused the explosion?'

'Not yet but its early days. The burnt-out rig was only accessible to the investigators two nights ago and the first priority was obviously to recover bodies. From what I can gather some of the bodies were so badly burnt that identification will require dental records. The only thing that we can be grateful for was that it could have been an awful lot worse. Apparently, there were over 80 people on the rig when the accident happened.'

'Then let's be thankful for small mercies.'

'You know what is the saddest and most ironic aspect? The reason why the incident was not a lot worse, akin to the Deepwater Horizon incident that occurred in the Gulf of Mexico a few years back, was that the drill rig manager managed to shut the subsea isolation valve before the explosion took place. In doing so he put himself directly in the area of maximum risk. He was one of those killed by the explosion and whose body has yet to be identified. Without that action we would be looking at not only considerably more casualties but a pollution event that would make the Torrey Canyon look like a spill at your local garage.'

'I repeat, let's be thankful for small mercies. A brave man. It's all too easy to forget the dangers that the offshore industry has to manage in order that we can put petrol in our cars.'

A sad smile played across Frank's handsome face. Green shrugged his shoulders to indicate a change in the conversation.

'I know we said that we wouldn't discuss budgets this evening but have you been able to make any progress on the deficit reduction?'

'I've had discussions with the main holders of the UK debt and whilst they are pleased that there has been a change of government, they are also acutely aware of the mess of the UK economy. Much of the debt is held by foreign governments who are not particularly sympathetic to the UK so I am not expecting any charity from them. They'll play the game and quote the ratings agency as an excuse to demand more in interest. They know that eventually we'll have to default but by that time they anticipate that we would have paid so much in interest that they will have got their money back anyway whilst at the same time the UK will be a broken economy. The anticipation is that international companies at present based here, particularly financial companies, will desert the UK and relocate to more financially secure countries, i.e. those holding the UK debt. It's fair to say that even those countries who we consider friends are only too happy to use our predicament against us and for their own countries benefit. As in fact we would probably do if the boot were on the other foot. Of course, once these big financial companies leave, so do their taxes meaning we will be in an even bigger mess. So, at present no good news I'm afraid.'

'I wish I hadn't asked.'

Green ran his hand through his hair again. Just then Jason Bhatia wandered over.

'You two are looking rather glum. I thought that this was meant to be a celebratory party?'

'We were just discussing the North Sea incident.' Frank mentioned as a means of explanation.

'Ah I can see why the long faces then. Not good. I've just been talking to Cynthia. She's really under a baptism of fire over it. All I've got to worry about is another incursion into UK territorial air space by a Russian bomber. You know the Russians are getting more and more adventurous. That's the third time in as many weeks that they have entered the UK airspace. The last two times we didn't even send a fighter up to challenge them until they were almost over land. Knowing how much they have been spending on defence over the past few years I am getting very nervous of their intentions.'

Bhatia was wearing a blue pin striped suit with a white shirt and blue spotted tie. His shoes were black brogues polished to a gleam. He too was enjoying the Greenfield sparkling wine.

'Surely it's just the Russians playing their normal games. I know that President Khurin is always going on about the old Soviet Union and reclaiming Russian pride but that's just for internal consumption. The reality is that he can buzz the UK until the cows come home but I can't see him doing anything more as long as we have America on our side. We might have let our armed forces deteriorate but we do still have the ability to defend ourselves, don't we?'

Green turned to Bhatia.

'You may be right about Khurin but as to the state of our defences I am unable to answer that. Five years of under, or in fact no, real spending on defence has taken its toll. I am due to have a meeting with the joint chiefs of staff tomorrow to get their take on the state of our defences but I can already guess what they will say. In a nutshell, give us more money.'

At that Bhatia turned his gaze to Frank.

'The military might want more money but if we are cutting back on people's benefits, which I suspect we will have to do, then to be seen at the same time to increase spending on our military won't go down well with the electorate.

'Nor will seeing Russian troops walking down Whitehall.'

Bhatia continued to face Frank but Green interceded.

'I can't see it coming to that, Jason and at this time we just don't have the money to expand our armed forces. I am concerned about the Russian incursions into our air space and will ask Gary Davies to send a strong message about it to the Russian ambassador. It won't make the slightest difference I suspect but I can't see what else we can do. The reality is that Russia is not on our doorstep and will have to go through many other countries before it gets to us. Let the Europeans worry about Russia. They are not exactly being helpful to us regarding our financial position so why should we worry about Russia?'

'It's not really just the Russian threat that makes a strong defence force important as you are well aware. Apart from our NATO commitment to spend 2% of our GDP on defence, something we haven't done for at least the last five years and as a result of which, by the way, the Americans are not in the mood to bail us out if we do get into trouble, we also have the ongoing war on terrorism. Richard, I know that every minister is going to be clambering to get a bigger slice of a small pie but we are incredibly vulnerable at this time. We no longer have a nuclear deterrent and our conventional forces are rusting away. The number of people in the military has reduced to the lowest level since records began and most of those that are left are office bound warriors.'

'Tomorrow I'll get some real figures and then I'd like to talk again.'

Bhatia drained his glass and set it down on a nearby table.

'If you want to save money then how about stopping the overseas aid, stopping tax relief for charities and cutting all public sector salaries such that no one earns more than you do. And that includes everyone in that den of socialists, the BBC. That should save something like thirty billion pounds for a starter.'

Glancing between Frank and Green, Bhatia turned on his heels and walked towards the waitress to get another drink.

'I think the youngest member of your cabinet could be quite a firebrand.'

Franks had himself taken another glass from a nearby tray.

'But he does have a point about our NATO commitment. I recall a few years back when President Trump was in charge across the pond, he was very vocal that no one in Europe was spending enough on defence and why should America pay for the defence of countries that didn't want to pay to defend themselves. At that time the UK was just about meeting its commitments, if you included office furniture and paper clips in the calculations, so we had something of a moral high ground against our European neighbours. Since then we have lost that position and at the same time Europe has set up its own defence force to operate alongside NATO. As we are no longer part of the European project, we do not have any say in the running of the European army but in reality, it is useless. Just a vanity project by the European Community. It's as underfunded as the old NATO commitments and its run by a committee. If Russia walked into Poland tomorrow it would take the Europeans about six months to even consider mobilising. No, NATO is still Europe's only real defence and without the UK leading the way I fear America will withdraw its commitment and concentrate on the dangers coming from the East.'

The general hubbub in the room indicated that people were enjoying good conversations with just the occasional raising of a voice. With such an array of egos in the room it would not have been surprising if more raised voices were heard but so far everyone seemed to be behaving themselves. Perhaps it was the influence of the spouses being present or the general air of something new happening but the mood in the room seemed remarkably buoyant. As Richard Green looked around trying to recall everyone's name, he wondered how long such an air of optimism would last. Turning back to Alastair Frank he continued their conversation.

'Nonetheless just because there is a need to spend money on the military doesn't change the fact that we don't actually have any money to spend unless you can pull a rabbit out of the hat. What about the throw away items mentioned by Jason. Anything there?'

'Sorry, I can't answer that right now. I'll need to talk to the relevant departments but just as Jason will defend his budget so will all the other departments. I guess we'll just have to wait and see what the budget brings and then see where we can make savings. One thing we can absolutely be assured of is that the amount of money we are spending on the public sector is unsustainable and will have to be cut; but unfortunately, as the implementation of any public sector cuts will be in the very hands of the people that should be cut it will be a bit like asking a turkey to vote for Christmas.'

'It all comes down to time doesn't it?' Green shook his head before once again running his hand through his hair. 'To unravel years of growth in the public sector is not something that we can do over night. You know when I was doing a proper job, I often wondered why we were busily sending all our youngsters to get university degrees in statistic and media studies when we were short of plumbers and brick layers. No wonder Brexit was such a balls-up. The majority of British youngsters were coming out of their fine universities with their honour's degree with the promise of a well-paid job. The fact that those jobs didn't exist and so had to be invented in the public or charity sector was the brain child of a previous administration but in the meanwhile no self-respecting graduate would dream of doing the mundane jobs such as picking fruit, serving at tables or working in the low paid gig economy. So many industries got to rely on importing cheap labour from Europe. When that supply was threatened instead of trying to make it work with our own people the companies most affected put up such a noise barrier that Brexit became a mess and ultimately, we ended up with a communist government. Cue where we are today. Eventually we will have to address this labour imbalance and try and sort out the lousy Brexit agreement but meanwhile we need to buy time.'

'But enough of budgets and politics. I see that we have been neglecting Mrs Frank and Green so shall we join the ladies?'

Putting his hand on Frank's arm Green steered him towards their wives who were in deep conversation on the other side of the room. Richard Green felt sure that their conversation had to have been more cheerful than their husband's.

Chapter 16
April 2026

London Downing Street

The sunshine coming through the thick glass windows leant an air of comfort to the small living room in 10 Downing Street. Usually off limits to anyone but to the close friends and family of the prime minister the room formed part of his private apartment. The thickness of the windows was as a result of the reinforced panes having been installed following an IRA mortar attack on 10 Downing Street. The attack by the Irish Republican Army, whose aim was the separation of the United Kingdom, at the height of the terrorist campaign on the British mainland led to a considerable increase in protection for establishment buildings. The windows in 10 Downing Street as well as other government buildings were now bullet proof and could withstand a close proximity bomb blast. Not that this was in the minds of the present occupancy of the room who were only very young children when the IRA were taking their bloody battle to the heart of the British establishment..

Sitting in the comfortable chintz armchairs around a light oak coffee table was Richard Green, Cynthia Graeme, Jim Simpson, Jean Robertson and David Grant. Each had a cup of tea in a delicate Royal Doulton cup and saucer placed on a coaster on the coffee table. Sugar and milk were available but all participants took their tea without either. Many of the traditional ways of British life had changed as the younger generation found its own voice and one change that reflected the future, in the eyes of the young, was that drinking tea with milk and sugar was not considered cool. The down side of having tea with no milk was that it was served hotter and for the unwary could cause some discomfort if taken too early. Jim Simpson was only too aware of this. He had been summoned to Downing Street to give an account of the explosion on the Saebo drill rig and had nervously taken a mouthful of the tea when first placed in front of him. The subsequent scolded tongue was quite painful but ironically helped distract his mind from the grilling he suspected was coming despite the relaxed surroundings chosen for the meeting. The Prime Minister, unaware that his guest was suffering, opened the conversation having already dispensed with the initial pleasantries.

'First let me thank you for coming to this meeting at such short notice. Whilst I'm sure the legal beavers will be looking into who to blame for the tragedy that happened in the North Sea a few days ago, I wanted to have an off the record discussion with you first to try and get a better picture of what happened. I give you my word, if you can believe the word of a politician, that what is said in this room will remain private. I just want to understand how and why 19 people lost their lives and I would prefer to find out from you than read about it in the press.'

Green addressed Simpson and Grant from a seat directly opposite so he could better observe the reactions of his guests. Prior to becoming Prime Minister Green had been used to chairing important commercial discussions and had found it much easier to gauge the reaction of one's opponent if it was possible to look then straight in the eye. Robertson sat to the side next to Cynthia Graeme.

'I understand that whilst the drill rig in question, The Triton I think it was called, was not actually owned by OEC, it was contracted to OEC to drill on the Caratacus concession and on that basis OEC along with Saebo Drilling has a responsibility of care. Is that correct?'

Simpson glanced across at Grant before responding,

'Yes Prime Minister, that is correct. Whilst Saebo Drilling has direct responsibility for the day-to-day safety aspects, OEC is responsible for assessing the Saebo Drilling safety regime and ensuring it is robust and adhered to.'

'Good. I have looked at the report prepared on your two Companies and have to say that to date you seem to have an exemplary safety record. Saebo drilling has had nearly three years without a lost time incident and whilst developing the Caratacus field OEC has reported only four near miss incidents with no injuries. There have been a number of minor incidents which have led to schedule delays but to date no injuries. That all changed with the explosion on the Triton. The question is why did the explosion take place? I understand that the HSE are carrying out an investigation and in due course we will get a full report but that could take months. Meanwhile the press is calling this a terrorist incident and clambering for an independent enquiry. To help me determine the best approach I would appreciate if you could let me know your thoughts on the cause of the incident' Sitting back Green kept his gaze on Simpson but it was Grant, the CEO of Saebo drilling, that replied.

'Prime Minister, perhaps I can start the ball rolling.'

David Grant, a Norwegian despite his western sounding name, was 64 years old and a veteran of the oil business. Having started his working life as a tool pusher on the early American rigs that helped open up the North Sea in the seventies and eighties, he had worked his way into firstly a management role and then became a director of one of the world's biggest drill rig operators before starting his own company. He had a reputation for being a fair but tough employer. Saebo Drilling was his company founded at the height of the last big oil boom just in time to see the market collapse. That had not stopped Grant from ensuring his workers and equipment were well looked after and he had been known to forego his own salary when money got a tight. The Caratacus contract had been won against fierce competition but had been a life saver for the small independent company. The explosion had hit David Grant hard and would most likely be the end of his company. Nevertheless, he was not one to bemoan his lot and genuinely felt that looking out for the relatives of the casualties was his responsibility.

'First let me make my position absolutely clear in that my number one priority has always been the safety and wellbeing of my employees. I have been left devastated by this incident and want to get to the bottom of what happened more than anyone. To that end I can give you my assurance that my people are working with the HSE to find the truth.

'From preliminary investigations the explosion appears to have started on the drilling deck and was as a result of a release of gas that was then ignited. The source of the ignition is not known. Theoretically there should be no ignition source anywhere near the drill deck but there is always the chance of a rogue spark at the wrong time and wrong place. Even something as trivial as a small stone caught in someone's shoes catching the steel walkway can cause a spark. We will probably never know but what we do have a better understanding of is the reason for the gas leak in the first place.'

Glancing between Green and Graeme, Grant saw that he had their full attention.

'As you may or may not know, the Caratacus Field is quite complex. Most oil and gas fields in the North Sea are relatively shallow, something like six to eight thousand feet below the seabed. The Caratacus Field is considerably deeper at a depth of closer to 14,000 feet but equally as important to understand the cause of the accident, the field lies below the existing oil and gas bearing structures. Obviously, the geology is quite complex but I'll try and simplify it.'

'As someone that knows very little about geology that would be most appreciated,' Green interjected with a slight smile on his lips.

'Most people think that the North Sea is a declining region when it comes to oil and gas production and to be fair that is backed up by production figures. In fact, it was in 1999 that peak production was reached and ever since the amount of oil and gas produced from the North Sea has been in decline. Every now and then a larger field has been found such as the Buzzard field in the UK sector and the Johan Sverdrup field in the Norwegian sector but these fields have not been able to replace the fields that are being depleted. The Caratacus field is set to change all that.'

Grant turned to Simpson.

'Jim. I have a confidentiality clause in my contract with OEC so I'm not sure how much I am allowed to disclose so it would be better if you took over here.'

Simpson looked a bit uneasy but took up the story.

'There is nothing really too secretive about what we are doing but one thing I've learnt in business is to be cautious with reporting because the more is reported the more ammunition you give to your rivals, particularly when one is a minnow swimming amongst the sharks so to speak.'

Simpson leant forward to reach for his tea cup before remembering his scolded tongue and promptly sat back in his chair.

'What David wanted to tell you and was restrained by the confidentiality clause is that the Caratacus field is a real game changer in the fortunes of the North Sea oil industry. To put it in context the Brent Field, of which you will have heard, produced something like three billion barrels of oil equivalent in its near 45 years of production peaking at a production rate of something like 400,000 barrels of oil a day. The Caratacus field alone has estimated reserves of 15 billion barrels of oil equivalent and the plan is to be pumping 850,000 barrels per day starting from the middle of next year.'

Simpson stopped talking and glanced around the room. Green was the first to respond.

'I see that we are talking about a large oil field here but I fail to see how that explains the explosion on the Triton.'

David Grant took up the story again.

'The critical point here is that the oil is trapped below the normal oil-bearing structures so to get to the Caratacus Field we had to drill through that structure. What we think happened was that when drilling the last well, and we have already successfully completed ten out of our contracted twelve wells, we hit a shallow gas pocket. That is always a risk when drilling and normally we have safety devices from stopping the gas from going back up the drill pipes to the drill rig. In this case we think that the two safety valves that should have automatically shut failed. Why they failed we still don't know and that is what we hope will come out of the investigations. By the valves not automatically closing it allowed the gas to escape onto the drill floor where a rogue source of ignition ignited it. The drill rig manager did manage to close a manually operated subsurface valve that cut the feed of gas below the seabed which prevented an even bigger explosion. What I think I can say with a fair amount of certainty is that I would be very surprised if terrorists were involved. Everyone on the rig had been working for Saebo Drilling for at least three years and had been fully vetted prior to joining the company. Since the incident I have had the individual dossiers of everyone on the rig reviewed and none of them give any indication that they could have terrorist tendencies.'

'What do you mean by terrorist tendencies?' Cynthia Graeme interceded.

'We looked at their backgrounds. Obviously with the recent issues with ISIS we looked initially if any of the work force was a Muslim and hence could have been radicalised but that was negative. We are also aware that the radical Muslims are not the only ones involved with terrorist activities so we looked at everyone's background to see if we could find any signs of historical sympathies with the Irish IRA or even Scottish independence but drew a blank. In addition, no one has claimed responsibility for the explosion so what's the point of blowing up a drill rig if no one knows you did it? So, no I don't think that the incident was terrorist related.'

'Thank you for your openness but nevertheless 19 people have lost their lives as a result of this incident. I hope that you are right in your appraisal that terrorists were not involved. I really don't need that sort of complication right now. However, if not terrorism then it comes down to basic incompetence by someone. In my experience accidents don't just happen. They are as a result of someone somewhere making mistakes. Yesterday I was in contact with the Norwegian and Danish authorities and they are demanding answers as to what went wrong. After this discussion I will assure them that all concerned are working together to arrive at the facts of what caused this tragedy. This is the least that we can do for the relatives of those that died.'

Graeme's grim countenance expressed to everyone around the table of how serious she took the issue of determining the cause of the accident.

'Madam Foreign Secretary, no one regrets what happened more than I do. Many of those that died were personal friends. People that I have worked alongside for many years. I can assure you that finding an answer is just one step in the process. We also need to ensure that it can't happen again and that the relatives of the dead are adequately looked after. We are mindful that legal proceedings will likely follow so we have to be a little careful in what we can say and do at this stage but we have already set up a bereavement team to start the process. OEC are actively involved with this. There is no intention of a cover up.'

'I'm glad to hear it, Mr Grant. Thank you again for your openness and sorry that we are not meeting under more convivial circumstances.'

Green rose from his chair to indicate the meeting was over. After handshakes, Grant, Simpson and Robertson were escorted to the front door leaving Cynthia Graeme and Richard Green alone in the room. After pouring another cup of tea and noting that the three oil executives had barely touched their cups, Green turned to Graeme.

'I guess we can be thankful in that it doesn't appear to be terrorist related.'

'Indeed. One less thing to worry about but one thing that I did pick up on and which I hadn't really appreciated until this meeting was the size of this discovery. If what they are saying is correct, and I can't think it isn't, then not only are they looking at a massive windfall but also so should the British Taxpayer. I don't know what the tax situation is on the oil that comes out of the ground but I seem to recall that in the Thatcher years, when the North Sea was at its peak, the oil revenue was very helpful in allowing Thatcher to enact her economic reforms. I would suggest that we should have a chat with Alastair to see what this means. It could just be what we are looking for.'

'You may have a point but I can't see that this would be anything other than a drop in the ocean with regard to what we need to get us out of the hole. But I will raise it with Alastair at our next meeting.'

'Will you relay our discussions to the Norwegian and Danish authorities? I would also suggest that you mention that we are comfortable if they want to send a representative to join the accident investigation team. I don't want them to think we are trying to hide anything.'

'Will do.'

Graeme finished her tea and left the room noting as she did that, despite his reticence, Richard Green was deep in thought and she suspected that he was more interested in the possibilities that the large oil discovery represented than he was letting on.

Chapter 17
May 2026

Korea

After a build time of just three years the Kalevala semi-submersible crane vessel was complete. Proudly floating alongside the quayside, she towered over all the other ships in the yard. No one could call her a beautiful ship. Looking more like a floating car park with two large cranes at the stern and a large infrastructure at the port side bow, her yellow crane housings and blue hull gleamed in the afternoon sunshine. Strung between her twin cranes were flags of all nations of the world and a banner hung down from her top deck advertising the company that had built her. As was traditional in the Korean ship yard the ships naming ceremony was about to commence.

Alongside the great ship a platform had been erected with steps from the quay side. All along the quayside were hundreds of Korean workers who had contributed to the vessel's construction. Behind the quay, two marquees had been erected in which was food and drink for the after-ceremony party.

The ship's sponsor was David Saunders' wife, Madeleine. Having flown into Ulsan the night before along with the board of directors of Saunders Marine Solutions, Maddie, as she was known to her closest friends, was excited and a little nervous by the prospect of pulling the lever that would release the bottle of Korean C1 Soju to smash against the bow of the Kalevala. Stretching back hundreds if not thousands of years the tradition of baptising a ship was initially by using water and then latterly by using an alcoholic beverage, normally champagne in the west but over the years many different beverages had been used. The use of C1 Soju, Korea's national drink, was the idea of David Saunders as a sign of respect to the Koreans that had been responsible for the Kalevala's construction. One slight problem was that the Soju bottle was not made of glass but was an earthenware pot and although a small nipple had been added to the bow at the calculated point of impact the risk that the bottle would not break was considered greater than if the traditional Champagne had been used. If the bottle did not break the ship would not be baptised which would be seen as a sign of bad omen and bad luck which would be unfortunate for the ship's sponsor.

In the past the baptismal ceremony took place when a ship was launched; the process when a ship's completed hull would be allowed to slide from its place of construction into the sea before outfitting took place. The launch process put considerable strain on the ship's structure and was always a nervous time for the naval architect responsible for the launch calculations but in the modern shipyard, most vessels were constructed in dry docks and when completed the dock would be flooded allowing the vessel to gently float free. As a result, most modern naming ceremonies took place when the vessel had been completed and was ready to be put into service. The naming of the Kalevala was just such an occasion.

Once named, the Kalevala would be ready for its long journey from the Korean shipyard to start its first job in the North Sea, a distance of 12,500 nautical miles that was projected to take nearly three months with a stopover in Cape Town for refuelling. The vessel still had outfitting work to be completed so would sail with a construction crew of 200 HHI personnel as well as its sailing crew of 60 personnel provided by Saunders Marine. If all went according to plan the last of the outfitting would be completed before the vessel arrived in Cape Town allowing the demobilisation of the Korean construction crew and the mobilisation of the remaining Saunders Marine deck crew. The sailing time from cape Town to the North Sea would be used to allow the deck crew to familiarise themselves with the vessel so that once on location at the Caratacus field the Kalevala could go straight to work.

The naming ceremony was taking place at the end of May so it did not leave much in the way of contingency if the Caratacus topside modules were to be installed before the middle of September; but the fact that the vessel was in a state to sail at all was very much to the credit of her Korean fabricators.

As well as the Saunders Marine board of directors, also present on the naming ceremony platform were the board of Oceanic Energy Company, the HHI management team, various local dignitaries and senior members of the Saunders Marine construction management team all with their spouses. A total of 72 persons crowded onto the small platform to watch the proceedings. Maddie Saunders looked radiant wearing a single piece ivory dress of the finest silk with a delicate silk belt at the waist. Her shoes were dark brown leather that complimented the dress and on her head was a large brimmed sashed hat to keep her long blond hair in check. The perfect attire for the occasion and as the weather was clear and calm with a temperature of 24 degrees Celsius, the perfect attire for the weather conditions.

After a suitable address to the Korean workers, given in Korean by the HHI project Manager, Maddie stepped up to the lever that would release the Soju and after recanting the time-honoured address, blessing the ship and all that sailed in her, she pulled the lever forward. The bottle of Soju was released and under gravity but with its flight path dictated by the length of restraining wire, it swung towards the ship before impacting on the starboard bow exactly as planned. The earthenware bottle smashed into a thousand pieces and the Soju so contained cascaded down the side of the ship leading to a roar of approval from the gathered crowd and allowing David Saunders to start breathing again. One more potential hurdle passed.

As Maddie Saunders stepped back from the launch podium, a big smile on her face, David Saunders turned to the man standing next to him and shook his hand. Jim Simpson was equally as relieved as David Saunders and having grasped the outstretched hand gave his heartfelt and well-intended congratulations on reaching this important milestone. What David Saunders did not know was that whilst hoping for a successful outcome for the Kalevala, Simpson had secretly been working with Marco Paglia on an alternative installation option, one that Simpson hoped would not be needed but was nevertheless a back stop in case of further delays to the Kalevala. He also had a request to make and he considered that this was as good a time as any to raise this with Saunders.

'Well done, David. I have to say that I was beginning to doubt that we would ever see this day but hats off to all involved. It appears that you are still on schedule to get our work done before the end of the year. I think you know how critical this is and today is a big step.'

'Indeed. The phone call regarding the explosion of the bow section was a real bombshell and HHI have done an amazing job to get us back on schedule. We still have work to do during the sail but most of that is cosmetic. She'll be fully ready at the beginning of September to get the Caratacus deck installed, that is if it's finished on time. I heard you were also experiencing delays?'

'You shouldn't believe all you hear.' Simpson's smile showed that Saunders was closer to the truth than either would like to admit. 'but on the subject of the sail I was wondering if I could ask a small favour. As you know my youngest son is very interested in ship design. He is coming to the end of his Naval Architect course from Newcastle University and would love the opportunity to spend some time on the Kalevala. I don't suppose you have a berth for him to sail with the Kalevala to South Africa?'

'The Kalevala has 850 berths and we are using less than half that number for the crew and completion team so I can't see it being a problem. He will have to have undertaken his safety training of course and I assume that he will arrange his own travel to and from the ship but in principle it is not a problem. I'll get my secretary to email you all the details and I'll let the Kalevala's Captain know that it's been arranged.'

'That's great and much appreciated. He can also keep an eye on how the preparations are going and keep me informed.'

Simpson smiled to let Saunders know he was joking. Saunders went along with the joke.

'I knew there would be an ulterior motive. We'll just keep him in the lower decks and treat him like a mushroom.'

'Ah the keep him in the dark and feed him bullshit ploy. I'm sure he won't even call home if his time at Newcastle is anything to go on so I think your secrets will remain safe.'

'As you know we have no secrets from you. But let me leave you to enjoy the rest of your time in Korea whilst I go and have a word with a couple of people.'

The two men shook hands. Stepping down from the launch platform the various dignitaries and their wives made their way to the marquee specifically reserved for the launch party and invited guests whilst at the same time the work force made its way to the second marquee. Both marquees contained food, consisting mainly of vegetarian and seafood, and non-alcoholic drink although any observer would very quickly have noted that the quality of the food in the top marquee was considerably higher than that available to the work force. Not that this bothered the work force who were just pleased to have a half day off work and get a free lunch curtesy of HHI. Besides, in their society inequality based on status was accepted as part of their way of life. A purely western society may have felt aggrieved by the perception of inequality but not the Korean society.

Taking another portion of the fresh crab salad David Saunders found himself in conversation with Ron Thompson.

'Congratulations, Ron. I was beginning to wonder if we would ever see this day.'

'David, ye of little faith' – a big smile spread across the normally stern features of the big resident engineer – 'but between just the two of us, there were times when I thought exactly the same particularly after the explosion in the bow a few weeks back. You know the Koreans really pulled out all the stops to make good that fiasco.'

'Yes, indeed. I just said the exact same to Jim Simpson. They did a remarkable job but did we ever find out what caused the explosion? The last I heard they were still investigating.'

'I asked the same of Daniel Lee just yesterday but he was a bit non-committal. I have to say I got the feeling that he was holding something back but you know the Koreans, they are very good at hiding their emotions so I was probably just imagining things, but look, there is Daniel over there. Why don't we go and chat to him about it? I'm sure you would want to thank him personally anyway for the successful completion.'

Thompson turned and nodded in the direction of a small Korean standing apart from the other personnel, mainly westerners, in the marquee.

Daniel Lee was a little over five feet tall with black hair and an intelligent face that seemed to always be smiling. Wearing the overalls that was the uniform of the HHI workforce, even in such a ceremony, the impression he gave was that of a favourite uncle. In reality he was a very respected manager who had steered the project to a successful solution despite the difficulties encountered during the fabrication phase. He was also a formidable opponent when negotiating changes to the contract and one that had earned the respect of David Saunders for his perseverance and honesty whilst always retaining his loyalty to HHI. Saunders and Thompson wandered over to join him.

'Mr Lee, a very nice ceremony you have organised here. Many thanks and of course many thanks for getting the Kalevala into such a shape despite the many problems.'

Although Saunders had known Daniel Lee for over three years, he still used the formal Mister address rather than the American way of using the first name.

'It is my pleasure. And may I congratulate you on having such a lovely wife.'

Lee spoke English with a slight accent but unlike some Koreans the accent was not a distraction.

'Yes, getting married to Maddie was one of my better decisions. But I don't see your wife here Mr Lee. Are you married?'

'Yes, indeed but unfortunately she was unable to join us this morning. She had to work. So sorry.'

Lee did not think it necessary to add that his wife had been to many launch celebrations in the past and with her limited English found them quite stressful. He had given her the choice as to whether she would attend and she had declined.

'Work before pleasure. She is clearly a very dedicated lady. What does she do?'

'Actually, she works for the government helping to arrange the state elections. As you may know we have an election coming up shortly and so she is very busy. So sorry.'

Lee was not comfortable talking about his personal life and preferred to keep his business and his private lives separate. Steering the conversation back to more comfortable grounds he asked Saunders how long he would be staying in Korea. After a few more minutes of general conversation Saunders raised the question that he had discussed with Thompson earlier in the morning. As Lee responded it was impossible to tell by his expression if he was concerned or not by the incident.

'You are of course referring to the explosion that took place about six weeks ago. We were very lucky that we were able to contain the flooding and that we had the right material on site to fabricate a new section. Normally we would have expected at least a three-month delay for such an incident. But the cause is something that we are still investigating. The problem is that we cannot see what there was in the compartment that could have caused the explosion. Two years ago, we had a similar explosion but that was quickly identified as being due to a worker leaving an oxyacetylene torch on when he went to lunch. On his return he went to light the torch not realising the whole compartment was full of gas. But this time there are no indications so we have sent some of the damaged material for analysis in the lab. The really strange thing is that I received a preliminary report yesterday but can't believe the findings so have asked for a re-analysis. The report I received indicated the explosion was caused by something called RDX which as I understand it is a military grade explosive. We certainly don't have any in the yard so I think the laboratory must have made a mistake.'

Lee's face remained impassive with the same fixed smile but his eyes betrayed the doubts. Lee did not like loose ends and so was determined to find out why the explosion had occurred.

'RDX. Can't say that I've ever heard of it but as you say sounds a bit strange that the lab has identified that as a cause if you don't have any on site. When do you expect to get the re-analysis completed?'

'I've asked for priority so hopefully tomorrow. I'm sure there is another explanation but if the results come back the same then we have a real mystery on our hands. From what I've read RDX is relatively widely used but is not the sort of stuff you go into the local Lotte store and buy off the shelf. As well as getting the sample reanalysed, I've also got one of my guys checking to see if any explosives have been used recently in the yard and if so perhaps RDX was used instead of our normal TNT. Even then the mystery would still remain as to how it got into that bow compartment which had been completed months ago.'

As Lee was talking something in the back reaches of Saunders mind started raising alarm bells. Perhaps it was the fact that he had been watching the film Die Hard on the plane the day before but the question that sprung to mind was what if the explosion had not been an accident; but that was crazy. This was not a film and as no one was hurt – it couldn't have been a terrorist act. Besides what would anyone gain by punching a small hole in the Kalevala? He decided to keep his opinion to himself. Thompson though had also come to a similar conclusion and was not as reluctant to avoid making a fool of himself.

'Mr Lee. To me this sounds more like an act of sabotage than an accident if it is proven that RDX is responsible for the explosion. Has HHI upset someone?' Thompson smiled to make an attempt at brevity but the message was clear.

'Please do not jump to conclusions until we know the facts. I will of course keep you fully informed as to the results of our investigations. In the meanwhile, I suggest we enjoy the rest of the celebrations.'

Lee was keen to discontinue the conversation into the accident but what he didn't want to admit to the two westerners was that he had reached the same conclusion. He had already instigated an internal security review and had raised his concerns with the yard senior management. Even as they spoke the head of security was looking through CCTV coverage and checking all Identifications for anyone that had entered the yard in the forty-eight hours prior to the explosion taking place. This was not as onerous as it sounded as the yard used facial identification software to match the individual to their pass photograph. Divers had also been deployed to recover debris from the seabed and interviews arranged for anyone that could be identified as having worked in the area of the damaged compartment. The head of security was confident that if anyone had been in the area of the damaged compartment that shouldn't have been there then they would be discovered.

Saunders and Thompson re-joined their wives and the rest of the party and as they got more into the spirit of the occasion soon put all thought of the explosion to the back recesses of their minds. Daniel Lee was not so easily distracted and as soon as was polite he made his excuses and on leaving the party went to find the head of security.

Chapter 18
May 2026

Somewhere in Europe

Jason Chadwell was not a happy person. His success at what he did was based on his ability to remain anonymous; to get the job done and get out without leaving any trail or evidence that could be tracked back to his door. As one of the world's most successful saboteurs, the fact that his name barely registered on the most wanted list of any of the police forces of the world was testament to his success in hiding his tracks. But he had let greed get the better of him.

Having returned from Korea after arranging the 'accident' on the Kalevala he fully intended to take a small holiday before taking on his next assignment. At this time of year, the Seychelles were pleasantly warm and his villa on the Eden Island development required his attention. He just needed to book his flights, Etihad Airways via Dubai to Victoria airport, and his hired car in the Seychelles to get him from the airport to his villa. Once on Eden Island he would not be able to use the car as only battery-operated golf buggies were allowed on the island, but he would need the hired car when he left the Island to go to the Seychelles capital of Victoria for his provisions and to sort out his paperwork. As an owner of the villa he was eligible for Seychelles citizenship and he intended to apply during this trip. One day it could very well be useful to be a citizen of a country that had low taxes and very few reciprocal financial disclosure agreements with other countries of the world.

That had all changed with the receipt of another urgent assignment to go back to Korea. According to his contact the sabotage of the ship had not been as successful as hoped and even though he had completed his assignment as requested the Koreans had been able to mitigate the effects to such an extent that the sail away of the vessel had not been delayed. Chadwell was unaware that the ultimate client was Marco Paglia and that Paglia was desperate for the Kalevala not to get to Europe until after the offshore installation season was ended. He didn't know the client and he didn't know the reason why the delay was a necessity but whilst no one was blaming Chadwell for the failed consequences of the initial sabotage attempt it nevertheless hurt his pride in that he had not achieved the planned goal. It also helped in making the decision that a lot of money was being offered to return to Korea and finish the job.

If Chadwell was honest with himself, and in his line of business this was a necessity, he accepted that whilst pride played a small part of him taking the assignment it was the money that had by far the biggest influence. It was greed and that was something he reflected on as he considered what had gone wrong.

The assignment had to be completed in the next two months as the Kalevala was due to sail by the end of May which did not give Chadwell enough time to make the normal extensive preparations. He would have to rely on the same contacts and false identity as he had used the previous time he had been in Korea. He did not think that this would be a major risk as he was confident that he had covered his tracks adequately last time and that the identity of James Cartridge was still anonymous. His main concern was that he would have to act just prior to sail away which did not leave him any time if things went wrong.

Initially all went well. He had no issues with clearing customs and making his way back to Ulsan. He checked into a different hotel and once again followed his routine of requesting the taxi to drop him off outside another hotel. His assignment this time was to cause significant damage to the crane vessel's support struts which would take months to repair. Again, the damage was based in an area that would ensure no loss of life whilst causing the maximum disruption.

Having acquired the RDX and the detonator/timer components from the same source as previously he made his way to the HHI site and after a brief check of his faked pass gained entry to the yard. All being well he was confident he could place the explosive during the lunch time break and be out of the yard by mid-afternoon. His flight out of Ulsan was planned for the next day with the flight to Europe from Seoul in two days' time. Unlike his previous time in Korea he did not intend to stay in the Ulsan area but was looking forward to having a free day to see the sights of Seoul. Walking towards the Kalevala his confidence grew until he caught site of the ship. Much to his surprise everyone was leaving the vessel and from his vantage point close to one of the access gangways he could see that no one was being allowed back on the ship except for the security guards. *Just his luck* he thought *that they had chosen today to hold an emergency evacuation drill.* He would just have to wait until the drill was over or find another way to access the vessel.

Making his way along the quay he found himself caught up in the mass of workers that had just left the ship. Using the crowd as cover he gradually made his way to the quay side and looked up at the side of the massive vessel. Due to the water depth at the quay side the Kalevala was fully ballasted up with the top of the pontoons above the water and about level with the quay side. A gangway went from the quay side to the top of the pontoons. The main deck support struts went from the pontoons to the underside of the main superstructure. All Cartridge, aka Chadwell, had to do was get onto the top of the pontoon, enter the pontoon via one of the water tight doors that at present were open for ingress and egress and place the explosives in a place just under the struts. The explosion would damage the strut and the pontoon having the desired effect of delaying the sail away. The problem was that the gangway to the pontoon was also covered by guards. Cartridge decided to wait and see if an opportunity would arise.

Four hours later things appeared to have settled down somewhat. The guards had left the ship after three hours and now at last the workers were being allowed back onto the vessel. However, Cartridge noted that all workers were having their security pass scrutinised in a much more disciplined way. It was almost as if they were looking for someone. For the first time since accepting the consignment Chadwell started to wonder if he had made a mistake. What if they knew he was in the yard? He started going back over his actions to see if he could detect if he had made a mistake but drew a blank. Perhaps then someone had stitched him up. The client? the agent? Or one of his suppliers? But to what end. What would they gain? No, whichever way he looked at it he could not determine how he could have made a mistake or been betrayed. They must be looking for someone else but to be on the safe side he decided perhaps it would be better to get another pass. Looking around he found another westerner of similar build and looks waiting in the queue to join the vessel. Manoeuvring into position next to the worker it was not difficult for Chadwell to accidently bump into him and at the same time cause his pass, which was on a lanyard around his neck, to be ripped off. Apologising profusely Chadwell adroitly gave the worker his own pass and pocketed the workers pass. Chadwell then made his way to the pontoon top gangway and having scuffed the pass to make the photograph look worn out joined the new queue to gain access to The Kalevala.

What he didn't see was the worker who had been given his fake pass being detained by the guards at the other gangway and then being taken away by the yard security team to be questioned. Had he seen this he would have immediately realised that his identity had somehow been compromised and he would have aborted the mission and found a way to leave the yard. Without this information he blithely continued with the mission. The guard at the gangway looked at his fake pass and then at Chadwell. As the guard had heard on the radio that they had got their man he was perhaps a little less attentive than he would otherwise have been but even so he noted the poor state of the pass and when handing it back suggested Chadwell get it reissued. The guard did not think to check Chadwell's bag but had he done so he would only have seen the tools of a rigger. The bomb was securely packed in a false base to the bag.

Moving onto the pontoon Chadwell made his way to the water tight door and soon found himself in a dimly lit part of the ship right under where one of the main support struts was connected to the pontoon. Looking around to make sure he was alone he emptied the tools onto the deck and accessed the hidden compartment to extract the bomb. The bomb was a simple device with a magnetic base to attach it to the steel hull, a small amount of RDX with a pencil detonator attached to a timing device made from a digital clock. It was compact and once the bomb had been attached to the hull it would be hard for anyone not specifically looking to see it. Unfortunately, this was where things started to go seriously wrong for Chadwell. Having attached the bomb, he was in the process of setting the timer when he heard the approach of running feet. Not one to panic he dropped from his position but not before activating the device and found a suitable hiding place just in time to avoid being discovered by two security guards who seemed to be searching for someone. As Chadwell looked out from his hiding place he saw that the guards had stopped someone else about 20 metres along the corridor. To his chagrin he noted that the man the guards had stopped and were interrogating was a westerner. Even more of a concern was the fact that the two Koreans in the vicinity were not questioned. It was clear to Chadwell that the guards were looking for a westerner and for the first time it dawned on him that he was the intended target. Still not knowing how, he was now convinced his cover had been exposed and it was time for self-preservation to kick in. He recalled he had activated the timer on the bomb but had not actually set the time. He had been interrupted before finishing the set up but he couldn't get back to the site of the bomb without being seen. At least he thought the device was live and would eventually explode hopefully not when there were people around. But in reality, he didn't really care. It was his client that insisted on no casualties. In Chadwell's line of work casualties were to be expected and Chadwell had no intention of losing any sleep over a few Korean workers. His priority was to get off the ship and out of the shipyard without being caught.

Leaving the ship turned out to be easier than he thought. Because so many of the guards were tied up with searching the ship, only a skeleton crew manned the gangways and these were more intent on preventing anyone from getting on the ship rather than getting off. A full evacuation of the ship was once again in progress and so Chadwell just joined the throng leaving, kept a very low profile as he passed the guard post and soon found himself back at his original vantage point. The next problem would be to leave the yard. Back at the main gate it was apparent that all passes of westerners were being scrutinised carefully and that getting past the guards would not be possible. Another way to leave the yard would have to be found. If he couldn't leave by road perhaps the sea offered an escape route. Once again lady luck was on his side. Making his way back to the quayside he noted a small motor boat had just come alongside. The boat was only twenty-foot-long, open to the elements and with a small Hyundai 20 hp outboard motor. Its owner had left the boat alone whilst he went to the toilet. Chadwell didn't hesitate. Jumping into the boat he soon had the outboard hot-wired to start and was leaving the dock area before the hapless owner had finished pulling up his pants. From there it was a simple matter to find a suitable part of the coast where he could land, find a taxi, retrieve all his belongings and leave Ulsan by rail. Not wishing to risk using the false identity of Cartridge for fear that it was not just in the yard that it had been compromised he reverted to his own passport, not having any other to fall back on, and so it was that Jason Chadwell left Seoul and returned to Europe with many questions unanswered not least was how did HHI find him out.

Whilst Chadwell was making his way by train to Seoul, in the HHI yard Daniel Lee was deep in conversation with the yard security manager, a man named Sang-Don Jang. The conversation was convivial but there was a clear sign of tension between the two men.

'Mr Jang, please start from the beginning. I am confused regarding the fact that twice you cleared the Saunders Marine ship of all personnel causing considerable delay to the finalisation for sail away. You may not know but it is very important to the yard to get this ship ready to leave.'

'Then let me explain. You recall the explosion in the ship about eight weeks ago.' It was a rhetorical question and Jang continued, 'well you may remember at the time we were suspicious of the fact that we found traces of RDX when we do not use that explosive in the yard. We sent down divers and recovered most of the debris from the explosion which we had analysed. The results were over 90% certain that the explosion was not an accident.'

'What makes you so sure? The last time we spoke you were still investigating' the smile was no longer on Lee's face.

'The type of explosive was the first pointer but what confirmed things was the discovery of small parts of a timing device amongst the debris. We probably wouldn't have found anything had we not been looking as the bits were very small and could easily have been mistaken for parts of the ship, but the laboratory confirmed the bits to have come from a digital clock. That certainly would not have been in that compartment by accident.'

Jang lit a cigarette and inhaled deeply. His doctor had told him many times that he should quit but he basically didn't care. He had read about all the risks but that would not happen to him. After all his father had smoked every day until he died at the age of 93 so why should he worry. If he could have seen the small lump beginning to form in his left lung, perhaps he would have been slightly less sanguine.

'So, it was sabotage? But why would anyone want to blow a hole in the Kalevala. It doesn't make any sense.'

'No idea but having determined it was sabotage, the question was who was responsible. We looked through the security cameras that record everyone entering and leaving the yard through the main entrances and using facial recognition we linked the faces with the information on the individual passes. This was simpler than it sounds as the computer does most of the work. The system was only installed last year so this was a good opportunity to see how effective it was. The original idea was to have a fully automated system by this time which would have flagged up any discrepancies in real time but we're not quite there yet.'

'The search flagged up twenty-three cases where we had no record of the individual. That is where the face of the person caught on camera did not match our records for passes issued. We were then able to look at each pass in turn and determine how and when the pass was issued. This narrowed things down to three individuals, two Koreans and a westerner. We immediately programmed the security system to flag up if any of the three individuals entered the yard again. We also looked at CCTV coverage around the yard to see if we could identify if any of the three entered the Kalevala. On this latter check we did not get any conclusive identifications but the day after we installed the flag in the security system, we managed to get a positive identification on the two Koreans. It turns out that one of them had lost his pass and had borrowed someone else's to save the trouble of replacing his own pass. He has been reprimanded but no further action has been taken. He now has a new pass. The second man was a scrap dealer that had somehow got hold of a pass and used it to gain access to the shipyard and was stealing scrap metal. He has been handed over to the local police and will be charged. That left the westerner, a man named on his pass as James Cartridge. According to the yard records no pass was ever issued to a James Cartridge so he immediately went to the top of our list of suspects. As we didn't know the reason for the sabotage, we had to assume something might happen again so we briefed the security guards to report back to me personally if anyone answering the description of James Cartridge entered the yard again. We didn't inform the police as all we had was circumstantial evidence.'

Jang stubbed out the cigarette and reached for the packet on the desk in front of him. Absently he extracted another cigarette and placed it in his mouth. He continued to speak as he lit the cigarette.

'We didn't see any sign of Mr Cartridge for many weeks and I really thought that this would be the end of the matter but then this morning one of the guards on the main gate made an identification. To my surprise Mr Cartridge was not only back but using the same name and same pass. Unfortunately, by the time I got to the gate he had disappeared into the yard. My mistake for not telling the guard to apprehend the man. My immediate concern was for the Kalevala so I ordered an evacuation and a check on everyone that was on the vessel. I also ordered the vessel to be searched. Nothing was found and so we let personnel back on the vessel but we increased the guards on the gangways and this time left instructions that Mr Cartridge was to be detained if he tried to access the ship. Within half an hour we had our man, or at least we thought we did. A man using the pass of James Cartridge was detained at the main gangway onto the ship and brought to my office. He is still sitting outside but whilst he has similar features to the photograph on the pass it is not difficult to see that it is not the same person. Somehow the real Cartridge must have got wind of the fact that we were looking for him and switched passes. This is borne out by the statement of the man sitting outside who stated he had his pass ripped from around his neck, ostensibly by accident, whilst queuing to get on the ship. Having a different pass our man could now easily get access to the ship so once again I ordered an evacuation and a check on everyone on the ship but again, we drew a blank. We are still on high alert but a few moments ago I got a report that a small boat was stolen from dock number three this afternoon and has been found abandoned along the coast. It looks like the bird has flown but what he did when he was in the yard and where he went, we are still investigating.'

Jang leant back in his chair having finished his report.

'A pity you didn't inform me of this earlier.' Lee was clearly upset to have been kept in the dark. 'What about the Kalevala? Was there any sign of further sabotage?'

'Sorry that we were unable to inform you earlier but you were in a meeting and this was a yard security issue.' Jang did not look sorry. 'As for the Kalevala, as far as we know Cartridge never got on board but we are reviewing CCTV of the gangways. When does she sail?'

'The tide is right for early tomorrow morning so hopefully you are right because in 12 hours' time we will no longer have any control over the ship.'

Lee stood up from his seat eager to leave the smoke-filled room. The habitual smile was still absent from his face.

Chapter 19
May 2026

Aberdeen

Jean Robertson was just about to get into the shower when her phone rang. She was at first tempted to ignore the call but as the nominated spokesperson for Oceanic Energy Company on the subject of the Saebo incident she instead turned off the shower, grabbed her robe and made her way to the bedroom where the nearest phone was situated. At 36 years old Robertson was slim and attractive. The fact that she was still single surprised most people but Robertson was her own woman and was comfortable with her own company. Of course, she had had boyfriends, some quite serious, but always when it got too serious, she would back off. As the Human Resources Director of OEC she considered her career to be more important than any personal involvement and she was very good at her job.

Robertson was acutely aware that with the push to recruit more female executives in order to meet quotas the standard of some of the recruits was less than top class. As head of HR she oversaw the recruitment process for OEC which like most large companies had a positive discrimination policy in place. If a woman applied, they were given priority, but she also knew this meant sometimes accepting second best. So be it. This only balanced the inherently unfair advantage that men had enjoyed over the years. Ironically there was no way anyone could have accused the company of recruiting second best when it recruited Robertson. She was simply excellent at her job and it was expected that one day she would take over the role of CEO when Jim Simpson eventually decided to retire.

She got to the phone just before it would have reverted to the answering service and answered in her normal manner.

'Jean Robertson.'

The tone of voice unconsciously asked the called to state their business. At first the phone was silent except for a few clicks in the background. All the signs were there that the next voice would have a distinct sub-continent accent and declare that they were not selling anything but would just like to ask a few questions. Why did these calls always come at such an inconvenient time? Preparing to replace the receiver on the phone she heard a male voice. The voice was accented but it was an Eastern European accent not an Indian one.

'Irena, how lovely to talk to you after all these years.'

Although she hadn't heard the voice for nearly 21 years, she immediately recognised it. It was a voice she would never forget, a voice that brought back such grief and loneliness but also a voice that brought hope from despair. It was the voice of Dmitri Rostov, the nearest person that Jean Robertson had to a father. In shock she sat down on the bed and didn't know what to say. Rostov continued,

'I hope that you are well?'

'Yes, very well, thank you.'

At last Robertson found her voice and answered in a formal manner in order to regain her equilibrium.

'It's been a long time.'

'Over 20 years since you left Russia to start a new life in the west. In all that time your mother and I have heard nothing from you. But now the time has come for you to repay the kindness shown by the Russian state to a helpless orphan.'

Rostov's voice was devoid of emotion just as Robertson remembered from her childhood years when she had been forced to call Rostov papa even though he would never be her papa. Her mind involuntarily was transported back to that cold and misty day when her whole life had changed. The car crash that had killed her parents, the discovery by a passing cyclist who pulled her from the wrecked car, a frightened and freezing four-year-old, the subsequent ambulance ride to the local hospital and the kind doctor that had to tell her the awful news that her papa and mama were not coming home. Thereafter the series of foster parents until at the age of six years old she was adopted by Dmitri and Greta Rostov. But whilst she was now expected to call the Rostov's papa and mama, they were never real parents to her. More like guardians, they had made sure that the young Irena was well fed and looked after but never showed real love. She was sent to a special school that taught her only in the English language and expected her to spend ten hours a day on her studies. She learnt the history of Russia and the Soviet Union and was taught that the west was the enemy. Being above average intelligence, she was a quick learner and soon went on to learn other less conventional subjects such as how to operate a radio, how to code a message and how and what to listen to that may one day be of interest to Russia. In short, she learnt how to become a spy for Mother Russia. Knowing no difference and being at school with like-minded children she did not see that her upbringing was anything different from anyone else's. That all changed when she reached her 15th birthday.

On that day, instead of having birthday presents to open her "papa", Dmitri Rostov, had called her to his study and handed her a passport and a one-way ticket to Manchester Airport leaving in two days' time.

'The time has come for you to start the next phase of your training,' was all he said. 'Go and pack your things and be ready to leave tomorrow morning at first light.'

She could still recall the anguish and fear. Whilst growing up with the Rostov's had been very formal and with little or no love it was at least a stable life and she wasn't treated badly. Why was she being sent away and why to Manchester, a place she had been taught a lot about in her school, so a place she knew was one of Great Britain's biggest cities. She pleaded with Rostov not to be sent away but her cries fell on deaf ears. She was just told that this was what had been planned for her all those years before and gave her the great honour of maybe one day being of great service to the motherland.

She would be met at Manchester airport by Mr and Mrs Robertson and thereafter she would be called Jean Robertson. The Robertson's would provide all her paperwork including a new passport and a new identity. She was to call the Robertson's mum and dad and she would live with them as their daughter. No longer was she a Russian but she was now to become an English school girl who would be steered by the Robertson's.

And so it was that the next phase of her life started. Arriving at Manchester on a wet and windy evening she saw for the first time her new parents. They were a working-class family from Liverpool that were affiliated with the British Momentum movement, effectively the old communist party of Great Britain re-modelled for the modern world. As with the Rostov's the Robertson's were not unkind but showed very little affection to the newest member of the family which consisted of Mr and Mrs Robertson and two cats. Jean later found out that the Robertson's were paid via a secret account to raise her and steer her through university such that she would be able to find a job eventually in government. It was clearly stated that although she would be mostly free to steer her own course; eventually Russia would expect the vast expense put into her training and upbringing to be paid back. The call from Rostov, papa, after so long indicated that the payback was due.

Jean had always dreaded this day but knew it would come. Whilst her English father had steered her to a university degree in politics his attempt to put pressure on her to join the local conservative party in order to eventually become a Member of Parliament met with less success. Jean had argued that she needed experience outside politics if she was to remain above suspicion particularly with her parents known left wing political tendencies. Being very strong willed she got her way and having left Durham University with a first-class honours degree she went to live in Aberdeen where she got a job with Shell Oil in what was called the personnel department. Gradually she made her way up the ladder and made the right contacts until she found herself recruited by OEC as head of Human Resources.

'What do you want?'

Her fear made her response a bit too abrupt.

'Ah, Irena, whilst we haven't spoken for a long time that doesn't mean I haven't been keeping a close eye on you. Your English father supplies regular reports on what you are doing and particularly where you are working. I have to say that I was getting increasingly frustrated by your refusal to start your political career. Do you know how long it takes to infiltrate the British parliament but how useful it is to have, shall we say, people of authority who share Russia's interests. As I said I was very disappointed when told that you were resisting but do you know what the English word serendipity means?'

'Of course. It means a lucky accident.'

'Exactly. A lucky accident and that is what we have here. The serendipity in this case is that you are working for OEC who have become a company of interest to the Kremlin. No less a person than Boris Romanov has expressed an interest in you. Whilst you are still to remain in deep cover for a future infiltration of the British Parliament, something has come up that you are in a unique position to help us with. I am not privy to why the information is required but the Kremlin is very interested in the Caratacus development. I assume that you are fully aware of what this is?'

'Of course. It is the main reason for OEC's existence?'

'Good. Then perhaps you can tell me when it is likely to start producing oil.'

'Why do you need me for that? Its public knowledge that production is due to start next year.'

'But public knowledge and reality are not always the same thing.' Rostov's voice had an edge to it that made Robertson very nervous. 'I want to know what the reality is. How likely is it that the development will be on time and what are the weak points? Understand that it is not in Russia's interest for this development to go ahead next year and so we need to know where is the Achilles heel. How can we ensure the development is delayed without anyone being able to point a finger at Russia?'

'I work in the Human Resource department and don't have that information. I only know what everyone else knows which is that first oil is due on 1 July next year.'

'Then find out what I have asked for. I will ring again tomorrow at the same time.'

The phone went dead.

Chapter 20
May 2026

Naples

Marco Paglia was seated behind his desk preparing a presentation to his financial backers when the phone rang. Removing his reading glasses, he picked up the receiver and placed it to his ear.

'Ciao, Marco?' He answered in his normal way.

'Ciao. This is Constance. I have news.'

Paglia immediately forgot about the financial presentation and gave his full attention to the speaker on the other end of the line. Constance Luigiano was his contact at the Camorra.

'Good I hope.'

The brief pause before Luigiano answered should have acted as a warning but this was missed by Paglia.

'Shall we say it is not all bad.'

'Has the Kalevala sailing been delayed. That is all I need to know.'

'Regrettably the Kalevala sailed yesterday at 06:00hrs Korean time and is now on her way to South Africa.'

'Then you have failed?'

Paglia almost shouted down the phone but he knew better than to antagonise the man at the other end of the phone. Luigiano continued to talk in a calm and precise way.

'Failed? Our agreement was that we would only have failed if the ship arrives in the North Sea earlier than 15 September 2026. By my calculation that means we still have over three months to complete our side of the deal.'

'But for most of this time the ship will be at sea and with a sailing time of three months that is the time you have left. How can you stop it now?'

Paglia hadn't told Luigiano the reason that he wanted the ship delayed and in hindsight he realised he should have based the contract on a delay to the sailing rather than the arrival date. It was not in his interest for the ship to arrive later than mid-September if OEC was not 100% certain of this fact. Only then would they issue a contract to Rostella and trigger the non-compliance clause in the contract with Saunders marine.

'Perhaps we have already stopped it.' Luigiano answered rather cryptically.

'Please explain,' said Paglia.

'Let me first explain that eight weeks ago we thought that we had delayed the sail when we arranged for an explosive to be placed in the ship. Everything went to plan and damage was caused that should have done the job. Unfortunately, because of your insistence that no one gets hurt we had to use a small quantity of explosives and the subsequent damage was not as great as we had hoped. The Koreans were able to rectify things in time to meet the sail away date.'

'I am aware of your past failure. You assured me that the next time would be different.'

'And so it should have been, but due to the timing we had to use the same operative for the most recent sabotage attempt as the one of eight weeks ago. He had assured us that he had been undetected the first time so should be able to easily repeat his actions but this time with a larger quantity of explosive and by placing the explosive in a more vulnerable place on the ship. It appears that his confidence was ill founded. The Koreans seem to have been waiting for his return. They must have somehow realised that the first explosion was not an accident and that it was our operative that was responsible.'

'Are you telling me that the man has been arrested?'

Paglia had a sudden vision of the Carabinieri arriving at his front door even though he had been very careful to distance himself from the actual sabotage operations.

'Do not worry. He was not detained and is back in Europe. The Koreans were not as efficient with their security as they are with building ships so it was not difficult for our operative to avoid being captured. He even got onto the ship and placed his explosives in the agreed place but before he could properly set the timer he was interrupted and had to get out in a hurry.'

'What does that mean? You say he did not properly set the timer?'

'Let me explain. The detonation of the charge is controlled by a timer. In this instance the timer should have been set such that the explosion would occur at five o'clock in the morning when everyone was getting ready for the ship to sail. The explosive would have been right under one of the main support struts and would have meant the collapse of one of the vessels main structural elements preventing the sail away for at least the rest of this year. Unfortunately, as mentioned, our operative did not have time to set the timer properly and so whilst it was activated, he does not know on what time it was set when he left it. The explosion will take place we just don't know when.'

Luigiano paused whilst Paglia digested this information. It was only when he started to understand what he was being told that he began also to understand the full implications and the thought made his blood turn cold.

'How long could the timer be set for?' He asked in a quiet voice.

'It was a one month timer so any time in the next 30 days.'

'And your operative has no idea what was on the timer when he activated it?'

'Correct. The bomb could detonate tomorrow or in thirty days' time. We don't know when but I am assured that detonate it will. You see, we will have fulfilled our part of the contract so will expect to be paid the full agreed amount.'

Luigiano's voice was still calm but now contained an element of menace.

'Our agreement also stipulated that no one was to be hurt. If this bomb detonates when the ship is in the middle of the Indian Ocean and structural failure occurs how can you be sure it will not be catastrophic. The whole ship could sink. Who knows how many people will be killed? This was not our agreement.'

Now Paglia had put all caution aside and was shouting down the phone. He just stopped himself from calling Luigiano a name that would have questioned his parentage.

'People that play with fire can sometimes get hurt.'

Paglia could almost detect the shrug of shoulders from the tone of Luigiano's voice.

'When the bomb is detonated the ship will not reach the North Sea and we will consider our part of the contract fulfilled. If a few people are killed so be it. You knew that this was always a possibility and so we will still expect full payment. I do not need to spell out what happens to people and their families who do not honour an agreement.'

The phone went dead. There was no doubt that the menace was real. Paglia realised his naivety in thinking he could stipulate conditions in such a contract and that he would have to pay what had been agreed. The money was not his biggest concern. The fact that he could be responsible for the death of hundreds of innocent people only just began to dawn on him and whilst he was certainly not averse to bending and even breaking the law to get what he wanted he drew the line at murder. Putting his head in his hands with his elbows on the desk he leant forward and desperately started thinking what to do next.

Over 8000 miles east of Naples, Sang-Don Jang was also hunched over but he was hunched over a video monitor. The picture in front of him had been taken on top of the Kalevala's hull on the day of the intruder and the day before the sail away of the ship. It clearly showed the man known to him as James Cartridge entering the water tight door that led into the bowels of the ship. In his left hand he held a tool bag. Jang also contemplated what to do next.

Chapter 21
May 2026

Kremlin

'Good evening, gentlemen.'

Alexander Khurin opened the conversation having first ensured his guests all had a drink in their hands and were seated comfortably in the front room of his Odintsovsky accommodation. An early start to summer had bought an unusual heat wave to the Russian capital so the windows were open to allow a refreshing breeze to blow away some of the heat of the day.

'Igor, perhaps you can start by explaining what happened on the streets of Moscow yesterday?'

'You of course mean the demonstration and subsequent riot.' Khurin nodded and Antipov continued,

'The original demonstration was against the increase in food prices and the youth unemployment. It was instigated by a small but vocal group calling themselves the Voice of Russia. The name of the organisation has been taken from the since renamed Voice of Russia radio station now called Radio Sputnik. Its leader is a nobody from Kostroma who we have been keeping a close eye on for a number of years. the decision to allow the demonstration to go ahead was jointly taken by myself and the mayor of Moscow on the basis that it would be better to allow an outlet for the frustration of the people than to attempt to bottle up the tension. We also saw this as an opportunity to identify and remove the ring leaders. It was whilst arresting them that things got ugly. The mob turned on the police carrying out the arrests and half a dozen police officers were injured, none seriously so. Looting of shops occurred which rather played into our hands as we were able then to portray the mob as nothing more than a bunch of thieves. The police sent reinforcements and soon had the situation under control. As well as the ring leaders 50 arrests were made. The press has been instructed to report that the riot was nothing less than an attempt to steal from the hard-working people of Moscow and that those responsible have been arrested. The Voice of Russia has been declared a criminal organisation. We will ensure that the ring leaders are found guilty and disappear for a long time.'

Antipov looked relaxed as he came to the end of his report.

'Thank you, Igor. As always you have handled the situation well but the incident does show that we always need to be vigilant to what is happening within our own borders. Whilst we plan for the expansion of Russia, we must not lose sight of the fact that there are people within our own society that would rather Russia remained weak and went the way of the western democracies. People that are not willing to make the sacrifices needed to make Russia great again.'

Khurin glanced around the room. Briefly making eye contact with Antipov, Nikolaev and Romanov he did not see the irony of his statement. The sacrifices were being made by ordinary Russian people who were finding it more and more difficult to make ends meet so he and his associates could carry on living the high life. Satisfied that he had reinforced his point he turned to other issues.

'Let's hope that the lesson has been heard and that others that perhaps would like to follow on from our friend from Kostroma will in future think twice.' Khurin smiled but the smile didn't extend to his eyes.

Shifting the subject Khurin turned to Nikolaev.

'Vitali, how goes our preparations to destabilise the NATO alliance?'

Sitting in a high-backed chair directly opposite the Russian President, the Russian foreign minister briefly consulted his notes before answering.

'Things are going well, Mr President.'

Even though Nikolaev had been in the inner circle for over two years he still could not call Khurin by his given name. Khurin for his part did not feel the need to change this. Only those people that he had known for over a quarter of a century and who had proven their loyalties time and time again had that privilege.

'If we are to take back the territory of the old Soviet Union, we need to neutralise NATO and for that we need to exploit its weakness.'

'To understand NATO's weakness, we first need to look at its history. NATO was originally founded in 1949 and it had a very clear objective. To counter the strength of the Soviet Union and its allies in the east. As the Soviet Union was part of Europe any future battle was expected to be fought on European soils; and so, the NATO alliance was very much seen as a European endeavour which was reflected in the make-up of the original alliance. Out of the twelve founding countries, ten were European. Later as the Soviet Union went into decline the influence exerted over the eastern European countries that once formed the basis of the Warsaw Pact waned and eventually the Warsaw alliance ceased to exist. Many of the ex-Warsaw pact countries applied and were granted the right to join NATO such that today NATO consists of 29 separate nations all committed to come to the defence of each other in case they are attacked. It is important to note that it was always European countries that joined such that today all members are European except for Canada and the USA, that is if we accept that Turkey is European.'

Looking around the room Nikolaev saw that he had everyone's attention.

'The irony is that the original reason for NATO's existence no longer exists. The Soviet Union is no more and as I said most Warsaw Pact nations have now joined NATO. This has not been lost on the Europeans. The rules of the club are that each country must spend at least 2% of its GDP on defence as part of its commitment to other nations. But while America looks world-wide and continues to spend close to 3.5% of its GDP on defence, most European countries spend less than 1%. The old Soviet Union has been defeated and Europe is incapable of seeing any risk from countries outside its borders so why do you need defence? In addition, with the European Union's combined army now in place and America no longer interested in the defence of Europe NATO is seen by many as antiquated and unnecessary. There is some concern about the rise in Russia's strength but insufficient to convince the citizens of Europe to spend more on defence.'

'I mentioned that there are 29 nations in NATO but the only ones we need to consider are America and Turkey.'

'But what about France, Great Britain and Germany?' Antipov interrupted.

'France and Germany are members of the European Union and have turned over their armed forces to the European army. This is a typical European Union venture, great in theory but useless in practice. Great Britain has been previously discussed and will not be strong enough to give the necessary leadership. No, it is the interplay between Turkey and America that we have been exploiting. If either left NATO our analysis is that the whole alliance will fall apart. We thought we'd achieved our goal a few years ago when America and Turkey found themselves on different sides in the ISIS conflict but at the last minute a compromise was worked out without solving the underlying issues.'

'We have continued to work on Turkey and more and more they see Russia as a natural ally rather than America. In addition, we provide Turkey with most of its energy needs. We are already in advanced discussions with President Demir to set up an alternative defence pact between Russia and Turkey. Included in the pact will be Belarus, Georgia, Moldova, Azerbaijan and Ukraine. We anticipate that the discussions will be concluded as early as next month in which time Turkey will formally leave NATO. America will use this as an excuse to also leave NATO.'

'We anticipate that within weeks the NATO alliance will cease to exist.'

Nikolaev reached for his glass of water and took a long drink whilst waiting for a reaction from the other occupants of the room.

'That will certainly scare the shit out of the Europeans.' Romanov was the first to respond. 'But have we got our timing right. Won't the collapse of NATO just make the Europeans increase their defence spending to compensate for America and Turkey leaving? As we won't be ready to launch our attacks to restore our borders until late next year wouldn't we have been better to leave NATO intact for another three months at least?'

'You may be right, Boris, but we cannot control the timing of these events to the hour and minute.'

Khurin stepped into the conversation.

'Despite what Vitali has said, we cannot guarantee that Turkey leaving will cause NATO to collapse even if we think that this is the most likely outcome. If NATO doesn't collapse it will definitely be weakened but we will need some extra time to exploit these weaknesses to ensure our ultimate goal.'

'Excellent work, Vitali. What about our preparations in the target countries?'

'The primary countries that we are targeting are Poland, Bulgaria, Romania, Hungary, Slovakia and the Baltic states. We also will be looking to bring the 'istan' countries back into our sphere of influence but as we already have sympathetic governments in these states, we are of the view that once the western buffer zone is secure these countries will easily be coerced into re-joining a Russia dominated alliance. We see the pact being prepared with Turkey as the basis for this new alliance and will use the Turkish Islamic card to convince the other Islamic nations that joining such an alliance will be in their interest. This is an area that will have to be handled with great care but by the time the Islamic states realise that the alliance is controlled by Russia it will be too late for these countries to change their allegiances and they will become to all intent and purpose Vassal states to Russia.'

'Finland is the outsider but it has always retained its neutrality. Even though it is in the EU it has not joined NATO for instance. We do not expect that it will change its position and we expect that we will be able to negotiate a non-aggression pact similar to that which was in place throughout the Soviet era.'

'Our proposal for the next two years is to concentrate on the western buffer zone and the first phase will be to take back the Baltic states. These states are seen as a relatively easy target because of the large percentage of Russian speaking citizens as a consequence of the previous Soviet domination of these countries. We have embarked on a mis-information campaign in all interested countries but we have put most effort into the Baltic states. The consequence is that the main opposition parties in all three countries are already strongly pro-Russia. In addition, whilst the Baltic states are members of NATO, neither Finland or Sweden are members. There is only limited co-ordination between NATO and non-NATO countries and with the collapse of NATO any western country that feels the urge to go to the support of the Baltic states would not have a land border to utilise except for a small border with Poland. By the time any sea borne defence force could be arranged we would have consolidated our position on the Baltic coast and we will use the Kaliningrad enclave to counter any Polish support. We anticipate that once our troops enter the Baltic states it will only take eight weeks to fully subdue any defences and a further four weeks to build the missile defence system to deter any counter invasion. We will issue the usual propaganda that we are only protecting Russian speakers from nationalist aggression. We have already arranged for a series of terrorist attacks targeting Russian speaking individuals to give us some legitimacy in this. The west will know exactly what we are doing but not wanting or being ready to intervene, they will just make meaningless political noises.'

'When will the attack on the Baltic states take place?' Antipov interjected.

Romanov who was responsible for the Russia armed forces stepped in.

'We are planning on having all our forces in place at the end of this year. By launching our campaign over the Christmas period, we buy ourselves a week or so extra whilst the western states get over their Christmas hangovers.'

Romanov smiled at his own joke. Nikolaev took up the narrative again.

'Boris has assured me that preparations for a Christmas campaign are well under way. But that is just the beginning. Assuming that everything goes according to plan...'

'Which it will,' Romanov interrupted.

Nikolaev glanced in the direction of Romanov before continuing,

'As I was saying, assuming everything goes according to plan then by next March we will have completed the annexation of the Baltic states and the first phase will be over.'

'The second phase is seen as more difficult as it will involve annexing Poland, Bulgaria, Romania, Hungary and Slovakia. The take-over of the Baltic states will cause concern to these countries and we would expect that they will start to strengthen their armed forces. We don't see Hungary, Bulgaria and Romania as real problems as they have governments that, shall we say, are open to persuasion that is in their best interest. They are already at loggerheads with the Brussels dominated EU and are only remaining within the EU because they get a net contribution in funds. If Russia is able to at least match that contribution without the straight jacket of having to comply with the many human rights restrictions that being a member of the EU entail, we fully expect that these three countries will agree to leave Europe and join our alliance. We will at the same time cut their access to the gas going to these countries via Turkey which will be a good bargaining chip when it comes to setting up the terms of the alliance. We fully expect that this will neutralise any threat from these three countries whilst we deal with the main problem which is Poland. I have ignored Slovakia as being too small to cause any concerns.'

As Nikolaev paused to take a drink of water Khurin continued.

'Poland has always been a pain in the side of Russia. Its people are fiercely nationalistic and its government whilst anti the bureaucracy of the EU has prospered considerably by being allied to the west. It has been careful to keep its relationship with Great Britain strong despite the latter leaving the EU a few years ago. It also has a half decent armed force looking very much towards Russia. Also, let's not forget that it was the German invasion of Poland that triggered the Great Patriotic War when Great Britain and France eventually saw through the subterfuge of Hitler's Germany and said enough was enough. Poland will be our biggest challenge.'

The three other men in the room all nodded before Nikolaev once again took up the narrative.

'Mr President is absolutely correct in his assessment that Poland has been the biggest headache and is the reason why we cannot put in place our plans any earlier. It is a big country and one that we have been unable to make many inroads into the political system. If we launched an all-out invasion, we are concerned that we could be bogged down before the other European countries got their act together and started to put up a defence, particularly as we would be getting too close to Germany. Our plan therefore is to only take half the country. We propose to advance as far as the Vistula River before swinging to the south of Krakow and hitting the Czechia/Slovakia border at a place called Trójstyk. At the same time, we will invade Slovakia. By limiting our territorial gains to only half of Poland we estimate that we can be at the Vistula River within 12 weeks of starting the campaign. Immediately after we start the campaign we will open a dialogue with Germany to seek a peace agreement. We are still under discussion of the reason we will give for the invasion but our intention is to play on the guilt that still prevails in Germany regarding the Great Patriotic War. We know that the far right in Germany is making political gains so our thoughts are to express our concern that this far right movement is infecting Poland to the extent that we fear a repeat of 1939. We will state that our annexation of the east of Poland is our only territorial ambitions to reinstate a buffer state and to give assurances that we will stop at the Vistula. Hopefully this will slow any Western European response and give us time to set up our defences on the Vistula.'

'You seem to be putting a lot of reliance on the missile defence system to consolidate our position before any counter attack can be formulated.'

Antipov had a look of concern on his face. Whilst he was aware of the plan, this was the first time he had heard the details. It was Romanov that answered.

'Whilst ostensibly complying with the medium range missile limitation treaty we have quietly been developing a new system, one that is far in advance of anything the west has. This missile has the range to deliver a nuclear war head to any city in Europe. We have over 200 mobile launch sites for these missiles and each launch site has four missiles. A few weeks prior to putting in place our operations we will leak the existence of these missiles which should slow down any immediate response from our European neighbours. We have also developed a missile defence shield which consists of anti-aircraft and anti-tank capability far in advance of anything the west has in its arsenal. We will use this shield in the same way that the Egyptians used their missile shield during the Yom Kippur war but we will ensure that the shield stays intact and that it remains solely defensive. We have over 4000 of these missile defence systems which we will deploy along the entire new border. That way we will show that any counter attack will be met with a potential massive nuclear offensive if it succeeds but first it will have to break through the defensive shield. By making it clear that having regained the territories of the old Soviet Union we have no further territorial ambitions; we fully expect the Western Europeans nations to abandon the Eastern European nations for the sake of a peaceful end to any further conflict.'

Antipov had a thoughtful look on his face.

'I see now the importance of neutralising the threat from Great Britain. Your assessment of German impotent as a result of their guilt for the last war reflects my understanding that the only real threat to our expansion plans are Great Britain and France. And without Great Britain, France will be powerless to act alone. Igor, I commend you and your team for a well thought out plan. I'm sure that, as always, the devil will be in the detail but I cannot on the face of it see any major flaws provided the execution is as well enacted as the plan.'

'You can leave the execution to me. All will be as planned I can assure you.'

Romanov had a wolfish look on his face as he relished the thought of being the instigator if not the architect of making Russia great once again.

'What about the strength of our armed forces? Are they good enough to achieve the initial conquests? A lot has been said about what happens after we have taken over the territories but not a lot about how.' Khurin aimed the remark at Romanov.

'Apart from identifying strategic targets we have been strengthening our armed forces by spending over 6% of the country's GDP on the military for the past five years. Our army and air force are the strongest and best equipped in Europe. Our navy is weaker but we have deliberately been channelling our resources into the army and air force for obvious reasons. To keep up with this level of defence expenditure would be crippling for the country and as you have seen by the recent rioting our people are beginning to feel the effects of insufficient spending in other social areas. But once we have consolidated the territorial gains, we will be able to considerably increase our GDP using the resources of our new territories and also reduce our military spending to a more sustainable level. The extra money can be channelled into social issues and should go a long way in settling the internal unease that we see today.'

'But I assume that even if America does not come to the defence of Europe it will not just ignore what we are doing and let us get away with it? I would expect them to impose economic sanctions that would make what we saw a few years back look like a breeze. Wouldn't that mitigate any positive effects on our GDP?'

Khurin shifted his gaze from Romanov to Nikolaev.

'We have been cultivating our relations with China and Japan for the last few years as well as consolidating alliances in the Middle East. Western Europe is still dependant on Russian gas so we do not expect that American led sanctions will come to much. Our analysts have estimated that within a few months of any sanctions being imposed the Americans will realise that the only one being hurt is themselves and when they see the Europeans continuing to trade with us, they will soon drop the sanctions and accept the new world order.'

Silence descended on the room as the four colleagues mulled over what they had heard. The plan was audacious, brave and calculated. The rewards were great and at least to the people in the room the risk of failure was low.

'Thank you all,' Khurin at last broke the silence. 'Needless to say we need to maintain the strictest secrecy on this until we are fully ready for implementation. I assume that Vitali, you and Boris will put together a detailed timed plan for the operations ensuring all critical junctures are well highlighted. It does seem to me that there are particular things that you have assumed will be achieved that if aren't could have a significant effect on the outcome of the plan. An example would be if we are unable to get Turkey to break from NATO or if they do, NATO remains intact with the full backing of America. I'm sure there are many more such junctures which need to be identified. When do you think that such a plan will be ready?'

'We are working on just such a plan, Mr President. It should be available for your review within the next two months.' Nikolaev answered.

'Good. Please keep us all informed of the progress and I look forward to seeing the final plan when ready. Does anyone else have anything to report or should we call it a day?'

Khurin went to rise from his chair expecting the meeting to be over but Romanov continued talking.

'Just one further item to report. You may recall our concerns at the last meeting of the effect that Great Britain's new oil find could have on the ability of Great Britain to expand its armed forces.'

Khurin sat back in his chair and indicated Romanov to continue.

'As fortune would have it, we have a deep asset in Great Britain that we have been cultivating to eventually become a member of their parliament. The asset in question has been in Great Britain for a number of years but has not yet made a move into politics, something that has been a bit annoying for the asset's handler. Annoying maybe but fortunate for us. Coincidently the asset is at present in a senior position at OEC, the energy company that is the operator of the Caratacus field. Last week I ordered the asset's controller to contact the asset to find out where the weak point was regarding the development of the Caratacus field. It would appear that most of the infrastructure is in place but still outstanding is the offshore production platform. If we can delay the completion of this platform, we would delay the project. Our asset has identified two ways in which this could be done. The first is to stop the installation vessel which is the only one in the world that can install the main platform. The second is to delay the fabrication of the accommodation unit presently under construction in Norway. We could also strike at the onshore processing plant but that would be more difficult to disguise as an accident. As the installation vessel is already sailing to Europe it is outside our reach, at least until it gets into European waters, but the facilities building the accommodation unit are easily reached and not particularly well guarded. On that basis we have decided our best option is to sabotage the accommodation unit. We are working on a strategy to implement which should be finalised within the month. The unit is due to leave the fabricators and go offshore in three months' time but we have enough time. By taking action against the accommodation unit we will delay the Caratacus project for at least a year, delaying the subsequent tax benefit to the British economy. One more risk neutralised.'

Romanov looked pleased with himself as he glanced at the other faces in the room resting finally on Khurin's face.

'Well done again, Boris. So far so good. And now to bed. Thank you all gentlemen.'

This time Khurin left no opening for anyone to continue the discussion. He had a girl young enough to be his daughter waiting in his bedroom and he didn't want to keep her waiting any longer.

Chapter 22
May 2026

Korea

As Daniel Lee gazed out of the window of his third-floor office the shipyard seemed somehow empty without the massive profile of the Kalevala to dominate the view. He knew the yard was as busy as ever with 16 ships in various stages of production but none of the new ships came anywhere close to the size of the Saunders Marine crane vessel. He still had the final contractual issues to resolve and the final bill to get paid relating to the work performed on the Kalevala but he was already considering his next project when there was a knock on the door to his office. Before Lee could respond the door opened and Sang-Don Jang walked in and sat down in the chair on the opposite side of Lee's desk. The look on Jang's face told Lee that this wasn't a social visit. Jang started talking without any niceties.

'Mr Lee, I believe we have a problem with the Kalevala.'

Whilst Lee was not particularly friendly with Jang, he did not dislike him and respected his position so kept his response neutral.

'Good morning, Mr Jang and what sort of problem do we have? The ship has sailed and apart from a few minor contractual issues and the completions that will be performed on the sail to South Africa the ship is no longer our concern.'

'The problem relates to the intruder incident that occurred just before the ship sailed. You will recall that we detected that the same man who we now consider responsible for planting an explosive device on the Kalevala eight weeks ago had returned to the yard?'

'A, Mr Cartridge, if I recall. You also advised me that you had been unable to detect the man had left the yard but presumed that due to a missing boat that eventually turned up along the coast that he had stolen the boat and left by sea. Are you now saying that this wasn't the case?'

'Not at all. We still believe this to be true. What we didn't know was why he decided to leave by sea rather than through the main entrance as previously. We had to assume that somehow, he realised that we were looking for him and couldn't risk going through the security checks at the main gate. His efforts to avoid detection indicate that he had a nefarious reason for being in the yard but the question is what was his reason. Taking into account the damage he caused on the Kalevala the last time he was detected in the yard it would be logical to assume his target was once again the Kalevala.'

'But you told me there was no evidence that he had got access to the Kalevala this time?'

Lee's suspicions of where this was going were raised.

'The last time we spoke there was no evidence but since then my colleagues and I have been looking through the video recordings of the CCTV cameras that we still had on the ship. As you know most had been removed due to the proximity to the sail away date but we still had three in place. It was on one of these cameras that showed our assumption that Mr Cartridge did not get access to Kalevala was wrong. He was detected walking along the top of one of the pontoons and seen entering the hull via a worker access door.'

'Are you sure of this. It couldn't be a mistake like the last time when the wrong man was apprehended?'

'I'm afraid there is no mistake. Whilst his face was visible for only a brief moment it was enough for the face recognition software to make a positive identity. There is no doubt that our potential saboteur gained access to the ship and what's more he was carrying a large tool bag. The camera also caught him exiting the same door way; it has to be said seemingly in a hurry but more of a concern he was no longer carrying the tool bag.'

'This is not good.'

Lee leant back in his chair and steepled his fingers whilst he digested the news given by Jang.

'Who else knows about this?'

'At the moment just myself, the security guard that found the match on the video and now yourself. I wanted to talk with you before elevating the news to senior management.'

'Thank you for that, Mr Jang. I appreciate you keeping me informed but the question now is what do we do about it? The Kalevala sailed three days ago and as far as I know there have been no indications of sabotage in that time. Is it possible that Mr Cartridge was disturbed before he could cause any further damage? You say he seemed to be in a hurry when he left the ship so perhaps he noticed that he was the target of a manhunt before he had the chance to cause any further sabotage actions.'

'My initial thoughts as well but the time between him entering the ship and leaving again is 15 minutes. That is plenty of time to plant a bomb and make his escape if we assume that this was his intention. Even if he didn't have time to position any explosive device, I think we have to assume that he would have had one with him and as he did not have his bag when he left the ship, assumedly the explosives must still be somewhere on board. In my view the Captain of the Kalevala has to be informed and a search of the ship carried out. That would be my recommendation to the senior management.'

As Jang finished speaking, he reached into his pocket and extracted a packet of cigarettes. Korea still hadn't adopted the western policy that smoking was only allowed in the open air and not in confined public spaces. Lee, as a non-smoker, prayed for the day when such legislation was also enacted in Korea. Until then he had to endure the inconsideration of such people as Jang who seemed to have no thought to the fact that his smoking deeply annoyed Lee and to light a cigarette as he was now doing in Lee's own office was even more intolerable. But not wishing to cause a fuss he just got up and opened the window before returning to his chair and again addressing Jang.

'If we inform Saunders Marine, we have to also inform them the reason for our suspicions and that will not reflect well on HHI or for that matter on you. They will want to know why, when we knew the vessel had been sabotaged, they had only now been informed. They will also want to know why the same man that carried out the sabotage was able to get back in the yard and potentially cause further sabotage.'

'You will not be aware but we are in the final stages of agreeing commercial terms for the construction of the ship. Saunders Marine have been trying to delay some of the payments with the excuse that the ship has not been fully completed in accordance with the specification. The payment schedule was not particularly good for HHI in the first place, we only get paid 70% of the overall cost of the build on completion, so at the moment HHI or at least HHI's banks are subsidising the cost of build. Any indication that there is a bomb on board placed there whilst the ship was still under HHI safe keeping will be all the excuse Saunders Marine needs to withhold payment of the outstanding amount. And if nothing has happened yet then the chances are Cartridge did not set any explosive devices, otherwise I would have expected it would have detonated by now. So why prod the bee's nest when we don't yet know if there is any honey?'

'But what if there is an explosive device and it detonates when the ship is at sea. It could cause considerable damage and loss of life. I think the risk is too great to not do anything.'

Jang was aware that he would most likely take a large part of the responsibility for the breach of security if it was reported but he was also conscientious enough to realise the potential consequences of doing nothing were too high. As he got up from the chair and walked over to the open window to flick the ash off the tip of his cigarette, he continued,

'We have to inform the Kalevala and instigate a search.'

Lee was not about to let a payment of over a billion dollars be delayed if he could help it. He had already told the yards financial director that payment would be received within the month and the yard lenders had been informed accordingly. Any change now would mean considerable loss of face for Lee but also would send the wrong message to the yard's creditors. If there was one thing that made banks very nervous it was uncertainty; and nervous banks meant higher interest rates on future loans. Whilst the security aspect would reflect badly on Jang, Lee knew that he would also be implicated.

'Perhaps, I can suggest a compromise.' Lee turned around to face Jang who was now standing by the open window. 'I think we both suspect that there is no active explosive device on the ship but due to the consequences if we are wrong, we need to instigate a search of the ship.'

Jang nodded in agreement as Lee continued.

'Then why don't we use our people to carry out the search? We have nearly 200 people on the ship finalising the outfitting. We can arrange for them to search the ship. We just need to find an excuse for the search that will not alarm the Saunders Marine crew.'

Jang, whilst conscientious, was also aware of the negative aspects on his career if management got involves so he was open to any alternative solution.

'That would work. Do you have anything in mind for the reason for searching the ship without going through Saunders Marine?'

Lee again took his seat and steepled his fingers with his elbows on his desk as he thought through the possibilities.

'It has to be something serious enough to allow the whole ship to be searched which means the Saunders Marine crew will need to be involved but they don't have to be looking for the same thing. We will clearly have to tell our people what to look for. The question is can we trust them not to blabber to the Saunders Marine crew?'

Whilst the question was meant to be rhetorical Jang answered,

'I think we can, particularly as most don't have any interaction with the ship's crew and anyway most don't even speak English.'

'Also, my thoughts. Our representative on board is Hoseong Park. I know him well. He can be trusted to keep quiet. Why don't we suggest that one of the HHI work force is missing and may have fallen over-board? A search would be necessary to ensure he hasn't fallen and hurt himself somewhere on the ship. We can tell Mr Park that he must look for a worker's bag or any sign of an explosive device whilst the crew will be looking for a missing worker. After Mr Park and his team can confirm that they have found nothing they can inform the ship's crew that the HHI worker has been located and it was a false alarm.'

'But what if they do find an explosive device? What do they do then?'

A second cigarette had appeared between Jang's fingers.

'Then we have no options. We will have to inform the authorities to get someone to the ship to deal with it but then at least we will know where it is. The fact that it hasn't detonated means it most likely hasn't been primed so it should be a quick and painless activity to disarm it. I'll get on the phone to Mr Park immediately. Meanwhile this stays between the two of us; correct?'

'Agreed. I'll send you a still photograph of the workers bag from the CCTV video which may help Mr Park to know what precisely to look for.'

With that Jang flicked the half-smoked cigarette stub out of the window and left the room. Lee reached for the phone and asked his secretary to place a call to Hoseong Park on the Kalevala.

Chapter 23
May 2026

London

The Palace of Westminster lies adjacent to the River Thames in the centre of London and next door to Westminster Abbey from which it derives its name. The Gothic style building that is seen today was completed in the 1860s and stands on the same site as a previous government building destroyed by fire in 1834. Today most people know the Palace of Westminster as the Houses of Parliament due to the fact that it houses the two parliaments of Great Britain, the House of Commons and the House of Lords. It is ostensibly from where Great Britain is governed and where legislation is enacted. Apart from the two great debating chambers, one for each parliament or houses as they are normally called, there are over one thousand other rooms in the Palace which are used for everything from offices, libraries, kitchens, dining rooms, bars, utility rooms, official accommodation for certain dignitaries and even a gymnasium and shooting range.

Today, within one of the hundreds of offices, Richard Green was sitting at the head of a long table chairing his first security meeting. Also seated around the table were Cynthia Graeme, The Home secretary, Gary Davies, The Foreign Secretary, Jason Bhatia, the defence secretary, Joan Stapleford, Director General of MI5, Duncan Smith, Head of MI6, Rachel Stewart, the Commissioner of the Metropolitan Police and General Sir David Jordan, Chief of the Defence Staff. Other lesser personnel representing various departments of the civil service and security services were also present but they were there primarily to carry out any decisions that might be made by their superiors.

Following introductions Richard Green addressed the room.

'Ladies and gentlemen.' He smiled and glanced around the room. 'Thank you for attending this first meeting of the security council under this administration. I am fully aware that most of you will be very familiar with the format and have served on this committee for a number of years working for the previous administration.

'The last few months have seen a big shift in the political make-up of our country. I like to see this as a result of my over whelming charisma but I think we all know that it was because the British people had just had enough of socialism or at least the form of socialism practiced by the previous administration. They voted for change and they voted in large numbers.

'As I said many of you worked closely with that administration and perhaps think that you owe them an element of loyalty, but I am here today to tell you that if you are harbouring such thoughts then please leave the room now.'

Green stopped talking and looked around the room briefly letting his gaze fall on each individual. No one moved to leave although a couple of junior security personnel dropped their gaze or were suddenly required to make a note on the jotter in front of them as Green's eyes reached them.

'Good,' Green continued, 'I am pleased that I can count on your full support to try and unravel the mess that we find ourselves in. You will no doubt be aware, more than most, that the finances of the country are in a dire strait. It was the defence and security budgets that suffered most under the previous administration as funds were channelled into social support. The exception for those around this table was the police budget which held up reasonably well.'

Green looked across at Rachel Stewart who nodded in acknowledgment.

'I would like to say that things will change; and it is my full intention that they will change, but I have to be realistic in what can be achieved. There is no magic wand that can be waved to suddenly find the resources we need but hopefully the policies that we are introducing in areas such as taxation, business legislation, social services, education and the state sector in general will gradually mean that we will have more resources available to spend on our security services and defence. Having said that, what I would like to hear from around the table is what are the risks facing this country today and what is being done with the available resources to counter those risks? I hope when responding you will take into account what I have said about the availability of additional resources and not use this forum to pass around the begging bowl.'

'Joan, let's start with you. Forgive my ignorance on who does what but I promise I'll get to know you all in the coming months. I understand that you, as head of MI5, are responsible for domestic counter intelligence and internal security.'

'That is correct, Prime Minister.'

Joan Stapleford was a rather stern looking middle-aged lady who could easily have passed as a head mistress rather than the most powerful person in the department responsible for counter intelligence. Today she was wearing a blue cardigan over a pale blue blouse and a knee length cream skirt. Her shoes were from Clarke's and were navy blue.

'My responsibilities are to look inward so I will concentrate on the risks within our borders. Duncan will be able to illuminate any external risks.'

'Internally the biggest risk that we see is the low morale and lack of diversity within our organisation. To attempt to quantify this I have instigated a 360-degree survey of all personnel including myself and have introduced a positive discrimination policy to try and attract more ethnic minorities and female operatives. Quite frankly it is a disgrace in this day and age that we only have 19% of personnel that are female and less than 15% that come from a minority background.'

Stapleford placed a pair of reading glasses on the end of her rather pointed nose and consulted the note on the table in front of her. Before she could continue Green interrupted.

'Before you go on, can I make one thing absolutely clear not just to you but to everyone else? I don't give a monkey's uncle about who you employ to perform your work. I expect you to employ who so ever is best for the task in hand irrespective of sex, colour or creed. I know that the previous administration has set targets for such things but this administration will be removing all such targets. That not only goes for those organisations that have, as you put it, positive discrimination recruitment but also all those organisations that employ based on the old boy's network.

'And whilst we are on the subject of expectations, I also expect that all managers are competent to do their job so this administration will not only be looking to do away with targets but will also do away with a lot of the reporting at present required which it seems to me is only being performed to either keep someone in a job or to ensure everyone has covered their backside. We have to find ways of reducing our costs and one area that cries out is to cut unnecessary bureaucracy. You have been warned that when budgets are set this is an area that we will be looking at very closely.

'But right now I would like to know what are the threats to UK Plc rather than whether you have implicated personnel surveys, set targets for the type of person you will employ or perform a risk assessment every time you go to the toilet.'

Running his hand through his hair he looked straight at the unfortunate Stapleford who was not used to being talked to in such a way and was quite taken aback.

'Er, precisely, quite,' she blustered, 'I was just trying to explain an area of concern that could prevent the optimum efficiency of the intelligence service.'

'Thank you. Your point has been made. Now perhaps you can tell me what are the biggest internal threats to our country.'

Still trying to find her composure Stapleford again consulted her notes before continuing.

'We have three main concerns. Firstly, and top of our list is the war on terrorism. After the Syrian conflict we saw a large influx of refugees but not all the refugees were genuine. Some were trained terrorists intent on not only causing mayhem themselves but also on radicalising local Muslims to commit atrocities. Already this year we have thwarted five attempts and identified a further 12 potential risks but even so we were not 100% successful as I'm sure you are aware.'

'I assume that you are referring to the Saebo incident?' Green interrupted.

Stapleford looked bemused.

'Not at all. As far as I'm aware there was no indication that terrorism was involved in that incident. No, I was referring to the damage caused to the New Semington Aqueduct that flooded the A350 resulting in five deaths and sever disruption.'

'I was not aware that this was a terrorist incident. I was under the impression it was an accident.'

'That is the story we put out. We didn't want to give the terrorists the advantage of publicity. We still do not know who carried out the attack but it most certainly was not an accident.'

'Why did you think the Saebo incident was terrorist related?'

'Just fishing. I had a discussion with the rig's owners a few days ago and he was of the opinion that the incident was nothing more than a tragic accident. You seem to have just confirmed that.'

'I have seen the preliminary investigation report and the cause is put down as a faulty valve and an overheating ventilation fan. When the shallow gas pocket was hit the valve did not shut allowing a gas release that was ignited by sparking from the faulty fan. Nothing to do with terrorism.'

'Thank you. That's good to know. You mentioned you had three concerns. What are the other two?'

'The second concern is that we are detecting a growing number of incidents involving Russian sympathisers. At the last count we were aware of at least 350 individuals that had a connection with Russian intelligence.'

'350?'

Green looked shocked.

'They are the ones we know about. We suspect that there are at least the same number that we do not know about. A worrying trend is that Russia has been placing sleepers in the United Kingdom for years before they are activated. As these sleepers lead a normal life until activated, they are next to impossible to detect. They have a bona fide history so normal background checks show nothing out of the ordinary. The reality is that, until activated, these people are invisible but could be anywhere. They are given specific tasks when first placed in this country, such as infiltrate the trade union movement or join the intelligence community, and we wouldn't know they were working for Russia. They could just get on with whatever job they had until Russian intelligence determined that they had a sufficiently influential position and started to use them to either get information or to cause disruptions. Only then do they potentially expose themselves and give GCHQ the chance to pick them up.'

'If you know about 350 people who are spying for Russia why do you not arrest them?'

'Because if we arrested them the Russians would only replace them with people we don't know. In addition, by monitoring these 350 persons we sometimes get lucky and get a lead to one of the sleepers who are our main concern. Only last week GCHQ was able to get snippets of a conversation between an unknown person in Scotland and someone from Grizodubovoy street.'

'Grizodubovoy street?' Green queried.

'GRU headquarters. The home of Russian intelligence. We spend a lot of time listening in on anything that comes out of that place. This particular conversation was of interest because it targeted someone that until then had not been on our radar. Most but not all of the Russian agents or sympathisers are in the south of the country, specifically within the London area. We know of only two sympathisers in Aberdeen and both were working offshore when the call was detected so we are trying to focus in on who the call was directed towards.'

'You mentioned that you were detecting an increase in the number of incidents involving Russian sympathisers. What sort of incidents are you referring to?'

'Nothing really specific. The level of communication between Moscow and the United Kingdom has increased considerably since the election. We assumed that this was the Russian government trying to learn more about you and your politics. After all you came from nowhere to being prime minster in 12 weeks so I am assuming that the Russians want to know who they are dealing with. But that doesn't cover all the additional chatter. For instance, we know of an agent in the heart of the treasury that has been leaking information to the Russians for the last four years. As I mentioned earlier, we leave him in place because that way we can keep track on what the Russians are getting. The individual doesn't know that we are on to him and we make sure that he gets access to sufficient material to keep his paymasters contented. Normally the agent just hands over information and the Russians pay him but just recently the Russians have been asking for specific information.'

'What sort of specific information?' This was from Cynthia Graeme who as Home Secretary was nominally Stapleford's boss.

'That's what has raised my third concern.' Stapleford turned to face Graeme before continuing. 'The information requested was to determine if the United Kingdom would be able to cover its upcoming debt payments or if it would be able to roll over the debt. More specifically they wanted to know how much the debt problems would affect the ability of the new government to fund its armed forces.'

'Why would they be so interested in that?' Green asked a rhetorical question almost to himself before continuing and directing his gaze towards Gary Davies.

'Gary, what's the message coming out of Moscow?'

Gary Davies looked uneasy as he responded.

'I really have no idea. I have not yet had the chance to speak to our Moscow ambassador. Too busy trying to determine how to fund the Foreign Office and how to balance the books. Alastair Franks is putting a lot of pressure on all ministers to fix their department budgets so he can determine the overall budget for the country which is due in a couple of weeks.'

'Perhaps, I can add something,' Duncan Smith interrupted.

As head of the British Secret Intelligence service more commonly known as MI6, Smith was the one person in the room that would have access to intelligence relating to Russia. A quiet man who would normally wait to be asked a question before offering an answer or opinion, he was sufficiently worried about some aspects of what he had heard from his sources in Moscow to raise his concerns. More so after what he had just heard from his counterpart in MI5.

'Please, go ahead. Duncan, isn't it?' Green turned his attention to the head of MI6.

'Duncan Smith, Prime Minister. I have had the honour of serving as head of the SIS for the past seven years both under the previous Conservative administration and then when the socialists were in charge. During that time, trying to maintain our network in Russia has not been easy. You mentioned that today was not a day to pass around the begging bowl but I have to say that the intelligence service has been starved of funds for far too long and this has had a serious effect on our ability to see what our potential enemies are up to. That and the perception that Russia is no longer a major threat when the likes of some of the Middle Eastern countries are taken into account. That being said we have been able to maintain some of our assets inside the government of Russia and what we are hearing is disquieting to say the least.' Smith looked at Green and got an acknowledgment to continue.

'The first thing to observe is that the Russian president has consolidated his power base and is now basically a dictator even though he still has to answer to the electorate every six years. The last election was five years ago and the main opposition candidate mysteriously disappeared just before polling took place. He hasn't been seen since but there is anecdotal evidence that President Khurin or one of his henchmen was involved in his disappearance. The next election is in a year and the result is a foregone conclusion. There are of course dissidents but Khurin is very clever in that he plays on the nationalistic tendencies of the Russian people and makes out the dissidents are enemies of the state. Only last week there was a demonstration in Moscow to complain about the high prices and unemployment levels. The demonstration turned nasty, probably instigated by the Russian GRU, and the mob started looting. This was the excuse the police needed to move in and arrest the ring leaders. But I digress.

'Khurin has made no secret of his desire to make Russia great again. Some in the west see this as playing to the Russian people rather than imposing any real threat, but there is more to it than that. From what little we have been able to discover about what is happening in Russia one thing is very clear; a large amount of money is going into the armed forces and particularly into missile technology. You may recall that America accused Russia of violating the 1987 Intermediate-Range Nuclear Forces treaty a few years back. The treaty banned the development of ground-launched medium-range nuclear missiles which are just the type that would be used if a major war ever took place in Europe. America was right to be concerned. Whilst ostensibly adhering to the treaty Russia was continuing to develop more and more efficient missile technology. Today we estimate that Russia has a major stock pile of short to medium range nuclear weapons aiming at the West. The West is way behind in this field and in nearly every other area of weapons development.

'Whilst we in Europe have been sitting on our hands Russia has been arming itself to a frightening degree. Their army and air force are twice the size of NATO forces in Europe and much more modern. If it wasn't for the American presence, Europe would be an open door. The question we should be asking is what will Khurin do with this superiority and that is where it gets scary.

'We know that the Russian economy is not in great condition but they are still spending a large amount on their armed forces. This is unsustainable as the old Soviet Union discovered. So why spend the money and risk internal disorder if you have no intention of using it? Signs are not positive. Already Russia has effectively taken back control of Ukraine and Georgia by using the internet to influence and manage the electorate after a concerted armed intervention in, particularly Ukraine. Next on their list are the Baltic states. We are detecting the same social media propaganda blitz in Lithuania and Latvia that was used in the Ukraine and Russia has been holding military exercises on the borders of these two countries. Estonia seems to be less under attack but perhaps that is because last year a pro-Russian or at least a more neutral administration was elected in that country. There is a very strong likelihood that Russia will make a move on the Baltic states within the next year.' Smith stopped speaking and looked around the room before continuing.

'What happens then is very much conjecture and dependant on whether the west will stand up to Khurin and that depends on America and whether they will honour their NATO commitments. As things stand, they are treaty bound to come to the aid of another NATO country under attack but how strong their commitment is has to remain under doubt particularly with the increase in Chinese nationalism which is causing serious concern to America's Pacific alliances?

'What I have just heard from Joan Stapleford fits in with SIS's interpretation of Russia's intentions and that is that Khurin is readying himself to take back territory he considers is rightfully Russia's. The only two European countries he would have concerns about are France and Great Britain so it would be in his interest to know what we are spending on defence and whether we could be considered a threat to his plans.'

Whilst speaking Smith had been leaning forward with his forearms on the desk in front of him. He now sat back in his chair and crossed his hands in front of his corpulent stomach whilst gazing over the top of his wire rimmed glasses that were perched precariously on his small, rotund nose.

'You paint a grim picture, Mr Smith.' Cynthia Graeme spoke quietly but there was clear concern in her voice.

'Positively scary, I would say,' Green interrupted.

'Duncan, how much of this is guess work and how much is backed up by facts?'

'Rearmament, use of cyber-attacks on sovereign states, military exercises and threats to ex-Soviet Union States are all facts. America's commitment to help Europe and Khurin's ultimate intensions are conjecture based on our analysis of what is coming out of Moscow.'

'Sounds a bit like 1938 all over again.' Jason Bhatia entered the conversation for the first time. 'If my O level history serves me correct Europe disarms after the first world war, nationalism rises in Germany and they rearm against the terms of the treaty of Versailles. The rest of Europe gets caught with its trousers down and they miss the danger until its almost too late. Germany first sees how far it can push by rearming the neutral zone on the French border, then takes over Austria followed by Czechoslovakia and finally Poland. Each time the rest of Europe makes excuses for not doing anything and only when it becomes absolutely clear that Germany is not going to stop, do Great Britain and France take the threat seriously? Five years of war follow. The question that can never been answered is what would have happened if Great Britain and France challenged Germany militarily as soon as Germany started to rearm instead of choosing to ignore what was in plain sight?'

Richard Green turned back to Duncan Smith.

'How much of what you have just told this room has been discussed with our NATO allies?'

'At the intelligence level we have shared all our material and analysis with other NATO countries intelligence services. Whether the information and conclusions have been passed on to the NATO command, I can't say.' Smith shifted his gaze to the one person in the room wearing a full uniform of the British army.

General Sir David Jordan was 57 years old and had been in her majesty's armed forces since leaving university at the age of 21. During his career he had seen active service in Afghanistan and in the two gulf wars before he had left the field for a desk job. He was well liked within the armed services, even within the navy and air force, which was unusual for an army officer. Considered to be what used to be called a soldier's soldier, his experiences in the field had brought home the full horrors of war but also had made him realise that there were some really nasty people in the world that if not checked would bring untold misery on their fellow mankind. The use of force was something the General would try and avoid if at all possible but if it was necessary, he would ensure his troops were prepared to their best ability. He addressed the meeting.

'Duncan has painted quite a bleak picture but it is one that I tend to support. In my opinion Khurin is by far the biggest threat to world peace since the end of the cold war. NATO is fully aware of the threat but the big problem that we in the military have is convincing the politicians that the threat is real.' Jordan looked directly at Richard Green as he spoke.

'The NATO alliance has contributed to world peace for the best part of 75 years. Some would say that it is the reason that world war three has never materialised although perhaps the prospect of mutual self-destruction as a result of the nuclear arsenals has also played its part. Instead of a major world war we have had a series of proxy wars around the globe where Russia supports one side and the west the other. The middle east has been the focus of much of this. Just look at Syria, Yemen and Iraq. People die or are made homeless every day; but because it is not right on our doorstep it just becomes a news item. The population of the west has taken for granted that war in Europe is a thing of the past. They depend on the United Nations, The European Union and NATO to keep them safe; and to date, despite some difficulties along the way, Europe has been successful in avoiding wars within its borders. The Serbian wars in the late nineties were an exception but this was almost the exception that proved the point.

'What this has meant is that we have an entire generation who have grown up believing that war is a thing of the past so why waste money on the military? But in my opinion, this is very naïve. It is rather like someone who has been paying their house insurance for all their lives. They hope they will never have to claim but only when the house burns down do they realise the importance of paying the premium. If you stop paying the premium and the house burns down you are left with nothing. Most Western countries stopped paying the premium many years ago and channelled tax payers' money away from the military into social programmes. This is to be commended as long as the other side goes along with it. I think we all agree that a world without weapons and without the need for a military is desirable but like so much of the idealist's viewpoint, it does not take into account human nature. By presenting a weak front we also present an opportunity to some of the nastier elements of humanity and Khurin fits that category.

'Going back to the original question, yes, NATO is aware of the threat but NATO is suffering from acute under funding and is a much-weakened organisation since the formation of the European army and the rise of China distracting America. In addition, Turkey is forming closer and closer political ties with Russia threatening its NATO commitments should a conflict with Russia arise. Without a much stronger political commitment across the NATO countries I fear that NATO will not be able to protect Europe should Russia attack.'

Jordan finished speaking leaving the room in silence whilst the implications of his last statement sank in.

Chapter 24
June 2026

Between Taiwan and Luzon

Captain Eric Beckman stood in front of the wall of glass that constituted the front window of the Kalevala's bridge. From his view point he was able to see the tug that was attached to the front of the Kalevala by way of a three-inch steel hawser. The tug was connected to supplement the Kalevala's own propulsion and achieve the most efficient fuel consumption on the voyage from Korea to Europe; even so Captain Beckman was well aware that at a fuel consumption of nearly 100 tonnes per day the cost of the voyage to Europe would be in the order of half a million dollars in fuel alone.

After leaving Korea, Beckman had set a voyage for South Africa passing between the islands of Taiwan and Luzon, then through the Straits of Malacca and directly across the India Ocean skirting Mauritius before heading into Cape Town where the refuelling tankers were already on order. A voyage time of 35 days was planned and Beckman was looking forward to it. For too long he had been based in the Korean shipyard as part of the commissioning team whose task was to check all the systems were working as they were intended but also to familiarise themselves with the systems. There was still plenty to do particularly in getting the lower cabins and wash rooms ready for inhabitancy but the Korean work force was well on top of the challenge. All Captain Beckman had to do was get the ship to Europe. The task of overseeing the work was the responsibility of Ron Thompson, the yard resident engineer who had sailed with the Kalevala to ensure all the outstanding items were completed to his high standard.

As Beckman gazed out of the window at the calm blue sea and reflected on how lucky he was to have command of such an amazing vessel he was joined by a young fair-haired man wearing trainers, a pair of jeans and a red polo shirt with an insignia on the left breast pocket that indicated it was from a French fashion house. At five foot ten inches tall, Robert Simpson had the same rugged looks as his father combined with the kind eyes and wavy blonde hair of his mother. Unlike his elder brother, Ted, who had been instrumental in the success of OEC, Robert was more interested in boats than in geology. An Olympic standard sailor at the age of 17 he had already represented his country in The Finn class, coming in a creditable 7th place overall. He had then progressed into ocean racing having crewed a 55-foot modern ocean racer in the Fastnet race from The Isle of Wight to the Fastnet rock off the coast of Ireland before taking part in the Clipper Round the World Yacht race. It was only natural that he should pursue a career either in the merchant or Royal navy but unfortunately, he had been born colour blind and not being able to distinguish between a green and a red marker post could have disastrous consequences, scuppering any chance he may have had of a seagoing future. Disappointed he instead concentrated on his education obtaining four grade A* in his 'A' Levels on physics, applied maths, pure maths and French. With such qualifications he could get into any university in the country. He chose Newcastle which had the reputation for being at the forefront in Naval Architecture, the science of ship design. Having completed his second year, he was already on course for a first-class honour degree. Normally during the university summer recess, he would have got a job crewing on a boat in the Caribbean or the Mediterranean, but when he heard about the Kalevala, he had asked his father for the opportunity to sail with the ship, a request his father was only too happy to facilitate. Having joined the Kalevala just prior to her departure from Korea he had soon earned the respect of the crew who had rather expected that the son of the owner of an oil company would be a spoiled brat. Robert's pleasant demeaner and willingness to try anything without a hint of arrogance endeared himself to the seasoned mariners and Robert soon found himself a popular addition to the crew.

Turning to address Captain Beckman he spoke with a slight Newcastle accent picked up from his time in the North East of England.

'Captain, we seem to be making very good time?' The question was just an ice breaker.

'Indeed. We have managed over 12 knots for each of the last two days having cleared the traffic around the coast of Korea. The next challenge will be getting through the Straits of Malacca. We have been informed that piracy is still a concern but I suspect that any pirate will think twice about trying to get on board this vessel. In our present ballast configuration, the main deck is 24 metres above the sea level which is an awful long way to climb from a small boat.'

Beckman turned his gaze from the scene out of the window and faced Simpson.

'How are you enjoying the cruise?'

'Early days yet but so far very enjoyable. Everyone has made me very welcome and I find it fascinating looking at what make this vessel work. Yesterday the first officer showed me the computer simulation for when lifting a heavy load. Part of my college work has been to determine how to calculate ship stability but with a ship like this one it takes on a whole different meaning. I never realised until it was explained that the moment the cranes lift a load it is equivalent to that weight being added at the top of the crane which has a dramatic influence on the ships metacentric height.'

Beckman laughed. 'Sounds complicated to me. That's why we have first officers and computers. I prefer to concentrate on the ships navigation and leave the clever stuff to others.'

Simpson knew from discussions with other officers that Beckman was one of the cleverest and most respected people on the ship and so he took this statement with the proverbial pinch of salt. As the two men continued their conversation a new comer joined them. Beckman turned to face Hoseong Park and raised a quizzical eyebrow.

'So sorry to disturb you, Captain, but may I have a minute of your time?'

Park was a small balding man in his mid-fifties, clean shaven and wearing an HHI overall. As he spoke, he constantly bobbed his head making Simpson think he looked a little bit like a hen pecking for food.

'Of course, Mr Park. What can I do for you? I trust that you and your colleagues are being made welcome.'

'Very much so, Captain. Thank you. But I do have one problem.'

Beckman by now was used to the difficulties in holding a conversation with the Koreans. Perhaps it was the language or the culture but Beckman's take was that the Koreans didn't do small talk and were always very business-like, at least when they dealt with him. Park continued.

'I regret that we seem to have lost one of our work force.'

Beckman became serious.

'What do you mean, Mr Park? How can you have lost one of your colleagues?'

Beckman couldn't have known it but Hoseong Park was playing out the scenario concocted by Daniel Lee and Sang-don Jang to avoid suspicion whilst the ship was searched. Even though Hoseong Park was lying through his teeth his face remained inscrutable and he kept his eyes on the face of the Kalevala's Captain.

'I am afraid I don't know how he got lost. The man's name is Ji Lee. He was working on the main deck painting the hand rails with two other men. When the coffee break was called the other two men noticed that Mr Lee was not there but all of his equipment was still in place. They went to the coffee shop to see if he had gone on ahead but he wasn't there. They tried the toilets but again nothing. They then came to me. I am fearful that he may have fallen overboard.'

'For his sake I hope that isn't the case. Anyone falling from the deck would not survive the fall. And even if they did the chances of them surviving for very long in these waters is remote. When did his colleagues first notice that he was missing?'

'About fifteen minutes ago. As I said they had a good look around before coming to me and I came straight here.'

Beckman turned to speak to Sydney Barclay, the officer of the watch sitting in a chair on the other side of the vast bridge.

'Sid. Please signal the Vigilante that we have a potential man overboard case and that we need to stop whilst we carry out a head count. After the Vigilante has been informed please sound the muster stations alarm.'

The Vigilante was the towing tug.

Turning back to Park, Beckman continued, 'Mr Park, we need to ensure that Mr Lee is no longer on board the Kalevala before we report a man overboard situation. Right now, time is of the essence. As I said, if Mr Lee has gone overboard, I suspect his chances of survival are minimum but we can't afford to miss any chance so I will instruct the Vigilante to slip the tow rope and precede back on our previous course. Meanwhile we will hold a full muster on board the Kalevala.'

As he finished speaking a loud alarm started with a recorded message telling everyone to report to their muster stations. For the Kalevala that meant everyone who was not in a safety critical function had to go to their designated life boat at the ships bow where an officer would tick off their name against a pre-prepared check list. After 20 minutes it was reported that everyone was accounted for except for Ji Lee. It had taken all of the twenty minutes for the Kalevala to come to a stop. Beckman ordered the tow line disconnected and requested the Vigilante carry out a man over board search. At the same time Hoseong Park suggest to Beckman that perhaps Ji Lee had gone somewhere on the ship and got lost or disorientated and fallen over. Park volunteered his workforce to search the ship. Beckman agreed. Park had manipulated the situation to perfection. The fact that he had caused as a minimum a day lost sailing time and caused considerable anguish to the officers on board the ship was not something that concerned him. He worked for HHI and HHI management had asked him to do his duty which he would do to the best of his ability.

Park gathered all of his work force together in the ships cinema and in Korean explained what they were really looking for. He showed a picture of the bag carried by Chadwell and made it clear that if anyone found such a bag, they were under no circumstances to touch it but were to report straight back. He did not say what was in the bag. Within a few minutes the ship had been divided figuratively so each search party could cover one part of the vessel but even with nearly 200 people it would still take over three hours to completely search the whole vessel.

On the bridge Robert Simpson asked Captain Beckman if there was anything he could do to help. Like most mariners Beckman was a religious man and his only response was to suggest Simpson prayed. Beckman had never before lost a man over board but he knew of other Captains that had that experience and he could still see the far away and haunted look in their eyes as they relayed their story. The sea is a cruel place even when the wind isn't blowing it into a frenzy. In the northern areas it is the cold that claims most man over board victims. In the North Sea hypothermia will kill anyone that finds themselves in the water within 20 minutes. In the warmer waters of the tropics, life expectancy is longer but the added danger is of sharks. In case someone fell from a ship it was unlikely they would fall without some injury that would inevitably mean a loss of blood. A shark is an amazing creature that can detect blood in the water at a distance of a quarter mile away or further if the current is in the right direction. Once detected the shark will zero in on the source of the blood when it will use its other senses such as sight, sound and electroreceptors to determine if the blood is from a source that is edible. Strangely most sharks do not find human beings a very tasty meal but they do tend to use their teeth to taste before deciding whether to eat. Unfortunately for the victim this bite to taste is often fatal and even if the shark subsequently decides it doesn't want to dine on human flesh it is too late for the poor victim who will bleed to death. Beckman knew all this which led him to a very negative impression on the survivability of anyone that went overboard. He prayed the search of the ship would find the lost Ji Lee.

Unbeknown to Captain Beckman as he worried on the bridge over the fate of one individual, he would soon have a much bigger catastrophe to worry about. Deep within the bowels of the great ship and 20 metres under the waterline the timer placed but not adjusted by Jason Chadwell four days before continued to count down until at exactly 13:21 hrs and ten seconds it reached the trigger time. Two Korean workers who were in the hull at the time were the first to die. The explosion tore a hole in the hull right where a strengthening strut connected. Being in the main part of the hull there were no water tight doors to hold back the inrush of water and the hull quickly began to flood. The two Korean workers were engulfed by the flood water and being unable to get to the emergency exit they drowned in the flooded hull.

On the bridge no one heard the explosion but the juddering that went through the ship was apparent to all. At the same time alarms began sounding on the damage control board showing the extent of the flooding. As Beckman and his officers tried to make sense of what the board was showing Hoseong Park rushed onto the bridge.

'The bomb has exploded.' He blurted out between gasps as he tried to catch his breath having run up seven flights of stairs in order to reach the bridge. Beckman looked at him in shock.

'What the blazes are you talking about?' He bellowed. 'What bomb?'

'The bomb that we were told to look for. I was told it was unlikely to be active but they were wrong.'

'Who are they and what bomb are you talking about?'

Beckman now had his voice under control and knew that he had to find out more before he could know how serious the incident was. Park, with his strange bird like bobbing continued.

'Earlier today I was told by my manager in HHI that they had a suspicion that a saboteur had accessed the ship just before it sailed. The saboteur was the same person who was responsible for an explosion in the bow compartment eight weeks ago so my management were concerned he could have set another bomb. As he was detected and chased from the ship and as no explosion took place within 24 hours of him being on board; my management assumed he hadn't had time to activate the bomb, if in fact there was one. However, he had been carrying a bag when he entered the ship and he didn't have it when he left, so I was asked to find the bag and if it did contain a bomb, I was then to tell HHI who would arrange for it to be defused. They told me it couldn't be active or it would already have exploded.'

Beckman looked at Park in disbelief.

'You're telling me that this whole thing about a man over board was just a charade to enable you to carry out a search of the ship? Why didn't you just tell me the truth so we could be forewarned and even help?'

Park shrugged his shoulders. 'So, Sorry. I was told that there was no real danger and that I wasn't to tell you.'

'No real danger. Then why is this board' – Beckman touched the damage control board – 'showing that we have major flooding in the centre hull?' Turning from Park, Beckman addressed his first officer.

'Sid, have you closed all the water tight doors in hull two?'

'All closed and the flood water is contained at present. We have also started to compensate for the flooding by deballasting water from ballast tanks two, three, eight and nine.'

'What about the Vigilante? Where is she? We need her back here.'

'I'll contact her immediately. Anything else?'

'Call a muster. Although there shouldn't be anyone in the hull whilst we are sailing, with Mr Park sending his people all over the place we don't know if anyone was in the vicinity of the flooded section.'

As he spoke another shock went through the ship.

'What the devil was that?' Beckman said to no one in particular. Before anyone could answer a large crack appeared in the middle of the main deck. The noise of steel tearing apart became deafening and the deck of the bridge started tilting towards the centre of the ship. To the astonishment and terror of all on the bridge it became clear that the ship was folding in half. Beckman was the first to react.

'Mr Barclay, sound the abandon ship signal and send out a mayday.'

The fact that he used his old friend Sydney Barclays correct address showed to all the stress that Beckman was under.

'Everyone else get to your muster stations. The way this is developing I don't know how much longer this ship will stay afloat.'

As he spoke one of the massive cranes on the stern of the ship teetered and fell into the water taking a large section of the upper deck with it. Without the weight of the crane the Kalevala rose out of the water in the corner where the crane had been causing the second crane to tilt crazily downwards until the crane housing broke free and followed the first crane over the side. It was clear that the Kalevala was breaking up at an alarming rate and that it would be only a matter of a few minutes before it went to the bottom.

The bridge was deserted except for Captain Beckman who had remained at his post and his first officer who was still transmitting the distress signal and keeping in contact with the emergency services of Taiwan as well as with the captain of the Vigilante. Beckman suddenly became aware of a third person on the bridge and looking around saw Robert Simpson walking towards him. Because of the slope of the bridge deck Simpson was struggling to keep upright but as he approached Beckman saw that he held three life jackets. Above the sound of the dying vessel Simpson thrust the life jackets at Beckman and Barclays before donning his own jacket.

'Time to leave, gentlemen.' He said in a very calm voice. 'All the lifeboats have got away and there is nothing more you can achieve by staying here. I just saw Vigilante off the starboard bow and already they are taking people from the life boats onboard. We are lucky that it is day light and the sea is calm but if you stay here you will go down with the ship for no purpose.'

Beckman looked at the younger man with new respect. Whilst most people would have been panicking Simpson was talking calmly and rationally. Taking the life jacket, he put it over his head before the three men walked out onto the bridge wing. By this time the bridge was no more than a few metres above the sea level as the Kalevala began her final voyage to the sea floor 700 metre below the surface. Beckman activated an inflatable life raft that was on the bridge wing and threw it over the side. Looking at Simpson and Barclays and determined not to be outdone in the calmness stakes by Simpson he stepped aside and just said. 'After you, gentlemen.'

Barclay did not have to be asked twice and holding on to his life jacket to prevent it from hitting him under the chin as he entered the water; he stepped from the bridge and dropped into the water that was rapidly coming up to meet him. Simpson followed suit and the last to leave the ship was Beckman. As the three surfaced and grabbed hold of the life raft they had a grandstand view as the last remnants of the once mighty Kalevala disappeared below the surface. They fully expected that they would be caught by the under current and pulled below the surface but the Kalevala just disappeared leaving a debris strewn ocean surface and a number of life boats and life rafts crowded with people.

As Beckman surveyed the scene from the low level of the life raft, he felt the anger beginning to rise. He had never lost a ship in all his time at sea and now to lose the greatest ship in which he had ever sailed due to an act of sabotage was more than he could bear. If it took a life time, he would find who was responsible and make them pay but in the meanwhile he had to get on board the Vigilante and start the process of assessing the number of casualties and preparing parents, wives, sons and daughters for the news that their loved ones would not be coming home. He bowed his head and steeled himself for what was to come.

Chapter 25
June 2026

Saunders Marine Headquarters Hartlepool

News of the sinking of the Kalevala reached David Saunders as he was preparing to leave for home. At first, unable to believe what he was being told, the awful truth gradually began to sink in. All his hard work and sacrifice over the last 25 years had come to nothing. What had he done so wrong in a past life that he deserved such bad luck? He paid his taxes and went to church every week. He didn't physically abuse anyone and always tried to treat people fairly; so why had God decided to punish him in such a cruel way? He could feel the self-pity welling up until it almost enveloped him. Sitting back behind his desk still wearing his overcoat he placed his head in his hands and fought to hold back the tears. It was all over.

Gradually he regained his self-control and with incredible slowness he reached for the phone and dialled his home number. His wife answered on the third ring. Used to getting calls at this late hour from her husband she fully expected either a confirmation that he was on the way home or just as likely that he had been delayed at the office and would be home later than expected. Having been married for nearly forty years they had developed an almost telepathic ability to judge each other's moods. Even before David spoke his wife realised something was seriously wrong. Having listened to the despair in her husband's voice as he told her what had happened and that he had to stay in the office to start managing the emergency she realised that this was not a good time for him to be alone. Having put the phone down she immediately put on her coat, left the house and made her way to the offices of Saunders Marine, a journey of twenty-five minutes. She didn't know what she expected to find or do once she arrived but she just felt that she had to be there.

What she found made her incredibly proud of the man that she loved and had been a constant companion with for such a long time and through so many experiences, both good and bad. Initially fearful that Saunders would do something foolish in his despair she found him in the company board room surrounded by his most senior personnel and closest advisers.

Having come off the phone to his wife, Saunders realised that self-pity solved nothing and no matter how bad it might seem at first glance there were very many people worse off than he was; and many of them had been on board the Kalevala when she went down. Those people expected him to look after them and needed his support. He was the company owner and it was in the service of his company that they had had their lives put at risk or, even worse, curtailed. Putting aside his personal concerns he started calling in his emergency response team. To his relief he was able to get through to everyone and within a few minutes the first of his team started to arrive.

The company board room had been allocated as the ER room and emergency response manuals were taken out of their storage units and placed on the table in front of each desk. These manuals contained critical phone numbers such as the coast guards, local hospitals, helicopter support services and the police as well as delegating responsibilities to each member of the team. The company Information Technology manager and his assistance had been the first to arrive and had immediately connected the phone lines and fax machines that would be needed by the emergency response team and the media response team. White boards were placed around the room for recording important information so all in the room had access to the same information and pens and paper were placed next to the ER manuals. The relative response team would be based in a different room where specially trained counsellors would respond to the calls from relatives trying to find out if their loved ones were safe once the story broke on the national news. A line of communication was set up between the ER room and the relative response room.

David Saunders never saw his wife looking into the board room door and didn't notice her quietly go back to her car and drive home. Only when she got back in to the house did she let her emotions take over and she broke down and cried. Not for herself but for all those people for whom Saunders Marine was their lives and who were even now fighting hard for the company and for their colleagues, the fate of whom were not yet known.

Back in the ER room David Saunders put a call through to the Taiwanese embassy and asked for the contact details of the Taiwanese coast guards who he assumed were co-ordinating the rescue of any survivors from the sinking. The call he had taken that started the nightmare had come from a reporter based in Korea who had received information from the Chinese about the sinking. He had explained to Saunders that he had been told that the ship had sunk close to the island of Taiwan and that he understood that they had mobilised their coast guards to assist with the rescue operations. Hence the natural starting point for Saunders to find out what was happening was to speak directly to the coast guards.

After a number of abortive attempts someone in Taiwan picked up the phone and answered in Chinese. Fortunately, English is very much a universal language and after realising that he was talking to a non-Chinese person the coast guard reverted to English. Gradually Saunders started to get a better picture of what had taken place. It was explained that a mayday had been picked up by the coast guards in the middle of the afternoon, that the crane vessel Kalevala had suffered an explosion on board that had led to a catastrophic failure in the hull and the vessel was sinking rapidly. The order to abandon ship had been given and the Taiwanese coast guards had mobilised a helicopter and search and rescue vessel to the location given. Not realising the size of the vessel or the number of people involved they had assumed they were talking about a crew of no bigger than thirty people but subsequent information received from the vessel stated the compliment was nearly three hundred people. Only then had they understood the potential extent of the tragedy and mobilised additional helicopters and support vessels. Initial reports from the helicopters at the scene indicated that there were a number of lifeboats and life rafts in the sea and that there was a support tug on location picking up survivors. Of the Kalevala there was no sign and it was assumed it had sunk. The location of the sinking was about 100 kilometres from the coast and survivors would be taken to Kao-hsiung harbour. A survivor processing station would be set up in the harbour area and it was expected that the first survivors would start arriving any time soon. Hospitals had been alerted and had called in extra staff to be prepared for any injured personnel. At this time the numbers of casualties were unknown. Saunders agreed to send through a crew list and to mobilise his operations personnel to Kao-hsiung harbour to help with the processing of personnel.

After coming off the phone all the information deemed was written up on the white board and a media response holding statement was prepared. Saunders also contacted his site team that remained in Korea and asked them, as the closest to the incident area, to get to Taiwan to give whatever support they could and also to arrange for personnel from HHI to go to Taiwan to give support to the Korean work force.

Eventually the news reached the ears of Daniel Lee. Aware of the enormity of the tragedy he immediately informed the yard management and told them everything that he had discussed with Sang-Don Jang. Neither man tried to hide anything realising that their failure to report the concerns regarding Cartridge could have been responsible for the loss of many lives. They were both distraught and very humble in front of the HHI management and even though both men realised that their careers were over they were determined to do whatever they could to make amends. To their surprise they were not sacked on the spot. The HHI management were pragmatic people who hadn't got to being in control of one of the biggest industrial concerns in the world by making rash and hurried decisions based on emotions. They realised that they needed both Lee and Jang, the first to handle the inevitable commercial consequences of the loss of the Kalevala and the second to co-ordinate with the police in finding the mystery man Cartridge. Whilst the rescue operation continued off the coast of Taiwan the hunt was on for the person responsible.

Chapter 26
June 2026

Aberdeen

Jean Robertson was following her normal breakfast routine. Having awoken at 06:30 hrs she showered, dressed and went down stairs for breakfast which consisted of a bowl of cereal and fruit juice. Sitting at the kitchen table, as usual, she turned the television to the news channel expecting the normal depressing stories revolving around whatever charity had managed to convince the BBC that their cause was the most righteous before the weather report, the main reason she watched the news, came on. To her surprise what she saw was a scene clearly taken from a helicopter showing a number of lifeboats in a sea covered by floating debris. Increasing the volume, she caught the end of the report saying that to date the death toll was unknown but that the vessel was known to be carrying over 250 persons. The story then shifted back to the studio where the news presenter continued the bulletin by including a number for relatives to contact for any further information. The number had an Aberdeen prefix.

Still unsure what the disaster was Robertson put aside her breakfast bowl and, reaching for her iPad, she went to the news page. The shock was elemental. The Kalevala had sunk. That was impossible. How could such a massive ship just sink? Not only had the Kalevala sunk but she had gone down so fast that it was highly likely that not everyone had time to get into the life boats. There was talk of considerable casualties. Pictures of survivors in life rafts and rescue vessels pulling people out of the water were all over the report and made her recall the Triton disaster of only a few weeks previously, the ramifications of which were still her main work load. She then recalled that Robert Simpson had been on the Kalevala and suddenly it became very personal. As she attempted to digest the news her mobile phone rang. It was Jim Simpson. Her finger hesitated over the answer button before, steeling herself, she pushed the green telephone icon and nervously said,

'Hello, Jim.'

Jean Robertson had worked with Jim Simpson for the last five years and during that time they had developed a close but plutonic relationship. Whilst Jean was not married, Jim had a wife, Sandy, who Jim affectionately referred to as the SS, and was a father to his two sons who Jean knew he doted on. The opportunity to take their relationship to another level had been there on many occasions. Sometimes when they were alone in a hotel after a meeting in whatever part of the world business had taken them to, they would discuss the thought of using one room, but always common sense would prevail and after a gentle good night kiss they would go to their separate rooms. The desire was there but they both realised that if they were to be able to work together anything but a pure business relationship would just get in the way. Besides, Simpson was very much in love with his wife who was also a close friend of Robertson. Neither was willing to cause hurt for the sake of a cure for loneliness or the quick thrill of illicit sex.

That didn't mean that they didn't care for each other. They did, and so when the phone rang and Simpson heard Robertson's short answer, he intuitively knew that she had heard the news of the Kalevala. Despite this and perhaps it was just to buy time before the really painful discussion started, he still had to ask the question.

'Hi, Jean. Have you seen the news yet?' Robertson could hear the pain in Simpson's voice.

'I've just been watching the morning bulletin. It is saying The Kalevala has sank but how can a ship of that size sink? It doesn't make sense. When we saw it last week it was the closest thing to an unsinkable ship that I have seen.' She paused before continuing, 'I am almost too fearful to ask but have you heard anything from Robert yet?'

'No, nothing. I've just come off the phone to David Saunders. As you can imagine he is absolutely devastated but holding himself together. He has confirmed that he is in touch with the Taiwanese coast guards and that many people have been picked up from the lifeboats but it is too early to know the names of the survivors. I just have to keep hoping that Robert is amongst them. He is a resilient character so I am hopeful. What else can I say? The SS is beside herself with worry as you can imagine. Ted is here with us and we are just like zombies sitting in the dining room looking at each other but not saying much. It puts everything in perspective when someone you love is in such danger. The company, Caratacus, material things; everything. It all means nothing.'

As Simpson's voice tailed off Robertson could feel his pain and just wanted to reach out to him. At the same time something in the darker recesses of her mind started to register – thoughts that gave her considerable concern.

'Do we know anything further about what caused the ship to sink?'

She kept her voice as neutral as possible but even to her own ears her internal fears could be detected in her tone of voice. Simpson was too distressed to notice.

'No. As I said, it is still early days. I have booked a flight to Taiwan and will be travelling with David Saunders in about six hours' time. Hopefully by the time we get into Taipei, the rescue operation will be over and we will be able to interview survivors to see if we can determine the cause. Also, I will know Robert's fate.'

'But I am ringing to ask a favour. I hate to leave the SS on her own and although she has Ted, I would very much appreciate if you could come over and sit with her at least until we know.'

'Of course. No problems. Let me get myself looking decent and I'll be there within the hour.'

'Thanks, Jean. I really appreciate this. God, what a mess.'

With that Simpson put down the receiver and returned to the dining room to do what he could to console his wife and eldest son. Jean Robertson meanwhile started to feel the raw emotion of guilt that came from the thought that her actions could have been responsible for the loss of the Kalevala and worse, for the loss of the son of one of her dearest friends. She thought back to the phone conversation with Dmitri Rostov.

After the initial conversation Robertson had facilitated an informal meeting with Jim Simpson. As head of Human Resources Robertson knew about the Caratacus field but she had been telling the truth when she had told Rostov that she only knew details that were in the public domain. Using her relationship with Simpson it wasn't difficult to determine that his two biggest worries were the installation vessel and the progress being made on the accommodation module. He was also concerned about the ability to continue funding the project but was confident that Sidney Bach would be able to convince the company creditors to increase the level of the credit facilities. Robertson had passed all this information on to Rostov. Now the Kalevala had sunk in mysterious circumstances and her closest friend's son was missing. Had the sinking been facilitated by the Russians to delay the Caratacus project, something that Rostov had indicated was in the interest of Russia? It seemed too much like a coincidence.

As she started to put on her make up to go and give support to Sandy Simpson, she couldn't get the thought out of her head that she was responsible for the sinking of the Kalevala and hence for the death of her friend's son. At that point she realised that despite her many years of propaganda during her childhood years she no longer considered Russia to be her home or the West to be her enemy. But what to do about it? She felt trapped and knew that she was no longer playing a game. Deep down she always knew that she would one day be asked to betray her adopted country and had tried to keep focused on the fact that she was Russian. Any help she could give to Russia was not a betrayal of Great Britain but a victory for Russian interests. She was helping her compatriots against a traditional enemy. Unfortunately, like a hostage that develops an affinity to their captives, something referred to as the Stockholm Syndrome, Robertson had become attached to her adoptive country. In particular she had become attached to Jim Simpson and his family. Perhaps it was the lack of love that she had experienced growing up in Russia and later with her English 'parents' but she had almost come to see the Simpson's as her real family, the loving family she had lost as a four-year-old. To think now that she was responsible for causing such pain to that family was almost too much to bear.

She tried to console herself by the thought that Robert would be found alive and well and that everything would be all right but she realised that this would just be the beginning. Rostov had made it very clear that being in OEC was fortuitous for the time being but when this latest issue had been resolved she would be expected to drop out of business and go into politics. No more procrastination would be accepted. She had already rationalised that the reluctance to start a political career was as a result of her doubt about what she was expected to do. The reality was that because of her upbringing she had never really integrated with the real Russia and so had no affinity for the country. The nationalism that most Russians develop by mixing with other Russians and being enveloped by the Russian culture had been missing in her upbringing. Instead she had gone to the West almost as an automaton but one that had not been fully programmed. Watching the western news and absorbing the western reaction to Khurin's Russia had had a profound influence on her and gradually her loyalty to Russia had weakened to be replaced by a loyalty to the West. The callous use of the information she had passed to Rostov which resulted in the sinking of the Kalevala made her realise that she could not continue to work as an agent of Russia.

Thirty minutes later Jean Robertson put on her coat and left her house on her way to sit with her best friend, Sandy Simpson, with the conviction that Sandy must never be allowed to find out her involvement in the sinking of the Kalevala. Robertson knew that any wavering of her loyalty to Russia would quickly be picked up by Rostov. It was what he was trained to detect. Once doubt had been sewn in Rostov's mind that Robertson was no longer totally reliable other means would be found to control her. The threat of exposing her involvement with the death of the younger Simpson would be just the leverage needed to keep her loyal. To protect that secret Robertson was going to have to convince the Russians that she was still working for them but at the same time she resolved to try and correct the wrong that she had already committed. She would work against Russia whilst ostensibly working for them.

Chapter 27
June 2026

Paris

It was a wet and windy spring day in Paris as the head of Interpol made her way to her office on Rue des 3 Fontanot, in the Nanterre district of Paris. Marie Lantieri was five feet three inches tall with long dark hair and an attractive face just showing signs of a few wrinkles around the eyes that gave a hint to her 53 years of age. Wearing a grey Austin tailored pencil skirt and jacket over a white blouse with flat grey Dalmain shoes and carrying a briefcase in one hand and an umbrella in the other she hurried from the bus stop to the front entrance of the building marked Ministere de l'Interieur. From the outside the building looked like any other modern glass and concrete office block. Apart from the sign over the doorway, the only other indication that the building was anything different was the presence of the armed National Gendarmerie standing outside. As Lantieri passed him he briefly glanced in her direction but recognising the most senior Interpol officer in France he remained strictly at attention and reverted his gaze back to the outside street searching for anything that may be out of the ordinary.

Once in the building Lantieri used her pass to first pass through security and again to take the lift to the fifth floor where she had her office. Waiting for her was her long-standing personal assistant. Having worked alongside Lantieri for the last 12 years Charlotte Reims knew her boss's routine and the first routine was a double cup of strong expresso coffee with a splash of skimmed milk. This she held in her hand as Lantieri approached. Taking the cup without any thank you Lantieri continued into her office followed by Reims.

'So, Charlotte. What have we got this morning? Anything new that needs urgent attention or just a continuation of the drudge from yesterday.'

Lantieri gave Charlotte a big smile that mitigated any rudeness that others may have felt from her abrupt style.

'There is something that I think will interest you.' Reims was the same age as Lantieri but in an attempt to hold back the years she was wearing a shorter skirt and an open top blue blouse that showed her ample cleavage exaggerated by a red push up brassier. She also wore heeled shoes and although not obvious to an idle observer she wore stockings instead of the usual panty hose favoured by most women for their practicalities. Recently divorced after 20 years, a mother and a wife she was now beginning to find her true self and quite liked the experience. Lantieri had noticed the change in her PA and also quite liked the new Charlotte and even found herself having erotic thoughts about her at all sorts of inconvenient times. She would have to be careful to keep her feelings hidden or risk losing not only a good PA but also a good friend. Lantieri knew that Reims was attracted to men not women which to Lantieri was such a shame.

'What would that be?'

Lantieri removed her suit jacket and hung it from a coat stand in the corner of the office before taking her seat behind a large teak desk. She carefully placed the coffee cup on a coaster depicting the Tower of London, something she had picked up the last time she visited that city a few weeks before, to avoid leaving a round mark on the desk.

'This has just arrived from South Korea.'

Reims placed a file on the desk in front of her boss. Opening the file Lantieri found herself looking at a grainy photograph of a man wearing a workman's overalls. The accompanying notes stated that the man was wanted for sabotage in South Korea and went under the name of James Cartridge or Jason Chadwell. The file went on to report that the man had twice entered the HHI shipyard in Korea and planted explosives. The second time he had almost been caught but had eluded the yard security services. At that time, he had been using the name James Cartridge however a man of the same description who had left South Korea bound for Frankfurt had used a passport under the name of Jason Chadwell. Interpol in Germany had ascertained that the man had only stayed in Frankfurt for a few hours before boarding a plane bound for Paris. As far as it could be determined he had not been registered leaving Paris so it was likely that he was still in the area. More interesting, whilst there was no record of a James Cartridge living in or around Paris there was a Jason Chadwell. Whilst the report expressed the opinion that it was highly unlikely that someone of such professionalism would use his own name when travelling it was still a lead that needed to be followed up. Coming to the end of the report Lantieri closed the buff coloured folder and looked up at her assistant.

'Looks rather run of the mill from what I've read. Why did you say you thought I would find it interesting?'

'You haven't made the connection to the big item on the news right now?' Reims posed the question. 'The sinking of that big ship in the Chinese sea?'

'Of course I've seen the news story. Who could miss it? There's nothing like a major disaster when it comes to selling papers. Are you saying that this Cartridge or Chadwell had something to do with the sinking? As far as I can tell from the news the cause of the sinking is still unknown.'

'That's what the newspapers have been told but we have heard from Korea that HHI have video evidence that puts this man on board the Kalevala, as the ship is called, just before an explosion caused severe damage to a part of the ship. It was later ascertained that the explosion was deliberate. The damage was repaired but the same man was seen on the ship the day before sail away and there is considerable circumstantial evidence that he left something behind, most likely a second bomb. Having failed to sink the boat the first time the theory is that he returned to do the job properly the second time. South Korean police have asked the Taiwanese authorities if they can interview the survivors of the vessel to see if there is any corroborating evidence but meanwhile, they have requested our assistance in checking out Mr Jason Chadwell.'

'That makes it interesting I agree. The press is reporting multiple fatalities as a result of the sinking. If our, Mr Chadwell, is responsible, we are dealing with a mass murderer of the worst kind. Someone that has no consideration for human life. My main concern would be that people who normally carry out such atrocities are professionals that work for money. They move in the shadows and nearly always work under aliases. I would be very surprised if the Mr Jason Chadwell mentioned in the file living in a small town south of Paris is the same man that carried out this act. But we have to act on the assumption that he is and take all necessary precautions. Please arrange for an armed response unit to be assembled and then I think I'll pay Mr Chadwell a visit.'

Charlotte Reims left the room to make the necessary arrangements whilst Lantieri re-read the files before turning on her office television to get the latest news of the tragedy being acted out on the other side of the world. As she sipped her coffee, she wondered what sort of person could commit such an atrocity and still be able to live with themselves.

Thirty-five kilometres to the south of Paris is a small town called Gif-sur-Yvette. As Charlotte Reims made preparations for an armed response team, Jason Chadwell was sitting in the front room of his comfortable house on the Allee de l'Etang watching the news. If he felt any guilt at the carnage he had caused, he didn't show it. His main emotion as he watched the drama unfold was one of concern that he hadn't covered his tracks as well as he would have liked. It most certainly was time for that holiday in The Seychelles, and quick. Not under the name of Jason Chadwell, though. He had other aliases and it was time for Mr Chadwell to disappear once and for all. It would be sad to leave Gif-sur-Yvette as he had become fond of the life style compared to his native Great Britain but he had not survived in the business he was in by being sentimental over anything or anyone. Finishing his cup of tea, despite his fondness for all things French he could still not stomach their coffee, he stood up and turned off the television. His study was in the back of the house and he quickly made reservations for the evening flight from Charles de Gaulle airport to Victoria on the Island of Mahe, the largest of the Seychelles Islands. The booking was made under the name of Charles Pritchard, an alias he had developed many years ago for just such an eventuality. All that was left for him to do was pack a bag of his most personal belongings, make sure all his bank accounts would still be accessible when he needed them and make arrangements for his house to have a mysterious fire destroying any forensic evidence. Hidden in the attic of the house was a skeleton belonging to someone that had crossed him many years before but who was roughly the same build as Chadwell. Although all flesh had long ago fallen off the skeleton, Chadwell was confident that when the accident investigators found the skeleton remains in the burnt-out house, they would not look too closely but just assume that poor Mr Jason Chadwell had died in the blaze.

Having made his preparations he arranged for a taxi to pick up Mr Charles Pritchard from a hotel located 15 minutes' walk from his house and set the timer on the incendiary device to detonate in six hours' time, about the time that his plane would be leaving the stand at Charles de Gaulle airport. Picking up his suitcase he closed the front door of his home of the last 12 years and walked up the garden path.

Half an hour later Lantieri accompanied by six, armed Gendarmerie arrived outside the house. The armed officers quickly split into pairs and moved to positions that covered all aspects of the house as Lantieri approached the front door. Still convinced that the whole thing would turn out to be a case of identity theft she was not particularly concerned as she knocked on the door only to get no reply. Indicating to the armed officers to remain as they were, she started around the house peering into windows as she went. Nothing seemed out of the ordinary until she looked through the window of the back bedroom when she saw what looked like someone lying in the bed. Looking closer she saw that the figure lying in the bed was covered in a duvet except for the head and that was when she realised that this was not going to be routine. The head was not that of a person, at least not a live person, but clearly someone that had been dead for a very long time.

Using her radio, she called for back-up and within minutes the front door had been broken down and the house was being searched. The incendiary device was found next to the bed containing the skeleton and it became clear that an elaborate scheme had been planned to burn down the house and make it look like Chadwell had died in the blaze. The bird had flown but he can't have left too long ago. The timer on the incendiary devise showed it had been set only 45 minutes before so they had missed Chadwell by a very small margin; but it meant he was still in France.

As the French bomb disposal squad and forensic analysts arrived Lantieri issued an all-points bulletin to detain and apprehend Jason Chadwell. Fully expecting that such a person no longer existed she made it clear that the fugitive would most likely be using a different name and that picture identification would be needed. The picture from Korea was circulated to all forces, ports and airports. Within four hours Jason Chadwell, aka Charles Pritchard was picked up at the Charles de Gaulle airport trying to board a plane to the Seychelles. The French police had got their man.

Chapter 28
June 2026

Taiwan

Jim Simpson and David Saunders arrived at Taoyuan International Airport after a two-hour stopover in Hong Kong at 09:45 hrs in the morning. Despite the 15-hour journey they went immediately to the reception centre in Kao-hsiung harbour. Normally entering the docks would require either a pass or a letter of invitation but due to the situation the rules had been relaxed particularly when David Saunders explained that he represented the Kalevala's owners. Having been directed to a large building near the centre of the dock area, Saunders and Simpson walked through the big open doors to find what can only be described as organised chaos – or at least they hoped it was somehow organised.

Scattered around the hall were hundreds of people, some clearly Taiwanese officials but also many westerners and Koreans wrapped in blankets either standing, sitting on the floor or in some cases lying down. Clearly these were the survivors from the Kalevala. Many of the lying had a medical orderly beside them and stretchers were being used to take the worst cases to a number of ambulances pulled up outside the reception centre.

Glancing around the large room Simpson began to get a feeling for how many people were on the Kalevala. Unlike Saunders he hadn't really appreciated the number of Korean workers that sailed with the vessel from Korea. Looking at the official looking Taiwanese he noticed that one man seemed to be in charge of proceedings and having nudged Saunders the two men approached the Taiwanese official. Waiting until there was a break in the seemingly never-ending stream of personnel vying for the man's attention, Saunders at last manged to catch his eye and introduced himself and Simpson. Kuan-lin Chi was the Kao-hsiung harbour master and had been allocated the task of co-ordinating the rescue efforts and making arrangements for the injured. He was clearly relieved to have someone senior from Saunders Marine to assist in the efforts and lost no time in explaining to Saunders and Simpson the situation. It wasn't good but it could have been a lot worse was the best that anyone could say. Kuan-lin was able to explain that a crew list had been received from Saunders Marine head office and HHI had provided a list of their personnel that had sailed with the Kalevala. Using this information Kuan-Lin has determined that of the 279 personnel on board at the time of the accident 263 had been accounted for. Off those five were confirmed dead and another 23 seriously injured. Of the 16 that were missing, it had to be assumed that they would not now be found alive. Dreading what he would find Simpson asked to see the list of survivors but Kuan-Lin did not have a copy with him and directed the two men to an administrator sitting behind a desk at the back of the room.

Simpson and Saunders thanked Kuan-Lin and, after giving assurances that they would do all that was necessary to assist in the repatriation of the survivors, moved towards the back of the room passing between the Kalevala's crew as they went. All through his working life Saunders had been involved with the sea and knew the dangers that it held but this was the first time he had been confronted by the reality of such a tragedy. The faces he saw would haunt his sleep for many years ahead. Afterwards when asked to explain what was the thing he most remembered about the incident he would always say it was the look on the faces of the survivors as he passed by. People didn't look scared or disturbed, they just looked vacant as if they had somehow lost their way in a world that they no longer recognised and now didn't know what to do next. There were a few exceptions. In one corner Simpson saw a group of western faces deep in conversation with someone with Eastern features that could have been Taiwanese or Korean, his knowledge of Eastern facial features being insufficient to tell the difference. As he carried on walking past, one of the group broke away and approached the two men. Saunders was the first to recognise the Captain of the Kalevala but then he was more familiar with him, Simpson only having met at the launch ceremony, something that seemed a lifetime ago.

'David. I heard you were coming. Am I glad to see you?'

Eric Beckman reached out to David Saunders and gripped him in a bear like hug. Somewhat embarrassed Saunders embraced the big man back before extraditing himself and stepping back.

'Not half as pleased as I am to see you, Eric. What a mess. I've just been talking to Kuan-Lin Chi who seems to be in charge of things here. He tells me that we have 21 dead and another 23 seriously injured. What the hell happened?'

Beckman looked straight into the eyes of his boss and for the first time Saunders saw the anger behind the fatigue.

'Some bastard planted a bomb on the Kalevala that blew the bloody ship apart. That's what happened. One minute we were congratulating ourselves on a smooth voyage and the next the whole ship is convulsed by an explosion. The explosion must have occurred at a strategically weak point because under normal circumstances if the hull were breached then the watertight doors would contain the flooding. In this instance the whole hull just folded in half. She went down in less than 15 minutes. And when I find the murdering bastard responsible, I'll rip their head off.'

'Just a minute. How do you know it was a bomb? This is the first I've heard that it was anything other than a tragic accident.'

Saunders felt himself go cold despite the 30-degree centigrade ambient temperature.

'Because our Korean friends told me just before the ship went down. Would you believe it but the HHI management knew that a bomb had been planted but still allowed the ship to sail. I've just been talking to Hoseong Park who was the HHI representative on the ship. I suggest that you and he have a tete-a-tete at the earliest possible opportunity. HHI have a lot of explaining to do.'

'Captain Beckman?' Jim Simpson could not contain himself any longer and for the first time Beckman turned his attention to him.

'Jim Simpson, isn't it? We met at the launch ceremony I believe.'

'That we did, under much more pleasant circumstances I have to say. But I am not here in an official role. I am here as a worried father and was wondering if you could tell me what has happened to my son. His name was Robert and he sailed with the Kalevala from Korea.'

The anger that had been showing in Beckman's featured were immediately replaced by a look of concern.

'Of course. Robert Simpson was your son. I somehow forgot that with all that has been happening. A remarkable young man. You should be very proud of him. He kept his calm when all around were losing theirs and was a tremendous help in organising the pick-up of survivors. When we had to abandon the ship, he was one of the last to leave and after getting himself, and in fact helping me, into a life raft he spent the next hour searching the sea for anyone in the water. By the time we were able to transfer to the Vigilante we had picked up another ten people from the water, largely thanks to Robert. I haven't seen him lately but I can confirm that he survived and was still helping the injured after getting back to the beach. My guess would be that you will find him at the hospital.'

Simpson felt his legs go weak as the stress of the past 48 hours dissipated. On the spur of the moment he grabbed Beckman's hand and pumped it up and down. All he could say was thank you over and over again.

Saunders placed a hand on the shoulder of his client and said nothing. He didn't have too. He was also feeling that out of the awfulness of the last few days there was one piece of good news on which he could gain solace. He was under no illusion regarding what the next few days would bring. Visits to the relations of the dead, the constant questions from the media and the inevitable official enquiry ostensibly under the guise of trying to find the cause of the tragedy but in reality, looking for the scape goat to take the blame. As he quietly reflected on the good fortune that Robert Simpson had survived, he started to prepare himself for the ordeal ahead and he intended to start with the Kalevala's Captain as soon as circumstances permitted. If the story he told regarding the Korean's knowing about an explosive device was correct then a certain Mr Lee was going to have a lot of explaining to do.

Chapter 29
June 2026

Paris

Deep in the heart of the Rue des 3 Fontanot is a small office that is used for interrogating suspects. Apart from a large two-way mirror that takes up an entire wall, the rest of the room was painted a light grey colour with only a clock to break the monotony. In the centre of the room was a small table and four wooden chairs. The table supported a recording device. The floor covering was a similar colour grey to the walls and was of a laminated fake wooden design. The room was anything but inspiring but then that was the intention.

Sitting on one of the chairs, James Chadwell was relaxed and sat with his legs crossed. He was wearing a grey jump suit supplied by the gendarmerie as a replacement for his cloths which had been taken for forensic examination. He was alone in the room but had seen enough TV to know that behind the large mirror would be detectives from the French police force watching his every move. He had been taken to the room from his holding cell about an hour previously and left on his own with just a cup of strong French coffee for company. The coffee remained untouched.

Since his arrest Chadwell had been desperately trying to formulate a story that would fit the known facts in such a way as to not incriminate himself, but until he discovered exactly what the police had on him, he knew he had to be very careful and only reveal the absolute minimum of information. And so, he waited, keeping his mind on anything but the present. Although he had been in police custardy before this was the first time that he had felt so vulnerable. He rightly suspected that being left in this grey room on his own for the best part of an hour was all part of the softening up process hence his attempt to concentrate on something banal. He was just thinking about a recent journey he had taken by car from Paris to the south of France when the door to the room opened and a lady and a man entered. Taking the two seats on the opposite side of the table Marie Lantieri introduced herself and her colleague, Detective Inspector Damien Remanan. Both police officers were dressed in civilian clothes and both had a cup of coffee which they placed on the table beside a small slim buff coloured file which Lantieri had brought into the room. Looking straight into the eyes of Chadwell, Lantieri began the interrogation speaking in English.

'Good morning, Mr Pritchard or should I call you Mr Chadwell?' She said.

Chadwell decided the best defence was to try and bluff his way out and replied in an indignant tone of voice.

'I don't know what you mean. I don't know anyone called Chadwell. And I don't know why I have been detained. What is it that I am meant to have done to be treated in such a disrespectful way?'

Lantieri ignored the outburst.

'Then I will address you as Mr Pritchard. That was the name you were using when you were picked up in Charles de Gaul airport so I assume that that will be the name you will continue to use. And before we start our discussion, I should advise you that we will be recording everything for future use. Do you have any objections to this?'

'I have objections to everything that is happening to me right now and will be expecting a serious apology when we are able to resolve whatever reason you think you have for arresting me.'

'Your objection is noted but we will still be recording everything.' Lantieri smiled and reaching for a button on top of the recording device pushed the record button. A small red light came on to indicate the tape recorder was working correctly.

'Good. So now we can start. First, I have to advise you of your right to have a lawyer present should you so wish. Do you wish to have a lawyer to represent you before we continue?'

Chadwell leant forward in his chair.

'I have been sitting in this room for an hour and it is only now that you advise me of my right to a lawyer. All I want is to get out of here and continue with my vacation. I do not wish to waste any more time waiting for a lawyer and as I haven't got anything to hide let's just get on with this. You will soon realise that you have the wrong man.'

'Very well. Your rejection of your right to have a lawyer present is noted. For the record please tell me your full name, address and date of birth.'

'Charles James Pritchard. Born 23 June 1973 and present address is 27 Edinburgh Street, Hornby, Lancaster Great Britain.'

'Thank you. And what were you doing in France Mr, er, Pritchard?'

'As I explained to the police officer at the airport I am on my way to the Seychelles and was just passing through France as it is cheaper than flying direct from the UK.'

Lantieri turned to the buff file on her desk before responding, 'Yes I see here that you mentioned this to the arresting officer. The problem is that we have no record of you arriving in France.'

'You wouldn't have. I came by car. I hitch hiked from Lancaster to Dover and then got a lift from someone who was travelling to Paris via the channel tunnel. The passport control at Calais never recorded my arrival as I was just a passenger in the car.'

'I don't suppose that you can remember the name of the driver or the number plate of the car that took you through the tunnel, can you?'

It was the first time that Detective Inspector Damien Remanan had spoken. From the tone of his voice it was clear he did not believe a word of the story and was just playing along.

'No, I don't. I just recall that it was a Black Ford Focus. The driver was not very talkative and as I was tired after my journey from Lancaster, I slept most of the journey.'

'Convenient,' but before Remanan could continue, Lantieri interjected.

'Mr Pritchard, we are both very busy people and I really don't have the time or the inclination to listen to any more of your fabrications. So, I am going to cut to the chase as the Americans would say. Yesterday morning we got a tip off that a suspected terrorist responsible for the death of many people had arrived at Charles de Gaul airport using the name Jason Chadwell. We tracked down Mr Chadwell to an address in Gif-sur-Yvette only to find that he had left about an hour before we got there. You not only fit the description of Mr Chadwell but your finger prints also match. We are still awaiting DNA results but we are certain that when we do get the results, they also will show that you and Mr Chadwell are the same person. You see, Mr Chadwell, or Mr Pritchard if you prefer, the incendiary device that you set was disarmed before it had time to explode and destroy all the evidence. We know that you are Mr Jason Chadwell who has resided for the last 12 years in Gif-sur-Yvette. We also know that the skeletal remains of an adult male were found in that house. The skeleton had clear signs of having met a violent death. The gunshot wound in the skull didn't need an expert to be identified although of course the body is as we speak undergoing a forensic examination. So, we have a body and a suspect and in due course we will identify the body and you will be charged with the murder. But that is not what I want to talk about today. We will have plenty of time to discuss your other activities later but right now I want to know what you were doing in Korea and who were your pay masters.

'We have looked at your bank statements; the Swiss banks were very helpful when we explained the reasons for our interest, and it is clear that you have been paid a lot of money over the years I assume to carry out other people's dirty work.'

Chadwell was stunned. How could they have found out so much in such a short space of time. Even if the incendiary device had failed to detonate; he knew he had not left anything incriminating in the house except the skeleton. He very much suspected that they would never be able to identify the remains making a murder charge hard to stick and whilst the forensic evidence would stop him from denying that he was in fact Chadwell, the real bombshell was that they had got access to his bank records.

Like most habitual criminals who had evaded capture for a long time, Chadwell over estimated his own intelligence. The reality was that once the police knew where to start looking it hadn't been difficult to track down the whole life story of Jason Chadwell. In the digital age we all leave a trail of our activities that tells our life's history. Jason Chadwell, for all his attention to detail, was no different and in fact the police had already narrowed down the identity of the skeleton to two or three possible individuals. DNA testing would quickly give the police a name and once they had a name it would only be a matter of time before they had a motive and all the evidence they would need to convince a jury of Chadwell's involvement. But Lantieri knew that that trail would be cold and it would be difficult to find out who had ordered the murder if in fact it had been ordered. Lantieri was convinced, from looking at the bank records particularly but also other evidence, that Chadwell was a gun for hire and she wanted to know who had ordered the sinking of the Kalevala. Who ultimately was responsible for mass murder of innocent people on the high seas?

Chadwell stayed silent as he frantically tried to concoct another story that would fit the facts without incriminating himself.

Lantieri took the opportunity to turn the knife.

'You know, Mr Chadwell, you don't mind if I call you that as we have now determined that you are in fact Mr Jason Chadwell?' Lantieri looked straight into the eyes of the man sitting opposite. 'No I didn't think so. As I was saying, you know, Mr Chadwell, we have a lot more than you seem to realise but what I really want to know is who are your pay masters and why did they want the Kalevala sank? We also want to know what other atrocities you are responsible for but that will come later.'

Chadwell tried to compose himself.

'I don't know what you are talking about. I've told you that I have just arrived from England to start a holiday in The Seychelles. I do recall staying in a house in the south of Paris last night as a guest of the driver that had taken me from Dover but I can't remember where it was. Clearly if it had been the house of this Mr Chadwell then you would find my finger prints and DNA but that doesn't mean that he and I are the same person.'

Even to the ears of Chadwell this sounded weak but it was all he could come up with in the short time available.

'What a load of bollocks!' Remanan couldn't help himself. 'You must think that we are really stupid to believe such a pile of horse shit.'

Quickly interrupting Lantieri continued the interview.

'I think what Detective Inspector Damien Remanan means is that we do not believe you and have evidence and eye witnesses that will very clearly demonstrate to a jury that you and Mr Jason Chadwell are the same person. So, it might be in your interest to be honest and co-operate with our enquiries.'

'What do you mean by that?'

Chadwell had lost all of his previous self-assurance and was showing clear signs of distress. Lantieri continued.

'I have asked Interpol to start tracking down where the various payments into your bank account originated from. That is a tortuous operation as many of the payments have been channelled through a number of holding accounts but the days when banks in such places as the Cayman Islands refused to co-operate are long since gone. It is only a matter of time before we find where the money originated. And when we know where the money comes from, we can find out who and why you were paid. For old cases we will have to first find the crime based on the dates of the payments which might not always be easy if you refuse to co-operate, but for the sinking of the Kalevala we know the crime so it shouldn't be difficult to find your paymasters and then eventually find the reason you were paid to sabotage the boat. The thing is, I would not be at all surprised if your paymasters don't turn out to be, shall we say, people who like their privacy and anonymity. Such people don't take kindly to individuals that expose them and such individuals often have a short life expectancy, even when locked up securely in a French prison.'

Lantieri took a sip of her now cold coffee whilst continuing to hold eye contact with Chadwell.

'So, what's it to be, Mr Chadwell? You can help us with our enquiries which will enable us to get to your paymasters before they get to you. They never need to know how we found them. Or we can continue with our enquires without your help in which case we are unable to give any guarantees that your involvement won't become general knowledge.'

'You can't threaten me like that.'

Lantieri thought that this was beginning to sound like a poor detective series on television. She also noted that Chadwell had stopped his denial that he wasn't in fact Jason Chadwell.

'I am not threatening you, Mr Chadwell. Please accept my apologies if it seems different. I am just pointing out that by co-operating we will be able to get to the real perpetuators quicker and without having to make it obvious where we got the information from.'

'Get smart, Mr Chadwell. Believe me I've seen what happens to people in prison when a contract is put on them. It's not pretty.'

Remanan tried with little success to make his features show compassion.

Chadwell looked like he was going to be sick.

Chapter 30
June 2026

London

'Good morning everyone and thank you for attending this meeting with such short notice. I'm sure you will appreciate that I would not have called the meeting if I didn't have important information to disseminate.' Richard Green looked around the room at the members of the security council gathered for the second time in as many weeks.

All eyes were on the prime minister as he opened the meeting.

'There is only one item on the agenda and that involves information recently received by MI5 so I'd like to hand over to Joan Stapleford to explain to the rest of you what she told me last night. Joan, over to you.'

'Thank you, Prime Minister. You may recall the last time we met we discussed the Russian threat in some detail. In particular we discussed the specific request for financial information that would give an indication of the amount of money the United Kingdom could use to fund its armed forces. Duncan particularly raised his concern that Russia was preparing to take back the territories it lost with the break-up of the Soviet Union and that the question of funding for our armed forces may in some way be related to that concern.

'The information that recently came into our possession would indicate that it is not content to just determine our ability to fund our armed forces, Russia is now actively engaged in trying to damage the financial and economic strength of the United Kingdom.' Stapleford paused and looked towards Richard Green who gave a brief nod of his head indicating Stapleford should continue.

'Yesterday morning we received a phone call from an unknown source that purported to be a Russian agent. As you can imagine we get all sorts of crank phone calls every day so the initial reaction was to ignore the call and file it under not proven. However, this caller mentioned one thing that made our analysts sit up and take notice. The caller mentioned the name Dmitri Rostov who just happens to be known to us.

'Dmitri Rostov is a senior agent of the GRU who specialises in controlling deep assets in the United Kingdom. You may recall that I mentioned that we know of a number of such assets and in fact have managed to turn a small number to act as double agents. At least two such assets have mentioned the name Dmitri Rostov as being involved with their recruitment. Not a name known to many people even within MI5, the fact that the caller used the name made her of particular interest.'

'Her? The caller was a woman?' Gary Davies interrupted.

'Yes. The caller was a woman. We know very little else about her. As would be expected her English was perfect and our linguistic experts have indicated she had a slight Liverpudlian accent but the call originated from a phone box in Peterhead.'

'A phone box? I didn't think such things still existed.' again it was Gary Davies that interrupted.

Stapleford looked over the top of her glasses in a school mistress sort of way and continued.

'The advantage of a phone box is that whilst it is traceable it is also anonymous. This particular box is located on the outskirts of Peterhead in a location devoid of the normal plethora of CCTV units. It was carefully chosen and it is highly unlikely that it will be used again. We have of course now installed surveillance units but as mentioned if the caller was an agent of Russia they would have been trained to never go back to the same place or use any form of communication that could be traced. The interesting thing though is that the call came from Scotland. Most agents that we know of are based in the south of the country and it is unlikely an agent would travel all the way to Scotland just to make a phone call so we suspect that the caller is based in Scotland. Two weeks ago, we intercepted a call from GRU headquarters to an unknown location somewhere in the Aberdeen area and this week we get an anonymous call from Peterhead. Perhaps a coincidence but I don't think so. I think that our caller is the same person that has recently been contacted by Moscow particularly in the light of the information she passed on.'

'Which is?' Davies's voice carried an edge of frustration as if to say get on with it.

'I'm just coming to that.' Stapleford again regarded Davies with an element of disapproval before continuing.

'The woman, let us call her Tanya for want of a better name, stated that she had been groomed all her life to serve Russia by Dmitri Rostov. Her role was to keep a low profile until such times as she could enter politics and potentially work her way into a senior political position. This ties in very much with the modus operandi of the GRU that we are aware of. Tanya went on to mention that she had become disillusioned with the Russian state and in particular that she considered the present Russian leaders to be a serious danger to world peace. She confirmed that she had recently passed on information to Dmitri Rostov which in hindsight and knowing the consequences she now very much regrets. She wants to try and make amends by informing us of the nature of the information requested in order, as she put it, to try and stop the madmen in the Kremlin.'

'What information did she pass on?' This from Duncan Smith who had been following the conversation with interest.

'Tanya told her handlers where the vulnerability existed with the development of the Caratacus Oil Field. She mentioned two areas where it was most vulnerable. The first was the fabrication of the accommodation unit at present under construction in a Norwegian yard. Without that module the whole development will be delayed. The second is the more interesting. It was the installation vessel Kalevala. Apparently, it is the only vessel in the world capable of installing the main production facilities and without the vessel the whole development could be delayed by years.'

'Kalevala. Isn't that the vessel that...' Before Duncan Smith could finish, he was interrupted by Stapleford.

'Yes, it is. The vessel that has just sunk off the coast of China.'

'Then you may be interested to know that we are getting strong indications from international sources that the Kalevala sinking was no accident.'

Smith's quiet statement certainly got the attention of the whole room. Richard Green was the first to respond.

'Are you sure of this, Duncan? It's the first that I have heard it was anything but a tragic accident?'

'The Koreans have as much as admitted that they knew a bomb had been planted on the ship before it sailed from Ulsan and Interpol have arrested a man in Paris as a result of intelligence received from Korea. The man in Paris was caught trying to leave the country under a false name having left an incendiary device in his house to destroy evidence. The house was searched before the incendiary device exploded leaving enough evidence to determine that the man had been paid to perform the sabotage on behalf of others. He is still being interrogated in Paris and to date is not admitting to anything but from what Jean has just told us it is quite feasible that his commission originated in the Kremlin. But why would Moscow want to delay the Caratacus project? What would they gain?'

These last two questions were more addressed to himself than to the rest of the room. The answer came from an unexpected source.

General Sir David Jordan had been listening intently to the conversation and suddenly looked up as if having an eureka moment.

'By delaying Caratacus, they delay the flow of funds to the UK treasury and hence weaken our ability to fund our military. Last week Duncan and I explained our thinking regarding Khurin's long term aim to reunite the lands of the old Soviet Union under a new Russian empire. If this is the case then it is very much in his interest to keep the UK as weak as possible at least until it is too late. Prime Minister, what would be the effect on the United Kingdom economy of bringing Caratacus on stream?'

'We are still trying to assess the effects. Alastair Franks is working the figures but it is fair to say that it will be substantial. The size of Caratacus took everyone by surprise and only really came to light following the drill rig incident of a few weeks ago. Early indications are that it the biggest oil reserve ever found in the North Sea and is on par with the bigger fields of the Middle East. Even with today's relatively low oil prices it would still bring in many billions of pounds to the UK exchequer every year for the next forty years at least. A word of caution though. The UK finances are in such a dire state that most of this windfall will have to be used to pay back the debts incurred by the previous administration or to fund expected welfare benefits, unless of course there is a national emergency. The big advantage of the additional revenue is that we would at least have the ability to make a choice whereas without it we are in survival mode only.'

Richard Green's reply was met with a courteous silence which was broken by Duncan Smith.

'If Russia is behind the sinking of The Kalevala then the only explanation is to try and delay the Caratacus project. They must have a good reason for doing that and the only one that makes sense is to delay the additional funding that such a project would bring in. We very much suspect that Khurin will make his move on the Baltic states in the next year so any delay in the revenue from Caratacus would, in his eyes, delay any increase in funding for the UK military meaning the UK would not be in a position to offer any resistance to such a move. We know that Russia is spending more than 5% of its GDP on the military. Khurin must be thinking what if the UK was in a position to do the same and have the Caratacus windfall to support such an expenditure? I'm afraid that the sinking of the Kalevala very much supports our fears regarding Khurin's intentions.'

General Jordan turned to Joan Stapleford.

'Joan. You stated the caller had identified two areas of weakness regarding the Caratacus development. The Kalevala was one but I think you said the fabrication of an accommodation unit was the second. Have we any indication if an act of sabotage has also been carried out on this module?'

'Nothing that I have heard of. The caller stated the unit was being built in Norway but I have no other information.'

'And you have no way of contacting this Tanya for more information?' This from Cynthia Graeme.

'Tanya made it very clear that she would contact us and not the other way around so the answer is no.'

'What does it matter about the accommodation unit? With Kalevala sunk hasn't Khurin already stopped or delayed the Caratacus project?' Gary Davies directed the question at Cynthia Graeme but the response came from General Jordan.

'My knowledge of the chaps that make their money getting oil out of the ground is that they are resilient types who don't have problems just challenges. I wouldn't assume that the sinking of Kalevala has stopped the project in its tracks. After all the only use of the Kalevala is to facilitate a lift which could be done by other crane vessels given the right circumstances and financial incentives. If I was Khurin I would want additional insurance and would still go after the accommodation unit. I would very much recommend that serious precautions are taken to prevent the unit from any further sabotage attempt.

'In the meanwhile, I would suggest we get more information from the operators of the Caratacus field regarding what the hell is going on. It worries me that a project which has such a critical influence on this country's, and in fact the world's wellbeing is in the hands of a bunch of civilians.'

The meeting continued for a few more minutes before being closed by the Prime Minister. An urgent meeting would be called with OEC to discuss the Caratacus project.

Chapter 31
June 2026

Paris

Marie Lantieri and Damien Remanan were sitting opposite each other in Lantieri's office. Both were relaxed but tired. The last few days had been busy trying to break down Jason Chadwell to get him to give information that may lead to the people behind the sinking of the Kalevala and hence responsible for the death of over 20 individuals. The fact that pressure on the two police officers had come from the Elyse Palace itself indicated how important it was for the perpetrators to be found. Not that such pressure made any difference to the way the Interpol inspectors went about their duties but it did at least mean that any resources they needed would be made available. To date there were over 30 officers working on the case. The house in Gif-sur-Yvette had been dismantled, almost brick by brick, without yielding much additional information. The house mentioned by Chadwell in Lancashire was indeed owned by a Mr Charles Pritchard but yielded as little information as the house in France. From what the officers had been able to gather the house in Lancashire had not been lived in for many years but had been maintained under a service contract with monthly payments for the service contract coming from Jason Chadwell's current account.

Door to door enquiries in Gils-sur-Yvette had found a number of neighbours that confirmed the identity of the man they had in custody as being Jason Chadwell and a DNA match completed the identification. Similarly, DNA and dental records had enabled the Paris police to identify the skeleton found in the house as belonging to a low ranking French official who had long been suspected as having links to an international drug operation and who had disappeared 12 years previously just as the police were closing in on him. The man's disappearance had sparked a low key but nevertheless intensive investigation but as no body was ever found the case had been closed as unsolved five years ago. At the time of the disappearance it had been suspected that the official would have been open to a plea bargain that would have led the way to higher ranking individuals being detained. The disappearance had stopped the investigation into the drug ring in its tracks. Now that the body had been found the police had managed to identify payments made into Chadwell's bank account at the time of the disappearance and were very interested to find that the original payment had come from a company that at the time was owned by a very senior member of the French political establishment. The files from the original investigation had been retrieved from the archives and the investigation had been reinvigorated.

In Korea the authorities had identified the hotel and room used by Chadwell on his visit as James Cartridge and although the room had been cleaned a number of times since Cartridge had used it, the authorities were still able to find a partial finger print identifying Mr James Cartridge as being the same person as Mr Jason Chadwell. Video footage of Chadwell entering the Kalevala before the initial explosion and again just before the Kalevala sailed had been sent to Paris, copies of which were on the desk in front of Lantieri.

Whilst the search of the house in Gils-sur Yvette was not particularly fruitful the electronic search of Chadwell's bank records had yielded considerably more information. Apart from the information that had led to the re-opening of the investigation into the international drugs ring there were a number of other unsolved murders, acts of sabotage and disappearances that when matched to payments into Chadwell's account had opened up many new lines of enquiry. But what most interested Lantieri, and where most of the political pressure was focused, was on the Kalevala case. Unfortunately, the bank records had not yielded quite as much information as initially hoped. Whilst 12 years previously the electronic banking system was still in its infancy and hence the ability to hide transaction history was not as well developed; with modern computers and sophisticated security systems, it was possible to pass a single transaction through as many accounts and as many countries as you wanted. With each account being password protected and some accounts in the few countries that still signed up to the "mind your own business" school of banking, tracking the source of the payments for the Kalevala sabotage was not proving as simple as they had hoped. Some progress had been made. All indications pointed to a start point somewhere in Southern Europe most likely France or Italy but the authorities had hit a major obstacle in their investigations. One of the accounts used to transfer the money to Chadwell was owned by a company called World Island Specialist Investments registered in a small Caribbean Island called Nevis. Nevis was one of the few countries that still considered the secrecy of its clients was more important than co-operating with world authorities. It took the secrecy issue so seriously that even the authorities in Nevis often had no idea who really owned many of their registered companies. Many attempts by foreign law enforcement agencies, and even by the St Kitts administration that theoretically had political control over its smaller neighbour, had been made to force the Nevis government to be more open but to no avail. What was generally known was that the island of Nevis was a favourite spot for individuals who had something to hide whether it was from ex-spouses seeking out the family fortune or individuals who would rather the tax authorities did not know about some of their dealings. It was also an ideal location for the criminal world to hide its illicit gains. In the past it had been associated with everyone from ex-presidents to boiler room scammers. As other so-called tax havens such as the Cayman Islands, Switzerland and Jersey were forced by international pressure to become more transparent, so more and more clients flooded to the remaining havens of which Nevis was one of the most successful. Lantieri was optimistic that Interpol would eventually find out who actually owner World Island Specialist Investments but was under no illusions that it would be a long drawn out process.

'We seem to have hit a brick wall with following the money, Damien. Where do we go next?' Lantieri opened the conversation.

'Good question. Chadwell is still refusing to even admit that he is Chadwell despite all the evidence to the contrary. He is clearly a professional and I very much suspect that we won't get anything else out of him. He knows that he is going down for a long time but he also knows that if he speaks his life expectancy is not very good.'

'Can we use that against him? Can we threaten him that we will tell certain individuals in the French underworld that he is talking unless he does actually talk?'

Remanan smiled. 'Apart from that being not very ethical and most certainly illegal I suspect that he would rather call the bluff than break his word. Some criminals have a strong code of honour which considering they don't hesitate to kill innocent people for money does seem rather ironic.'

'True. but I am getting a lot of pressure from on high to find out who is behind the Kalevala's sinking. Nobody has said anything but I have a strong feeling that there is much more to this than we have been told. Why for instance would our beloved leaders in government be taking such an interest if there wasn't a strong political angle? That's rhetorical by the way.' Lantieri returned Remanan's smile before continuing. 'We need to find some way of moving this investigation forward which doesn't just rely on following the money. The search of both the Gilf-sur Yvette and the UK property yielded no real information but Chadwell must have had a record somewhere of his activities. He has obviously been in business for over 12 years and in that time he would have amassed a considerable client base. If his financial records are anything to go on, he has been paid at least 50 times for what must be assumed to be criminal acts. He must have records somewhere. How are the checks progressing on the potential for other properties either in the name Chadwell, Cartridge or Pritchard?'

'So far, nothing. We have searched land registry records both here and in the UK, but unfortunately the names he has been using are fairly common and going through every record is taking a long time. That is of course assuming he used any of those names. We know that he had multiple identities so we could be looking in all the wrong places.'

Lantieri looked thoughtful.

'What did you just say? We know he had multiple identities? Of course. If someone has multiple identities it stands to reason he would also have multiple passports. But we haven't found any other passports so he either doesn't have any further identities, which I find very surprising, or he has other hiding places. To find the other hiding places we need to find the other identities.'

Lantieri suddenly sat up straight in her chair and stared straight at Remanan.

'Get onto the British authorities and see if they can do a facial recognition of all passports issued in the past 12 years. He may be able to change his name and details but he won't be able to change his facial features.'

Chapter 32
June 2026

London

There was an element of déjà vu about the small gathering in Downing Street's small living room. The only occupant missing from the previous gathering was David Grant who was still trying to manage the fall out over the Triton Drill rig incident. His attendance was also irrelevant to the discussion taking place. His place had been taken by General Jordan, today, and at the request of the Prime Minister, dressed in civilian clothing.

Richard Green had asked, summoned would perhaps had been a more appropriate word, the executives from OEC to come to Downing Street to discuss the latest problems with the development of the Caratacus oil field. Since the size and importance of Caratacus had come to his attention, Richard Green had become more and more convinced that its success was imperative if his own administration was to be a success. He desperately needed the revenues that such a development would bring to the UK exchequer and if what his security advisers were telling him had any basis in fact then he was in a race against the clock to ensure the UK defences were strong enough to meet the challenge from Russia. He was confident that given time he would be able to address the damage done to the UK economy by the terrible Brexit deal compounded by five years of a disastrous socialist administration; but what was now becoming increasingly clear was that time was perhaps not on his side. The initial idea regarding the windfall from Caratacus had given him hope that the debts becoming payable in the next two years would be either paid back but more likely rolled over without the need for serious austerity measures that in itself would have caused the economy to contract. The revelation that Russia seemed to be doing all it could to slow down or prevent Caratacus had focused his mind on the bigger picture. Whilst new to politics he was beginning to realise that a fast learning curve was required if he was to facilitate Great Britain taking its place once again at the top table of world powers.

Turning to his guests he gave them his best politician, 'you can trust me' smile before continuing. 'I have to say that after our discussion of a few months ago I did not expect that we would be sitting down again in this pleasant room discussing yet another major disaster related to the Caratacus Field.'

His eyes shifted from Jim Simpson to Jean Robertson and back as he spoke.

'But here we are, this time to discuss the Kalevala's sinking. Please tell me what you know.'

Simpson cleared his throat before responding, 'I'm sure that you are aware of the basic facts. The Kalevala left Korea two weeks ago yesterday bound for Cape Town. Three days into the voyage she sank with the loss of 26 lives, a death toll that may yet increase as there are still two Korean workers that are in intensive care. The ship sank close to the Island of Taiwan who responded efficiently and quickly to the emergency. I dread to think what the death toll would have been had it not been for the Taiwanese emergency response teams. You may not know but my own son was on the Kalevala when she sank. He survived not in a small measure thanks to the Taiwanese efforts.'

'We have had a full report on the sinking from the British consular in Taiwan and my colleague, Gary Davies, has passed on the personal thanks of the British government to the Taiwanese authorities,' Cynthia Graeme interrupted before continuing, 'the Prime Minister and myself are more interested in the details of the sinking. With the Triton incident our initial assumption that terrorists were involved proved to be false or at least that was our thought, perhaps our optimistic hope. Regarding the Kalevala incident we have received similar information that terrorists were involved this time substantiated by Interpol and the Korean authorities. First Triton and now Kalevala. It seems clear to us that someone wants to stop the Caratacus development and that with the sinking of the Kalevala they have succeeded. What we want to discuss with you is what you know about the sabotage of Kalevala and what affect the sinking will have on the Caratacus development.' Graeme addressed the question directly to Jim Simpson.

Simpson took a minute to get his thoughts in order before he answered, 'It is better if I start at the beginning. When I started OEC it was my intention to buy up nearly depleted oil fields which were uneconomical for the majors to keep going but which still had value for a smaller company with smaller overheads. I had no intention, or in fact any idea, how to go about developing a major new discovery particularly one the size of Caratacus. That all changed when my son, Ted, came to me with a theory that pre-salt oil deposits would be found in the North Sea.'

'Sorry. Pre-salt oil deposits?' Green interrupted.

'I don't know the full technical details but basically its very deep oil deposits that are to be found under a layer of salts that distinguish the shallow depth fields developed to date from much older deposits. First discovered in Brazil and Western Africa the quantity of oil is considerable. Brazil alone is thought to have reserves approaching 50 billion barrels in its pre-salt deposits. This compares with 14 billion barrels in the deposits above the salt layer. And its good quality oil which makes it suitable for refining into petroleum products at a minimum of cost. The only drawback is that in both Brazil and West Africa the deposits are in very deep water and a long way down.

'After Ted came to me with his theory about pre-salt being in the North Sea, I was at first sceptical but Ted persevered and so OEC decided to drill a test well. To our amazement we struck pay dirt in a big way which was the Caratacus oil reservoir. It is still a long way under the ground but it is in the relatively shallow waters of the North Sea so the cost of getting the oil from under the ground to market is a fraction of the costs in Brazil and West Africa. Once we had drilled additional exploratory wells to determine the size of the field, we had to make a decision as to whether to develop the field on our own or with partners. Rightly or wrongly we decided to go alone.'

At this point Jean Robertson interrupted. 'What Jim means is that the oil majors when approached weren't interested in just investing in OEC, they wanted to take it over or for OEC to relinquish control of Caratacus to them as the price for co-operation.'

Simpson continued, 'Jean is correct in what she says. The major oil companies would have made everyone at OEC very rich but this was Ted's discovery and he convinced me that we could do this ourselves. I think we were all a bit naïve but we went for it anyway. Along the way I have thought many times that we should have taken the offer from the majors, but then as challenges have been overcome and we have got closer to achieving first oil I've felt an incredible pride that a small company like ours has been able to achieve so much. But to get there we have had to take a few more risks than perhaps the majors would have been willing to take on board. One such risk was Kalevala.

'Money was always tight and we were always looking at ways to reduce the cost of development. In some ways finding the oil was the easy bit. To get the oil from the ground to the market requires a whole load of infrastructure. First the wells have to be drilled. Each well can only support a certain flow of oil so multiple wells have to be drilled. With each well taking between 45 and 60 days to drill using a drill rig costing £250,000 per day and needing ten wells just to allow start up you can see how quickly costs can add up. Then there is the cost of the support platform, the pipelines to get the oil to shore, the refinery and the onshore facilities.

'But I digress. Needless to say, as a small company we had to scrimp and beg for every penny so when the Kalevala came along with a story that meant we could knock £100 million from the development costs we were, or rather I was, dragged in. The problem with Kalevala in the eyes of my production director was that it was a one off and if anything happened to it, we would be in the smelly stuff. You see the £100 million cost saving came from being able to build almost the entire offshore production facilities as a single unit saving an awful lot of offshore completions. The reason that Kalevala was so important was that the offshore production facilities as a single unit became so big only Kalevala had the capacity to lift it into place. So, when Kalevala was lost, I thought that we were scuppered.

'Without Kalevala we can't lift the main production facilities as a single unit so we have to now go back to square one to build multiple but smaller units that have to be connected together after they get offshore. It will delay the project by years and means OEC will have to relinquish control.'

Jean Robertson was almost in tears.

General Jordan entered the conversation for the first time.

'Forgive me, but you said that you thought you were scuppered. I think they were your words implying that you may have had a change of mind?' Simpson turned his attention to Jordan.

Introductions had not been made but he recognised the General from previous television interviews. He had been surprised to see him at the meeting but resisted the temptation to ask why he was in attendance.

'Indeed. I should have mentioned earlier but this whole project has been plagued by bad luck and delays since inception. I have always assumed that this was just part of the problems associated with trying to bring such a complex project to completion. But a few weeks ago, we had an explosion on Kalevala that was a bit of a wake-up call. I always told my team that Kalevala was the only option in order to keep them focused but there was another option proposed by an Italian company called Rostella S.p.A.'

'Rostella are also in the business of offshore installation and operate the second largest crane vessel after Saunders Marine, the owners of Kalevala. Before we finalised the contract with Saunders the owner of Rostella came to me with an innovative installation concept that would enable his company to lift the Caratacus production facilities as a single unit but using two crane vessels. This had never been done before and given the choice between a proven concept and a new idea with all the associated risks I decided to concentrate on Kalevala.

'After the first explosion on Kalevala I approached Rostella and asked if the alternative lift concept was still feasible. Rostella confirmed that it was. Some small modifications to the production facilities will be required but this is manageable. My concern was that there would need to be work done on the Rostella crane vessels that would delay everything but I have been assured that the necessary modifications have already been carried out. Once we have completed the minor modifications to the production facilities, we are back on track to get the offshore installation completed this year.

'Yesterday I spoke to the owner of Rostella, a Mr Marco Paglia and advised him to start mobilising his equipment. As soon as I am back in the office, I will issue the letter of intent.'

This last statement was addressed more to Jean Robertson than the others in the room.

'Sorry I haven't had time to update you, Jean.'

Jean Robertson was taken aback. She had assured Rostov that sinking the Kalevala would stop the project and now she was being told that this wasn't the case. Rostov would think that she had lied to him which would put her in a very precarious position. Whilst she was pleased that the sabotage had failed in its goal, she was very nervous for her own safety. People that betrayed Rostov had a habit of disappearing.

As these thoughts went around her head Richard Green continued the conversation.

'Am I to understand that despite the loss of Kalevala the Caratacus project is still on target for completion?'

'Yes, Prime Minister, that is exactly what I am saying. The loss of the Kalevala is still a massive tragedy and I know from David Saunders that an investigation is ongoing to determine those responsible. As the Home Secretary mentioned earlier there is clear evidence that Kalevala was sabotaged and that the Koreans were aware that there was a bomb on board before the ship sailed. In my view this is criminal but not as criminal as the person that set the bomb and killed all those people. To find and bring the perpetuators to justice is a job for the police.

'Why the vessel was sabotaged I don't know but if it was to stop the Caratacus development it has not worked.'

Richard Green looked across at General Jordan. 'I think we need to take Mr Simpson into our confidence if we are to prevent further issues unless you have objections on security grounds?'

Jordan replied, 'I don't think we have any options. Go ahead.'

Green looked across to the two OEC executives before continuing, 'What I am about to tell you is highly confidential and I would appreciate your assurances that you will not tell anyone else.'

Simpson and Robertson both nodded their head in acknowledgement.

'As we discussed earlier, we initially thought the Triton incident was terrorist related. We discounted that after the investigation but what the incident did was highlight the importance to the UK economy of the Caratacus oil, something we hadn't been aware of until then. You may or may not know that the UK economy is in a bit of a mess and the windfall from Caratacus would be very helpful in helping to buy time until we can get the economy back on a firmer footing.

'A few days ago, we received an anonymous phone call from someone that stated they were a Russian agent that had been asked to provide information about where the vulnerabilities were for the Caratacus development. The agent, if in fact the person was an agent and we have no reason to think they were not, stated that they had advised Moscow that the two weakest points were the Kalevala and the accommodation units being fabricated in Norway. We have no idea why the agent should contact us with this information but the contact came a day after the ship was sunk and the number of people that lost their lives was becoming clear. We have had previous instances when individuals develop a conscience after a major tragedy and realise that they are serving the wrong master but at the time of the phone call we had no indication other than the Kalevala's sinking was anything but an accident. We now know the vessel was sabotaged and probably by the Russians and we strongly suspect the reason for the sinking was to stop or delay the Caratacus development.'

Jean Robertson was careful to keep her expression neutral as Simpson responded.

'But why would Russia want to stop Caratacus?' The doubt could be heard in the tone of Jim Simpson's voice.

'I'm afraid that I am not at liberty to answer that question but nevertheless it is what we believe. The question we now need to ask ourselves is if sinking the Kalevala will not stop Caratacus then what will Russia do next? As I said the Russian agent mentioned two weak points. The first was Kalevala the second was something about an accommodation module. Perhaps you can expand a bit on what they could mean by that.'

'Of course,' Simpson took up the conversation again. 'In fact, I was only discussing this with Jean two or three weeks ago. The accommodation module is part of the offshore development. The days of asking people to work offshore for four or even six weeks on the trot and live in spartan surroundings are long since gone. Nowadays the offshore workers are extremely well looked after and that means a two-week offshore shift with hotel like accommodation. The standard of accommodation has to be very high and there are only a handful of fabricators that specialise in building such units. Whilst we were able to build one large production unit the accommodation unit had to be fabricated in a separate location and will be installed separately to the production facilities. It is the only module separate from the production facilities which is complete except for the minor modifications needed to facilitate the new lift method. Without accommodation no one can work on the offshore production so it is as important that the accommodation module gets finished as it is that the production facilities are installed on time. The accommodation module is still in fabrication and whilst the planning is saying it will be ready on time, any delays could mean the offshore installation season is missed and first oil is delayed by a minimum six months. My concern regarding the module is mainly based on the fabricator getting everything finished on time. I was not thinking about sabotage.'

'If we are right and the Russians are behind the sabotage on Kalevala, the fact that this agent identified two areas of weakness and one has already been targeted, I think we would be foolish not to take precautions against the other potential target,' General Jordan addressed the room. 'I have made some enquiries and understand that the accommodation module is being fabricated in a yard close to Bergen in Norway at a place called Stord. I suspect the security in the yard is suitable to prevent minor pillaging but not to prevent a concerted sabotage attempt by Russia. I propose that we arrange additional security of our own. Specialists that are more adept at counter terrorism. We have people that fit the bill and can clear everything with the Norwegian authorities but will need your co-operation in getting our people into the yard without arousing suspicions.'

'Just let me know how we can help.' Simpson turned to Jean Robertson. 'Jean. Can I rely on you to give whatever support General Jordan requires? As I will be quite busy making arrangements with the Italians, I think it would be better if you acted as contact point for this.'

Jean Robertson kept a calm face but inside she was in turmoil. Not only had sinking the Kalevala not worked but now the second weak point that she had identified was being strengthened. In her own mind she began to question why she had made the phone call in the first place to warn the British authorities. At the time she had not considered the risk to which she would be exposed but now she wondered if her warning would not be her own downfall. Whilst she confirmed that she would help facilitate the incursion of British security personnel into the Norwegian yard she was desperately trying to think how she could retrieve her own position. The next few days would be crucial.

Chapter 33
July 2026

Naples

The last four weeks had been busy for Marco Paglia. After he had recovered from the shock of the sinking of Kalevala and the fact that over 20 persons had died, his attention turned to the future. The dead were dead and there was nothing that Paglia could do about that now, so just accept the reality and move forward. A day after the sinking he had received another phone call from Constance Luigiano requesting payment be made in full for the completion of the contract. Paglia knew better than to try and haggle the price on the basis of the number of fatalities, something that had been very specific in the original agreement. The type of people he was dealing with did not consider human lives worth anything as had been made very clear in the earlier phone call.

Using his own private Swiss account Paglia authorised the required amount be transferred to the account specified by Luigiano, an account also based in Switzerland. Within hours the money had been transferred automatically through a number of different accounts based in banks scattered around the world before it arrived at an account based on a small Island in the Caribbean called Nevis. The last contact that Paglia had had with Luigiano was to confirm that the money had been received and that the contract was considered complete.

A few days after the sinking Paglia received the phone call he had been expecting. Jim Simpson rang him personally having just returned from Taiwan with his son Robert. The formalities were kept to a minimum. Both men knew that with Kalevala out of the picture Rostella were the only company now able to lift and install the Caratacus Production deck. Negotiations were short but intense. Clearly Paglia could not tell Simpson that he was already out of pocket for the cost in hiring Luigiano but he could use the cost for upgrading his two crane vessels to make them suitable, a cost which Simpson would now have to pay plus the exorbitant day rate for the vessels starting from the moment Simpson agreed to their use. By the time the phone call was over Paglia had easily recouped all of his outgoings and made a very nice profit. In addition, he knew that without Kalevala, other clients who had been lining up to use the new vessel would now be knocking on his door. Life was suddenly good and the stress of the last few months dissipated as he realised his plan had succeeded. The loss of life was no longer anything that bothered him having rationalised that he had done all he could to prevent such a loss. It was not his fault, just an accident.

Three days after the call from Simpson the draft contract had been received and after some minor discussions on some of the terms and conditions it was signed two weeks later. There was no contract signing ceremony; in fact there was no actual meeting between the two signatories each having signed the contract and then passed the signed version to the counter party to sign. Both parties knew the contract was grossly one sided but both parties knew that there were no alternatives.

Immediately the contract had been signed. Paglia nominated a project team and gave instructions for his two crane vessels to start mobilisation to the North Sea. Assuming no further problems the crane vessels would arrive in the middle of August for an operation that should take no more than seven days weather permitting.

Meanwhile, unbeknown to Paglia, Interpol had identified the Nevis account used by Luigiano as World Island Specialist Investments. The ownership structure of the company was not yet known but once this was cracked the trail would very quickly lead to a Swiss bank account held in the name of Constance Luigiano.

Chapter 34
July 2026

Paris

After a brief knock on the door Remanan hurried into the office of his boss and gently placed three files on her desk. Surprised by the sudden interruption Marie Lantieri looked up from her computer screen with a quizzical look on her face. She had known Damien Remanan for more years than she cared to remember and knew that he would not have come into her office unannounced unless he had something important to tell her.

'You were right,' Remanan blurted out, 'Chadwell did have multiple aliases. We have just received information from the British police that as a result of the facial identification checks they have identified three other passports issued to a man with the same features as our Mr Chadwell. Not only have they identified that passports have been issued but by cross checking the names on the passports with other data bases such as land registry and car registration details, they have identified that Mr Chadwell had another 15 properties at his disposal of which all but two are in the United Kingdom. We are still checking the list but it would appear that the properties in the United Kingdom are all rented out and we can only assume that they are Chadwell's way of laundering the money he receives from his illegal activities. Some of the properties are in the centre of London and worth a lot of money. Our, Mr Chadwell, is a very rich man.

'But the most interesting properties are the two here in France. One is in Paris and the second is in Villefranche, just outside Nice. These do not appear to have been rented out and are likely to have been in regular use by Chadwell. We are arranging for the appropriate search warrants and I rather suspect that you would like to be present whilst the search takes place.'

A broad smile appeared on Lantieri's face as she quietly said to herself, 'Got you,' before addressing Remanan directly. 'Good work, Damien, and you are correct in your suspicions. I would very much like to see what Mr Chadwell has stashed away in his other properties. Whilst we mustn't get our hopes up too high, he has to have had a base somewhere where he kept his records. It certainly wasn't either the house in Lancashire or the one in Gils-sur-Yvette. If I were a betting person, I would suspect the property in Villefranche will be the most interesting but let's start with Paris. I assume that you have not told Chadwell about this discovery?'

'No, he is still being held under the counter terrorism act so we are able to keep him isolated from contacting anyone in the outside world. It is always possible that he has an accomplice somewhere so we need to ensure that he is not able to get word out. But the longer we leave it the more likely it will be that any accomplice will get wind of Chadwell's disappearance and destroy any records.'

Lantieri got up from her chair and reached for her jacket.

'Then we should move quickly. I'll arrange for Charlotte to get us on the afternoon flight to Nice and to have back up waiting for us. I'll also request the Nice police keep a watch on the Villefranche property until we arrive. Meanwhile let's go and see what Mr Chadwell has in his Paris apartment.'

Forty-five minutes later the two Interpol agents and a squad of armed police arrived at an address in an exclusive part of Paris. Having received the necessary search warrants, they made their way to the third floor apartment and after knocking the door with no answer, they forced an entry. The first impression was one of opulence. The front door opened onto a small hall and then to a large living area consisting of a solid oak parquet wooden floor and fine furnishings that could have come out of one of those expensive magazines that seem to only be found in dentist waiting rooms. The two bedrooms both had king size double beds covered by the finest linen. Both had fully tiled en-suite facilities of the finest porcelain and gold-plated fitting. To one side of the main living area was a kitchen, sparkling clean but with the best Miele appliances. A small study furnished with a small filing cabinet and a large desk and chair completed the layout. Disappointingly there was no sign of a computer and a thorough search of the rooms, including ultra-sonic checks of wall and floor spaces, yielded nothing. All indications were that the flat was ready but had not yet been occupied. Even the wardrobe was empty of cloths. The inevitable conclusion was that this was to be the bolt hole that Chadwell would return to after the dust had settled and he had adopted a new identity.

Disappointed but not disheartened Lantieri and Remanan left the Paris apartment with instructions to the local police to keep it under surveillance until further notice and made their way to Paris Orly airport in time to catch the 14:50 hr Air France flight to Nice. Lantieri had always suspected the Paris apartment would not yield very much based on what they had found in Gils-sur-Yvette, but she had much higher hopes for the Villefranche villa. Call it a hunch or whatever but somehow, she reasoned, it seemed more likely that Villefranche would be a safer place for someone like Chadwell than anywhere near Paris.

Arriving at Nice airport they were picked up by the Nice police and driven to an address on the Avenue Fernand Martin in the small seaside town of Villefranche-sur-Mer. The property was a small villa with its own swimming pool perched on the side of the hill. A steep road led to the driveway where they found the local police waiting for them. As the local police station was less than 500 metres away from address it had not taken the police long to reach the property.

Again, there was no answer to the polite knock to the front door so a forced entry was required but unlike the apartment in Paris the front door was considerably more secure. Taking this as a good sign Lantieri instructed the locksmith to be particularly careful. Her concern paid off as it was discovered that the door was not only alarmed but was rigged with explosives if the alarm was not deactivated in a certain time. Fortunately, the Nice police had come prepared and one of the squad was an expert in dismantling such devices. Within 15 minutes the alarm was deactivated and the explosive device removed but this was taken as a warning to take particular care. What other precautions were in place to prevent the small villa from giving up its secrets? The villa was furnished in a similar style to the apartment in Paris but there the similarity ended. It was very evident that the villa was in regular use. After the Nice bomb disposal unit had finished a sweep of the villa the detailed search could take place. In the master bedroom the bed was unmade and cloths were scattered about the room. The fridge was empty but the cupboards were full of non-perishable goods and whilst the villa was not dirty it had clearly been lived in.

Of much more interest to the Interpol detectives was the computer facilities found in the study and the large safe hidden in the attic space. Lantieri had no idea what would be found on the computer or in the safe. She had no intention of trying to open either herself, she had experts back in Paris who would be responsible for that, but it very much looked like her hunch had paid off. Care would have to be taken when accessing the safe and computer but Lantieri felt certain she would not be disappointed by the results.

Chapter 35
July 2026

Norway

Although it was nearly eleven o'clock at night the skies over the small fabrication yard on the Island of Stord in Norway were still not completely dark. Being only 1000 kilometres south of the arctic circle, at this time of year the sun only really set for about six hours which did not make the job of Major Vladimir Kornoukhov any easier. As the commanding officer of the four man Spetsnaz squad tasked with sabotaging the accommodation unit of the Caratacus project he would have wished for a darker night. Not that he was particularly concerned. This would be a routine mission. All he had to do was get into the yard undetected, set a fire in the main machinery space, making it look like an accident and leave equally undetected.

The four-man squad had travelled to Stord by road from their base in Murmansk, crossing the Norwegian border just outside a small Norwegian village called Elvenes. Making their way via the E105 they had followed the Norwegian/Swedish border before crossing over to the Norwegian west coast. The scenery was absolutely stunning and there was a relaxed feeling inside the Mercedes SUV as it made its way south to Stord. The four Spetsnaz officers were experienced personnel having served in Syria and Ukraine over the past two years. To them an excursion to an undefended yard on a small Island in Norway was like a holiday. Stopping off at Narvik and Trondheim they had made full use of their expense account and had even had the chance to chat up a couple of the local girls; although without much success. Despite their rugged good looks and well-toned bodies, they were still Russian and the Norwegians did not like the Russians. But never mind. That was their loss. Whilst they may not be overly friendly, they were still happy to take the drinks offered and whilst the drinks were flowing the Norwegian girls had stayed at the table laughing with the Russian 'tourists' but not getting too close.

Eventually the fun had to stop and the serious business had to start. After checking in at the Stord Hotel they had driven the three kilometres to the Kvaerner fabrication facilities to see what they were up against. After an hour reconnaissance they had seen enough. This was going to be easier than they had thought. The yard had a border with the road on one side and the sea on the other. A chain link fence surrounded the yard but the main entrance was large and open with only a manually operated barrier stopping the constant stream of heavy goods vehicles entering and leaving the yard. A single security guard sat in a small hut at the barrier issuing passes to those coming and going. Workers were seen to enter and leave the yard via a revolving doorway that was activated by an electronic pass. The doorway led directly from the yard to the large car park situated just outside the chain link fence.

Meeting back in Major Kornoukhov's room later in the day it was agreed that there was no advantage in waiting any longer than necessary and that they would access the yard tonight. They had identified a place where the fence was already damaged and all they needed to do was enlarge the hole to get access. Conscious of the need to leave no evidence of their involvement the fence would have to be opened in such a way that the enlargement would look like natural damage but this would not be an issue. Once in the yard one man would remain at the fence to keep the escape route clear and ensure the damaged section was not found whilst the remaining three men would access the accommodation module. The men would be dressed as Norwegian workers wearing the blue Kvaerner overalls, steel capped boots, hard hat and eye protectors. Due to the tight fabrication schedule the yard was working 24 hours a day at present, in order to finalise everything ready for the module to be towed to the offshore location in two weeks' time. Already the barge for the transportation was moored alongside the quayside waiting for the module to be loaded out and the module had been taken from the fabrication hall to the outfitting area just in front of the quayside.

Leaving the Mercedes SUV parked off the small perimeter road the four men had crossed over to the break in the fence and, having ensured there was no one in sight had enlarged the hole and were now crouched just inside the fence. It was eleven o'clock at night. Opening the fence using a set of bolt cutters had been easy. The men were not armed except with a commando knife, but carried a small detonator and a can of petrol. If the fire was to look like an accident, they could not use any of the normal explosive devices so this would be a low-tech sabotage.

So far so good. Leaving behind the look out the remaining three men scrambled down the slight bank to the yard access road and were just beginning to walk towards the accommodation unit when they suddenly found themselves challenged in an unmistakably military fashion – but more telling the challenge was in Russian. Turning to run they heard the unmistakable sound of sub machine guns being primed and again the order to stay where they were and drop to the floor. At the same time a bright light shone directly into their eyes instantly blinding them. With no other option available the three men did as they were told and lay on the floor wondering what had gone wrong.

No sooner were the men on the floor, their arms were seized and forced around their backs where cable ties were used to tie the hands together. Once they had been incapacitated, they were pulled to their feet and the can of petrol retrieved from the floor where it had dropped before the men were marched towards the accommodation module. On the way they were joined by the fourth member of the squad who was similarly incapacitated. No words had passed between the four men or from their captors since the original challenge and as they were led away Major Kornoukhov was desperately trying to make sense of what was going on.

Chapter 36
August 2026

London

Richard Green was alone in his office looking over the latest budget proposal when a gentle knock on the door interrupted his concentration. Annoyed, as he had specifically asked his secretary to advise any callers that he was not to be disturbed, he looked up from the report and brusquely asked the caller to come in. Joan Stapleford and Duncan Smith entered and made their way to the two chairs placed opposite Richard Green. After apologising for the interruption Duncan Smith was the first to get down to business.

'Prime Minister, you asked us to keep you informed on the Caratacus project and any further developments. As you know our security forces in the Stord yard apprehended four Russians who were clearly intent on sabotaging the module. They of course deny any involvement. They just say that they are tourists that wanted to get a better look at the yard and seeing a break in the fence took advantage to gain access. The fact that they were found with a can of petrol, a set of bolt cutters and most damning a small detonator makes their story highly unbelievable but they are sticking to it. As we would expect the Russian embassy in Norway is making a big fuss and is demanding the release of the men spouting the usual indignations about how badly Russian civilians are treated abroad by western fascist agencies.

'But to cut a long story short we have clearly identified at least one of the men as a Major in the Russian Spetsnaz, an offshoot of their GRU security services. So, it looks like the Russians are very clearly targeting the Caratacus project.

'In addition, we have heard from Interpol that they are zeroing in on the money men behind the saboteur of the Kalevala. They have found additional aliases for the perpetrator which led them to a Villa in the South of France where they found encoded files and a laptop computer. Interpol are working on both and we anticipate that the trail will again lead directly to the Russians.'

'Duncan, I am very busy this morning. In the next few days we have to announce the budget for next year and I am still trying to finalise things. Needless to say, by this time next week I will most likely be the most unpopular man in Great Britain but we all know that needs must. So far you haven't told me anything I didn't already know. Is there a specific reason for today's interruption?'

Duncan Smith remained placid and continued in the same even tone, 'It is because you are setting the budget that I felt the urgent need for this meeting. I have been told that the defence budget has not been raised apart from some inflation adjustments. Is this correct?'

'The details of the budget are still confidential and are not yet finalised but I think I can be open that right now; we don't have the money to increase the defence spending. It really is a question of priorities, and where we are today, we have to give priorities to reducing the deficit. The electorate will not accept any tax rises which anyway was a manifesto commitment that we gave, and we have already pared government expenditure as much as we dare without causing major hardship to large parts of the country. We have tried to at least ring fence the defence budget in the face of opposition calls to cut it further but unless there is a marked change in circumstances, I cannot see that we can change our present position.'

'And you don't consider the sabotage of the Caratacus project as being a marked change of circumstances?'

'On its own and without further evidence of the reason why Russia is involved, no I don't see this as being a marked change of circumstances.'

'At our last meeting before we deployed the SAS to Norway, we discussed the information that we received from agent Tanya. She made it very clear that Russia was intent on stopping Caratacus and it was this information that prompted us to give extra protection to the yard in Norway hence preventing an act of terrorism that would have delayed Caratacus.

'What more proof do you need? Russia wants Caratacus delayed at the least. You ask why. I would say that is obvious. They want the United Kingdom to remain weak.

'I didn't raise it at the previous meetings as I was concerned about security but we have very strong reason to believe that the previous administration was helped in their election campaign by the Russian state. We do not have clear evidence that the help was encouraged or even condoned by the socialists but the use of social media to target the young we do know was orchestrated by Russia.

'Russia wants a weak United Kingdom in order that it can carry out its ambition to retake the old Soviet territories.

'So, I ask you what is better? To have a balanced budget or have a Russian empire on our doorstep?'

'Russia won't do anything against a fellow NATO country without risking the full NATO alliance mobilising against them.'

Richard Green was beginning to tire of going over the same old ground.

'NATO' – Duncan Smith almost spat out the word "NATO" – 'is just about finished. It's as useless as a chocolate teacup. All it needs is for Turkey to announce its departure, and my information is that this may happen in the next week or so, and the whole alliance will collapse. America will go its own way and the Europeans are so dependent on Russian gas that even if they did want to resist the Russians, they could not without risking an acute energy shortage.

'The only country that can stop Russia is Great Britain. Perhaps even now it is too late but every day that we delay in improving our armed forces is another day that Russia has gained.

'I have just come off the phone to my counterpart in the CIA and he confirms that Russia has promised Turkey support in its fight against the Kurds as well as a significant reduction in the cost of gas if Turkey abandons NATO and joins an alliance with Russia and other ex-soviet states. America is not willing to support Turkey any more and sees Russia as a European concern; not something for America to worry about. If Turkey does leave NATO, America will follow unless Europe is seen to be carrying more of its share of the NATO burden.

'If the United Kingdom does not increase its defence spending by a significant amount then NATO will cease to exist within three months. Within six months, Russia will have annexed the Baltic states and within two years Russia will have regained all the old Soviet territories which includes many of the countries at present in the European Community.

'This isn't scare mongering; this is a very real likelihood.' Duncan Smith leant back in his chair and held the gaze of Richard Green until the latter dropped his eyes to his desk.

'But where is the proof? How can I tell the British public that they will have to go hungry because we have cut the benefit payments to pay for more tanks without something more tangible than hearsay?'

'Perhaps I can help,' Joan Stapleford spoke for the first time since entering the room.

At a nod from Green she continued.

'The information about the Norwegian yard and Kalevala came from Tanya. Tanya is clearly an important asset for the Russians. Dmitri Rostov is a senior soviet controller who only has direct involvement with agents of the highest importance. If Tanya has become disillusioned with the Russian system as she said then she may be able to get more concrete information about what the Russians are planning. It's a long shot but I would suggest that if she calls again and I fully expect that she will, we try and use her to our advantage.'

'What about if she doesn't call again?' Duncan Smith turned his gaze on Stapleford with a barely disguised look of contempt. 'From where I am sitting our domestic counter intelligence has constantly been caught with its proverbial pants down over the last few years and allowed almost free rein to foreign intervention whether it be terrorism or cyber security issues. Now you are proposing that we rely on the off chance that we may get a phone call from a source that we don't even know is reliable in order to determine if we should spend extra on our defences.'

Stapleford was taken aback by the intervention from the normally mild-mannered head of MI6 but what she lacked in ability she made up for in self-righteousness pomposity, a trait that had allowed her to use the politically correct charged public system to climb to the top of her profession. She responded in kind.

'If I'm not mistaken, foreign security is the responsibility of the Secret Service not counterintelligence. I was just raising a possible area where counterintelligence could be of assistance.

'You of all people should know how difficult it has been over the past few years with the budget cuts to operate a fully effective service. The police have been more and more stretched trying to be all things to all people which has meant that counterintelligence has had to give them assistance whilst taking resources away from other duties.

'The failures of the secret service in identifying returning Jihadists from the ISIL conflicts means that we have to monitor multiple suspects many of whom are probably not a security risk. We have prevented a number of terrorist incidents but if we miss just one, we get the press on our back.

'Please do not accuse my service of being caught with its pants down as you so inelegantly put it. I can assure you that without the diligent application of duty by my team the country would be in a lot worse position than it presently is.' Stapleford almost seemed to puff out her cheeks as she glared at Smith.

Richard Green stepped in before Duncan Smith had the chance to reply.

'Arguing about who is responsible does not help the situation. Duncan has raised a major issue which if true means that not only does the United Kingdom have a problem but Europe has a bigger one. Clearly if Tanya does ring back then any further information we can get from her would be of help but that is not something we can rely on, unless of course you are able to identify Tanya and so can go to her.' Green looked at Stapleford who shook her head.

'No, I didn't think so. Which leaves us back where we started which is how do we counter the threat from Russia?'

'It does seem to me that the most critical consideration is how do we prevent Turkey from leaving NATO and if Turkey does leave how do we convince America to remain loyal to Europe? NATO has been the key to European security for the past 50 years despite the illusion that the European Community was responsible.'

'Duncan, when is the next meeting of the NATO Military Committee?'

'The next formal meeting is planned to take place in three months' time but in the light of what is happening in Turkey and America I would be in favour of calling an extraordinary meeting as soon as possible.'

'I agree. I'll ask General Jordan to arrange and, in the meanwhile, we need to work out a solution to this threat.

'Regarding the defence budget, I can't guarantee anything at present but I'll discuss with the cabinet. If the threat is as real as you say then the only way that we will be able to keep the NATO alliance together is by reminding the member states why NATO was created in the first place. For too long we have taken peace in Europe as a given. If what you are saying is true then that might all be about to change and just when we are at the most vulnerable.'

Stapleford and Smith got up and left the room leaving Richard Green running his hand through his hair as he contemplated the conversation. Picking up the phone he asked his secretary to arrange an urgent meeting with General Jordan, Gary Davies and Jason Bhatia.

Chapter 37
September 2026

North Sea

The weather in the northern sector of the North Sea had been bad for the past three weeks but as Jim Simpson looked out over the stern of the Semi-Submersible Crane Vessel, rather unimaginably named "Biglift One", he was gazing over one of those rare sunny and calm North Sea days.

Where small wavelets reflected the sun's rays it looked like Christmas lights sparkling on the surface of the sea. Large areas of the sea were so calm that it almost looked like an oil spill had occurred only being disrupted by the occasional seabird bobbing about in the barely perceptible swell, at least barely perceptible from the deck of the Biglift One which was 22 metres above the sea level. All in all, a perfect day for the installation of the heaviest offshore lift ever performed using a floating crane vessel. Or in fact two floating crane vessels. Simpson moved from the stern of the Biglift One to the port side where its sister ship, equally as unimaginably named Biglift Two, was on station about 500 metres away. Between the two crane vessels was the top of the steel foundation structure that would support the topside production module. Simpson knew that although the top of the steel foundation was 30 metres above the sea level, below the sea another 120 metres of steel reached all the way to the seabed where it was anchored by enormous steel piles, designed to withstand whatever weather the North Sea decided to throw at it. As Simpson's gaze moved from the top of the foundations it rested on the heavy transport vessel or HTV, anchored a short distance from the two crane vessels. At 275 metres long and over 70 metres wide the HTV had been used to transport the massive Caratacus production facilities from the fabrication yard in Korea to the Caratacus location.

Earlier in the day a meeting had been held with the crew of all three vessels, OEC management and the marine warranty surveyors representing the insurers and all had agreed that everything was in place to allow the installation to take place. Thereafter it was the responsibility of the Biglift One superintendent to facilitate the installation.

His first task had been to transfer cutting and rigging crews to the HTV. To safe guard the facilities during the sea tow it had been necessary to weld steel tubulars between the underside of the facilities and the deck of the HTV. These steel tubes had to be cut before the lift could take place. Whilst this cutting took place, a 12-hour task for over 20 oxyacetylene wielding burners, the two crane vessels manoeuvred on either side of the HTV and eight preinstalled steel cable slings, each ten inches in diameter, were attached to the four crane hooks; two cables on each hook and two hooks on each crane vessel. The crane vessels were held in position using their dynamic positioning system. Each vessel had eight rotating propellers protruding from the underside of the hull. Each propeller was controlled by a computer based on signals received from a series of input devices that enabled the captain of the vessel to determine where he wanted the crane vessel to be and the computer did the rest. The system allowed the crane vessels to remain within a metre of the pre-set position in wind speeds up to 25 miles per hour. With the conditions in place today the propellers were hardly needed.

As Simpson continued to watch the preparations for the lift his mind drifted back to the events of the last few weeks. From the time that he had heard about the loss of the Kalevala to the emotional roller coaster that had been the dash to Taiwan to discover that his youngest son had survived. The sadness when he realised that others had not been so fortunate particularly the death of Ron Thompson, the Saunders Marine yard manager who had shown Simpson around the Korean yard after the launch ceremony had hit him hard. Then there had been the incident in Norway and the discovery that the Kalevala sinking was not an accident and all the while he was trying to keep his company from losing control of the Caratacus project. Even before the bodies of the Korean workers who had died in the Kalevala sinking had been repatriated to Korea the proverbial sharks had been circling. Calls from his banks and from other oil companies to offer condolences were in reality just a disguise to determine how vulnerable OEC were. Working 18-hour days and with no let up the pressure had been immense but he was still very much in business. He had to admit that it had been a close-run thing but the saviour had been the ability to rework the installation of the production facilities to use the two crane vessels provided by Rostella. The negotiations had been hard and there was no love lost between Simpson and the man standing next to him, Marco Paglia, but business was business. Paglia had extracted more than the proverbial pound of flesh to provide the Biglift One and the Biglift Two but he had at the same time saved OEC from the sharks. Simpson hoped that the perfect weather was a sign that his fortune was at last changing although having survived two sabotage attempts, he was not going to let his guard down at this stage. He felt grateful for the knowledge that discretely placed around the various vessels were members of the British armed forces provided by the British government who had woken up to the strategic importance of the Caratacus discovery. What he didn't know but which would have given even more of a feel-good factor was that a British naval vessel was just beyond the horizon monitoring every aerial movement with orders to challenge any hostile or unidentified aircraft that might approach the installation site. Richard Green may be struggling to be convinced that he had to increase the defence budget but he was sufficiently concerned to ensure no further sabotage could take place.

Nearly a day after it had been agreed the installation of the production facilities could go ahead everything was in place to start the lift. The steel tubular ties had been cut and the lift slings were installed. Personnel, whose task was to ensure the production facilities landed correctly on top of the foundation, had been transferred to the top of the steel foundation and communications had been established. The control of the lift would be critical. All four cranes would have to take up their share of the load whilst at the same time the two crane vessels would have to adjust their ballast to ensure they remained stable during the lift. Held on location either side of the HTV the crane vessels gradually took the load. It took over an hour of very slow and precise lifting before the deck foreman on the HTV was able to report that the production facility was no longer supported by the steelwork on the HTV and that the full load had been transferred to the crane vessels. It was a further hour of slow but controlled lifting before the facilities had been lifted to the height of the top of the foundation. This was the trickiest part of the whole operation. With a production facility weighing nearly 30,000 tonnes, the weight of nearly 3000 double decker buses, hanging between the crane vessels they now had to use the dynamic position systems to move the two-crane vessel in tandem either side of the steel foundation. Any sudden movement at this stage could be catastrophic by causing the deck to act like a massive pendulum.

Metre by metre the two crane vessels moved crab like until, either side of the foundation, they were in a position to start the lowering operation. As with the rest of the operation, patience was the precursor of success. In a reverse of the lifting operation the deck was lowered until it sat on the correct location on the foundations and slowly the 30,000-tonne weight was transferred from the cranes to the foundations. Only when the last lifting slings went slack and the production facility was fully supported by the steel foundation could Simpson breathe a sigh of relief. He had been on the deck of the Biglift One for the full 36 hours of the lift operation and was very tired but happy. Turning to Marco Paglia he shook his hand and congratulated him on a faultless operation before making his way to his cabin for a well-earned rest. He knew that there was still a long way to go before the Caratacus field would be producing any oil but today had been a major step in achieving that goal.

In the next few days the installation would be completed with the installation of the accommodation module and then there would be six months of offshore work connecting the accommodation module to the production facilities and connecting the production facilities to the pre-installed pipelines and pre-drilled oil wells; but a corner had been turned. Simpson would sleep easier that night than at any time over the last three months.

Marco Paglia was also feeling pleased with himself but as he turned to his own cabin, he would not have felt quite so happy had he known what was happening in an office in Paris at that precise time.

Chapter 38
September 2026

Paris

'We're still trying to get into the Nevis account to determine the principal who owns the account. Dealing with the authorities over there is like trying to pull teeth. Painful and incredibly slow.' Damian Remanan was once again in the office of Marie Lantieri.

'But we have got somewhere with the files found in the computer recovered from Villefranche.

'Our Mr Chadwell has been a busy man over the last 20 years but one thing he isn't is a computer specialist. He must have thought his files were secure from prying eyes but it only took our specialists eight hours to break through the passwords and cryptology to find the goodies hiding inside.

'And what interesting reading they make. Each time he took a job he carefully recorded the details on his computer. Contact details, how much he was paid, what the job entailed, the lot. It's an Aladdin's cave of information that I'm sure many police forces around the world will be pleased to receive. There are crimes recorded in the files that we didn't even know were crimes and interestingly there are some names mentioned that to date have been considered pillars of the community.'

Marie Lantieri was intrigued.

'Such as?'

'Such as a certain ex Foreign Minister of France and a certain serving Minister within the Italian parliament.'

'Interesting. Sounds like we are going to have to tread carefully on those cases. But what about the sinking of the Kalevala? What have we got on that?'

'Whoever employed Chadwell for that job was cleverer than the two ministers in that he was not contacted directly so we don't have a specific name. His files just refer to the organisation which is given as the Camorra.'

'The Neapolitan mafia?'

'The very same. The contact phone number mentioned in the files is a pay-as-you-go mobile phone with an Italian prefix. That plus the information we have managed to gather from the bank details relating back to a southern French or Italian connection all seem to tie down the principal as coming from somewhere in Italy, probably from the south of Italy.'

'What possible motive would the Camorra have to sink the Kalevala?' The question from Lantieri was rhetorical and she continued, 'what have you done to find the owner of the mobile phone?'

'To date nothing. As a pay-as-you-go phone it doesn't need to be registered to any individual and we are reluctant to ring it in case we alert the principal that we have it.'

'Can we track the phones signal?'

'I'm not an expert in this but I believe the only way we could track it would be to call the number and then try and determine where the phone is once it is answered. I believe we would have to keep the phone live for at least 30 seconds to get an adequate trace. The problem then is to get to the location before the phone's owner moves and disposes of the phone. That is of course assuming that the phone has not already been disposed of. It is highly likely that as soon as the job was finished the phone would have been thrown away.'

'We don't seem to be too much closer to finding the principal then.'

Lantieri was beginning to feel that they had hit a dead end.

'What do we know? We know that Chadwell was paid by a company called World Island Specialist Investments to sabotage the Kalevala. We know that he initially tried and failed so went back again. We know that Chadwell's principal was most likely based in Italy and was a member of the Camorra. We know that Chadwell had many aliases and has been responsible for many atrocities around the world although that latter point is not really relevant for our specific investigations. It's a start but after nearly three months it isn't very much. The question is where do we go from here?'

Remanan could sense his boss's frustration.

'We still have the Nevis bank account. It will take time but I am confident we will eventually break down the resistance of the Nevis government. In addition, we have another lead to the Italian connection from Chadwell's files. It would appear that he has been contacted more than once before by the Camorra. As with the Kalevala case there are no names mentioned but by cross checking these earlier cases we have come up with an interesting connection. Both previous jobs that Chadwell did for World Island Specialist Investments revolved around the Naples cargo handling trade. The first was to incite a peaceful strike of the Naples dockyard workers into violence and the second was to murder a minor Neapolitan official who was suspected of being a leader of one of the Camorra families. In my opinion it would be worth contacting the Italian police to see if they have any idea who would have benefited from these two incidents and if they have any connection to the Kalevala. As a last resort we also have the mobile phone.'

'What about, Chadwell? Now that we know all his dirty secrets can we use them to get him to co-operate?'

'We have been trying for weeks to get him to co-operate without any success and I can't see that changing now but I'll try again. Besides from what we now know I don't think even Chadwell will know who is the principal.'

Lantieri gave a sigh before answering, 'I suspect that you are right but please give it one more try. I'm still getting pressure from up top. It would appear that the British are convinced that there is a Russian angle somewhere but if there is, I can't see it. Waiting for the Nevis government to come through will be like waiting for hell to freeze over so it leaves us with the Italian connection. Who do we know in the Naples police that we can trust?'

'Off the top of my head I don't know but I'll find out. How much do you want to tell them?'

'At this stage just tell them that we are looking into the two historical cases to see if there is any linkage. You can mention that we have received intel that they are connected but don't mention Chadwell or Kalevala. If they press you just tell them that it is political. My experience with Italian police is that once you mention politics they back away from further questioning.'

For the first time that day Lantieri smiled.

Remanan got up to leave and as he placed his hand on the door handle Lantieri made one last comment.

'I still can't see what Naples has to do with the Kalevala? If we could just make that connection, I feel we would be a long way to solving this problem.'

Remanan left his boss to her thoughts.

Chapter 39
September 2026

Aberdeen

The phone call that Jean Robertson had been fearing came early in the morning whilst she was asleep in bed. Whilst it was nearly four o'clock in the morning in Scotland, in Moscow it would have been seven o'clock in the morning. Answering in a sleepy voice Robertson was immediately awake when she detected the slight pause in the connection followed by a series of clicks and then the voice of Dmitri Rostov. Such an early morning call was a sign that Rostov wanted to catch her off guard. Without preamble he demanded to know what had happened in Norway and why, when she had told him that the Kalevala was essential for the job its sinking had not stopped the project.

Taken aback by the tone of voice she hesitated before responding. Fortunately, she had been expecting such a call since she had heard of the arrest of the four Russian Spetsnaz and had been able to formulate a response. Composing herself she answered calmly that she had no idea what had gone wrong in Norway but had assumed that the men must have somehow given themselves away. All she had been told was that following the sinking of the Kalevala the security at the yard had been strengthened and that the attempt had been somewhat amateurish. Whilst Rostov would not admit any difference, this reflected his own thoughts having heard that the four men appeared to have taken very few precautions regarding secrecy during their trip through Norway but he still didn't like to hear members of Russia's elite forces being described as amateurish.

Continuing Robertson truthfully told Rostov that she had no idea that Simpson had identified another way that the production facilities could be installed and that when she had stated that the Kalevala was essential for the job that was very much the message that she had been told by Simpson himself just prior to her passing this information to Russia. Continuing she apologised and finished by expressing her regret that the efforts by Russia to sink the Kalevala had not led to the outcome expected.

The pause on the line should have warned her but the next statement from Rostov came like a bombshell.

'But we were not responsible for the sinking of the Kalevala so no matter that this information was wrong. By the time we had got the information the Kalevala had already sailed so we concentrated on the accommodation module. In our opinion the sinking of the Kalevala was just a fortunate accident. We were disappointed to find out that it was not quite so essential as you had suggested particularly after the attack on the accommodation module failed so miserably but we were not responsible for the sinking. Was the sinking not after all an accident?'

This was a most unexpected question and Robertson had to think quickly. How much should she say. Her training took over as she recalled the advice from Rostov himself. Always wherever possible tell the truth to disguise the lie.

'The sinking was a deliberate act of sabotage. Someone planted a bomb on the ship before it sailed from Korea. Interpol have arrested someone who they believe carried out the attack but he was just a hired hand. The police are searching for the principal culprit.'

'And you thought that was Russia and you didn't think to inform anyone.' The menace was back in Rostov's voice.

'I have no secure way of contacting you and going through the Liverpool route would just have led to a potential security leak. I expected a call from you and so waited.'

Reluctantly Rostov acknowledged the Liverpool conduit was not as secure as he would like and accepted Robertson's explanation. The fact that the Kalevala had been sabotaged and the British did not know who was responsible also went a long way to explaining why the security in Norway had been strengthened. Perhaps it was time to reduce the pressure on Robertson and see how best to move forward.

'You are right. My apologies for being harsh but you perhaps don't realise that delaying the Caratacus project has the attention of the president himself. It is very much in Russia's interest to prevent the British from getting the financial windfall from Caratacus at least for a year or so. The question is how do we now go about that? You are closest to the project. Now that the offshore facilities are fully installed how do we best delay things in such a way that suspicion does not fall on Russia?'

Robertson had to think on her feet, not easy as she was still feeling the effects of being woken in the middle of the night.

'I don't know off the top of my head. The British will now be on alert and my boss told me yesterday that security on all vulnerable parts of the project are being reviewed. The British are linking the sinking of Kalevala with the attack on Norway and as they know that Russia was involved in Norway, they are assuming that Russia was also responsible for sinking Kalevala. Any further acts of sabotage will immediately raise further suspicion.'

'We are not ready yet to show our hand so we certainly do not want any further suspicions. Those fools in Norway have done our cause no favours and when we eventually get them back from the Norwegian authorities, they will pay a high price for their irresponsible behaviour.'

'I'll discuss with Moscow what to do next but in the meanwhile put some thought into how best to delay the project without arousing suspicion. I'll ring you in five days.'

The phone went dead.

Robertson's mind was in turmoil. It was as if a large load had been lifted from her shoulders. Whilst Robert Simpson had survived the sinking Robertson still held herself responsible for the many Koreans who had died but more personally for the death of Ron Thompson who she had met on a couple of occasions. She now knew that the information she had passed to Rostov had not resulted in the ship being sunk. A bit light headed she tried to think how this affected her feelings for Russia. Did this change anything? Previously when she had contacted the British Security services it was as a result of the sinking of the Kalevala and the anger that she had felt at the wanton waste of life. Now that she knew the Russians were not responsible had this changed her feelings. Surprisingly she came to conclusion that it hadn't. She realised that even though Russia had not sunk the ship that was not because of a moral position but purely because the circumstances prevented them from making the arrangements in the time available. No, nothing had changed. She still felt the need to somehow do her small bit to stop the mad men in the Kremlin.

As she went back to bed, she knew what she would do.

Chapter 40
September 2026

London

Richard Green had many problems on his desk. The budget had been set for next week and it still hadn't been finalised. It had already been postponed once and any further delays would not be acceptable. Each department had put its budget together based on the guidance given by Alastair Frank a few weeks previously and since then there had been countless meetings to try and get the figures to match. The reality was that the British Government was spending too much money, much more than it was receiving in taxes. The borrowing limit was maxed out and payment of over £900 billion of loans were due in less than two years' time. What Green wanted to do was revitalise the economy by reducing the tax take, reducing the state control on every aspect of people's lives and hence stimulate the economy to grow such that an increased GDP would result in an increase in tax without increasing the tax percentage. To do this he needed to break away from the ties of Europe left over from the Brexit settlement, start to unwind some of the more damaging labour laws introduced by the last administration, reverse the nationalisation programme, start to reduce the hugely complex tax legislation, reduce the statute book and allow people to make their own decisions on those matters that did not affect others and generally wind back the nanny state.

He was fully aware that this went against every government since the late 1990s but in his view entrusting the individual to make the right decision and then making the individual responsible for the outcome of that decision was the right way forward. It started with education and ensuring that the right education was available for the skills the UK needed and it continued right through to the judiciary, health service and emergency services and all aspects of government spending. He knew it would be difficult but at every turn he had come up against the vested interest that was the present public sector. Grossly overpaid leaders of the public services were not about to see their empires dismantled and hence their importance reduced, particularly if that resulted in their own salary being reduced. Green had been shocked when he discovered that tens of thousands of public sector employees were getting paid more than he was. And every one of those salaries had to come from the tax payers' pocket.

Equally as bad was the charity sector. The state subsidised the charity sector to the tune of over £10 billion per year yet many of the leaders of the estimated 190,000 charities also paid themselves more than he was paid; and all charities were eligible for a tax payer handout in the form of tax relief or gift aid. Amazingly he had discovered there were ten individual charities just dedicated to looking after donkeys, each with its own management structure. No wonder the bill was so high. But how to reduce the bill without appearing to be heartless? The liberal establishment was very good at playing with the heart strings whilst ensuring they were adequately rewarded for their piousness. Of course, the public just saw the many volunteers in the charity shops or the carefully choreographed advertisements played on prime-time television without realising that the whole sector had been hijacked by individuals lining their pockets from the public's largesse.

Then there were the real big spenders. The benefit department, state pensions, the national Health Service, the armed forces, the emergency services and the increasing cost of caring for an elderly population.

Green knew that there were some things that were sacrosanct and which the public would never accept him changing but he also knew he had to do something. He couldn't carry on spending future generations money on today's expenditure. He knew how difficult it was going to be which was why he had such difficulties in agreeing the budget. He had to find the £900 billion in two years at the same time as reducing government spending. The last thing he wanted was to be forced into an emergency spend on the armed forces because of a resurgent Russia.

The windfall from Caratacus was a lifeline but only if it was used wisely. Throwing it all away on the armed forces would be a folly. And for why? Even if the worst-case scenario developed then Russia would just get back the borders the old Soviet Union had 30 years before and the world hadn't come to an end then. The European Union had been milking the UK ever since the abortive Brexit attempt and had been reducing their spending on their armed forces to support their European utopia, their European army their civil rights;, the disaster that was the Euro and their avalanche of regulations primarily intended to support the French or German farmers and manufacturers. Let them sort out the problem. When Hungary, Czech Republic, Slovenia, Rumania and the Baltic states were annexed by the Russians let Europe sort it out. Britain would not be under threat particularly since leaving the European Union a lot of its trade was now with countries outside Europe.

Green of course knew that it was not as simple as that. Even with the Brexit vote Britain was still very much part of Europe. Its geographical position placed it on the edge of Europe but its commitment was still at the heart of the continent. Whilst Green's politics were at odds with the rulers in Brussels, he felt connected to the real people of Europe, the people that just wanted to get on with their lives with minimum interference from the state. He felt honour bound to stand up for these people as much as he felt honour bound to stand up for the people of Great Britain. And that meant he couldn't ignore the threat from Russia.

With a deep sigh he picked up the phone on his desk and asked his secretary to arrange a meeting of the security council.

Two hours later he was sitting in a meeting room with Jason Bhatia, Gary Davies, General Jordan, Duncan Smith and Joan Stapleford. Cynthia Graeme and Rachel Stewart had not been available at such short notice. Green ran his hand through his hair and started the meeting.

'Thank you for joining me, everyone. I called this meeting to see where we are with the Russian threat. As you are all aware the budget has to be finalised and Jason has put in for a large increase in spending for the military.' Green looked across at Jason Bhatia who nodded in acknowledgement.

Green continued. 'If this increase were agreed to, it would mean we would have to divert funds from other areas which have already been pared to the bone.'

'And beyond,' Joan Stapleford muttered from the other side of the table.

'Thank you, Joan. Your objections to cuts in your budget have already been discussed. I don't intend to discuss them again at this table.' Green fixed Stapleford with a cold stare before continuing, 'Alastair Frank and his team at the treasury has assessed all the various department budgets and compared them to the expected tax take over a five year period taking into account a number of variables including inflation, GDP and growth projections. The normal stuff. He has also considered in his financial model the effect of the increase in revenue expected from the Caratacus discovery and it really is a life saver. Without

Caratacus we would either have to shut down large parts of the government or default on our loan repayments. With Caratacus we should be able to get through the next two years by which time the public debt will be a manageable proposition. I'm not saying in two years' time we will be able to take the hand brake off the public spending; I'm just saying we will not be on the verge of bankruptcy. It will buy us the time needed to get our other reforms in place which will hopefully in the long run improve our finances allowing us to generate the money to pay for much needed infrastructure investments.

'Unfortunately, the fly in the ointment is the defence budget.'

Green turned to address Bhatia directly.

'Jason, If I agree to what you are asking then the whole financial model collapses and we will have to call on the IMF. That I can't accept but at the same time I have to accept the Russian risk is real.'

Duncan Smith and General Jordan both leant forward on hearing this last statement. The last time they had been in discussion with Green he was in denial that the Russian threat was real. What had changed?

Green continued, 'Yesterday I heard from Jean that she had been contacted again by Tanya, who you may recall was the Russian agent that had warned us about Russian interest in Caratacus. Yesterday's call was similar to the last one in that it was made from a telephone box from a small Scottish village with no CCTV coverage, but there is no doubt it was the same person. What she told us was that the sinking of the Kalevala was not instigated by Russia but only because they could not get to it in time.'

Duncan Smith interrupted. 'That would tie in with what I am hearing from Interpol in Paris. I didn't want to say anything until we had more facts but all indications from their investigations around the suspected culprit are that he was paid and briefed from someone in Italy not Russia. Of course, subsequent investigations may find the trail goes beyond Italy but Interpol do not think that will be the case. It looks like Russia is in the clear on this one although the sabotage attempt in Norway is very much Russia's doing.'

Nodding Green continued, 'So we can assume that Russia is not responsible for sinking Kalevala but did want to delay Caratacus hence the attack in Norway.'

'Forgive me, Prime Minister, but if Russia is off the hook for the sinking of Kalevala why then are you now saying you consider the Russian threat to be real?' Gary Davies asked.

'Because of something else that Tanya said. She told us that she had been contacted again by Dmitri Rostov and it was Rostov that told her that Russia was not responsible for the sinking of the Kalevala. But Rostov also told her that the order to delay Caratacus had come from the Russian president himself and that it was very much in Russia's interest to prevent us from getting the increased revenues from Caratacus for at least a year or two. She went on to tell us that she had been requested to find out how the project could, even at this late stage, be delayed without any evidence being linked back to Russia.

'I might not be very bright but even I can see that Russia is up to something and with the other evidence presented by Duncan a few weeks ago it now looks very much like parts of Eastern Europe are in real danger of Russian expansion policies.

'The problem I have is no different from where we were at our last meeting. We do not have the resources to challenge or stop Russia and to agree to this large increase in military spending will push us into bankruptcy. We need to put our thinking caps on to avoid a disaster. Any ideas would be gratefully received.'

Green's attempt at lightening the seriousness of the situation was appreciated but everyone in the room knew the criticality of the situation.

Duncan Smith was the first to talk.

'At our last meeting we mentioned a number of things that were needed to allow Russia to have a clear run. The first and most important was that NATO had to be neutralised. Since that meeting I have been in contact with my European counter parts and we all see the same threat but also see that as long as Demir is in charge it is highly likely that Turkey will pull out of NATO. The Turkish generals, many of whom survived the purges of 2016 and 2017, are very much supportive of staying in the alliance but there is big political pressure for Turkey to quit. However, I am getting increasing evidence that opposition to Demir has dramatically increased since the elections in 2023 which many observers thought he had only won by fraudulent means. To put it bluntly the country is on high alert for a coup d'état. The people are fed up with the high inflation and the subsequent drop in living standards and the army is ready to take control. Unlike the coup attempt in 2016, this time the people will back the army. With the army in charge our information is that they will keep Turkey in NATO. If such an event were to take place it would be a big blow to Khurin's attempt to destabilise NATO.'

What Smith did not tell the room was that both MI6 and the CIA were actively supporting certain factions within Turkey. If all went to plan Smith expected that Turkey would have a military government sympathetic to the west and a secular administration within a matter of days.

'With Turkey remaining in NATO we fully expect that America will not want to abandon Europe but Europe has to show that it is an equal partner. As you know President Trump tried on a number of occasions to convince Europe to beef up its defences but most of the subsequent additional spending was just window dressing. The Europeans promised a large increase in spending in 2019 but when Trump lost the presidency in 2020 this promise was quietly shelved. Meanwhile the cold war between America and China had got to such a state that the incoming American administration were concerned that the cold war would turn hot. Despite their attempts to stabilise relationships, the Chinese were not about to back off over the South China Sea or their claims on Taiwan so America increasingly looked east when it came to defence spending. They were happy to leave the European arena to the Europeans and if Europe wasn't spending as much as they should on their own defence then so be it. Let that be Europe's problem. That isn't to say that America wouldn't honour its commitment to NATO but if it could find a way to back out, let's just say there are some across the pond that would welcome such a scenario.'

'Turkey staying in NATO would take away one excuse but more needs to be done. In my opinion there are a couple of options that would greatly help. The first would be for the European union to acknowledge that a European army is just a vanity project and is not going to work. The command structure is too complex and cumbersome. NATO should remain the mainstay of European defence.'

Green interrupted. 'We have been over this before. We have no say in the matter so how do you propose that we go about changing what is after all a central plank of European integration?'

'Let me first mention the second option. The French particularly are meeting their NATO commitments but other countries are not and that includes the UK. Germany particularly are spending much less than is needed. The reason that Germany is reluctant to up the spending is that they are so dependent on Russian gas that they are scared that any additional defence spending will be seen by Russia as an act of aggression and that in retribution Russia would either vastly increase the cost of the gas or even cut off supplies totally. If Germany could find an alternative source of gas then it would not be so dependent on Russia and perhaps could then be persuaded to do something about spending more on its armed forces. It would also be less supportive of a European army if it increased its expenditure to the same relative level as say France. I couldn't see Germany funding a large army only for it to be put under the control of Belgium.'

'That's all well and good but where do you propose Germany suddenly finds an alternative gas supply? I know Norway and the Netherlands are net gas exporters but the reason that Europe and particularly Germany are so dependent on Russian gas is that Norway and The Netherlands can't provide enough.'

Green ran his hand through his hair, a clear sign that he was getting frustrated with the discussion, a signal picked up by Duncan Smith who hastily continued.

'Correct, but there is a new source and its right on our doorstep. Perhaps you have not been kept up to date with the Caratacus project but my latest information is that it is not just an oil field but also contains vast quantities of gas. It is true that initially the gas cannot be extracted because it is needed in place to ensure the pressure in the field is high enough to extract the oil but after a couple of years new carbon capture injection facilities will be available that will be able to replace the methane gas with carbon dioxide. Projections are that the amount of gas is at least equivalent to the giant Groningen gas field that has powered The Netherlands for the past 60 years. That plus an expansion of Liquified Natural Gas facilities allowing Germany to import LNG from Qatar and Mozambique would mean Germany could cut its dependency on Russian gas.

'I know that Germany is concerned about its dependency on Russian gas and is even looking to see if it can use fracking techniques to extract gas but that would cause difficulties with the anti-fracking Green Party which has the balance of power in the Bundestag. The big advantage of using the gas from Caratacus would be that we could price the gas to be competitive with Russia but only on condition that Germany increased its military spending and dropped the idea of a European army. Germany would then take its rightful position at the top table of NATO alongside the UK and France from Europe.'

'I did not realise that Caratacus was also a gas field I have to admit.'

Green turned to Joan Stapleford. 'Joan, would that be something for the SIS to look into?'

Stapleford looked taken aback.

'I would say that is something for the department of energy rather than the SIS but if you would like me to instigate a security review, I am happy to put something in place.'

'Thank you, Joan. Please consider all the possibilities and prepare a policy document on the amount of gas that we could make available to not just Germany but also the rest of Europe and how that can be used to leverage the defence position. At the same time look at how it can be used to improve the trade agreements that were very one sided after the Brexit fiasco. I will inform all departments that you are to be given full co-operation and priority. I would like to see a draft report on my desk within 2 months.'

'Two months!' Stapleford almost spat out. 'that just won't be possible. It will take longer than that to prepare the briefing documents. Thereafter data will have to be collected and collated, scenarios will have to be modelled in computer simulations and risk assessed before a policy document can even be started. No, it just isn't possible.'

'Nevertheless, that is what I want and expect. If you are not capable of producing such a document then I will have to find someone who is.' Green looked directly at Stapleford to leave no doubt that he meant what he said. Stapleford held his gaze for no more than two seconds before dropping her eyes to look at the table. She did not like being talked to in such an aggressive way and was not sure how best to respond. In the end she just nodded and said she would prepare the report as requested. The others in the room could feel her embarrassment but secretly were pleased that Green's annoyance was aimed at her and not them.

'Good. Thank you, Duncan, for your input.' Green continued the discussion. 'All we have to do is assume that the Turkish president will be overthrown, that whoever takes over will be committed to staying in NATO, that Caratacus can deliver enough gas in sufficient time to supply Germany and the rest of Europe for that matter, that Germany will then more than double its defence spending whilst abandoning a key EU objective vis a vis the European army and America will remain committed to protecting Europe. Meanwhile the United Kingdom still doesn't have the money to increase its own defence spending. I don't think that we are any further forward.'

'I'm not so sure.' General Jordan had been following the conversation intently. 'It appears to me that what we have is a short-term problem by which I mean we have to get through the next two to three years. The issue therefore is to ensure that Russia does not make any move before the scenarios played out by Duncan can be put into operation. My understanding is that expectations are that the next territorial moves by Mr Khurin will be towards the Baltic states at present protected by NATO. Would I be right in my assumption that if Mr Demir is ousted it is likely to be imminent?' This latter addressed to Duncan Smith who just nodded in response.

'Then we will know in the near future if the coup d'état is real or imaginary. Assuming it is real then the proposal to influence Germany will most likely be sufficient to stay the hand of Khurin in the long term. However, in the short term it may also just push him to accelerate his territorial grab on the assumption that Europe is weak now and although he may not be totally ready, he is in a better shape than we are. It seems to me that we need to be able to demonstrate in the short term that we are stronger than we actually are and to deter an early land grab.' Jordan looked around the room for support and seeing a number of nods continued,

'Intelligence points to Khurin using a quick dash for territory and then building a defensive missile shield a bit along the lines used by Egypt in the 1973 conflict with Israel. If we can convince the Russians that such a tactic will not work then wiser heads in the Russian Dumas may be swayed to convince Khurin to rethink.'

'And how do you propose we do that?' This from Jason Bhatia.

'Ah. This is where it gets a bit embarrassing.'

Jordan looked anything but embarrassed.

'It has come to my attention that over the last five years when the defence budget was cut to the bone, a small group of individuals working for the RAF managed to syphon off some of the budget earmarked for social improvements in the armed forces to develop a new medium range fighter plane. Whilst the budget did not permit production, a prototype has been built and a few weeks ago it was flown to monitor a couple of Russian spy planes. All indications are that the plane was able to track the Russian planes without them realising they were being tracked. I'm told that had the RAF decided they could have launched air-to-air missiles and shot down both Russian planes without the Russians even knowing they had been targeted. If Russia could be fooled into thinking that we had a whole squadron of planes ready for action and they could somehow find out that the planes could not be detected by their radar defences they may think twice before launching any action that relied on a radar operated missile defence system.'

Jason Bhatia was the first to react to General Jordan's revelation. He did so with a smile on his face.

'So, General, the RAF's social improvement budget has been misappropriated to develop a superior fighter. Whilst I should be furious, I am incredibly relieved that we still have people in our armed forces that understand that their main function is the defence of the realm. I'm sure that we can leave you to take the necessary actions against the individuals but you have identified a course of action that may just work. But why not go further and just build a squadron of these planes?'

'Ultimately that would also be my suggestion but it takes a long time and a lot of money to go from a prototype to a full production run and as I understand it, we have neither.'

Richard Green took up the conversation.

'Your proposal has merit in my opinion but how would you propose that we go about the deception?'

Jordan answered, 'To show the capabilities would be quite simple. We just wait until the Russians mount another surveillance operation over Scotland and 'accidently' allow the stealth capabilities to be exposed. Only very slightly, a blip on their radar where a blip shouldn't be, but enough for them to realise that they have been tracked without their knowledge. But this would have to be followed up with false information being provided through the Russian intelligence service.'

He turned to Stapleford. 'Jean, how much do you think we can trust or use agent Tanya?'

Joan Stapleford was still smarting from her confrontation with Green but she composed herself to reply, 'Tanya has been very forthcoming so far without any prompting from us. She genuinely seems to want to help against Khurin but then again it could all just be a ploy to gain our trust. So far, she hasn't asked for anything from us and in fact we don't even know how to contact her. Both times she has contacted us.

'In my experience the best way to fool someone is to feed them a small trail of crumbs that altogether make a cake.'

Duncan Smith entered the conversation again.

'The first thing the Russians will do when they are made aware of the existence of the new plane will be to try and track down its base to determine as much as they can about it. Perhaps we can borrow a leaf out of the second world war. In the build up to 'D' day the allies wanted to convince the Germans that they were going to invade through Calais rather than Normandy. They did this by a number of ploys; the two most successful were to build an army of models close to Dover that they knew would be picked up by German reconnaissance planes and to drop a dead body in the med. with fake invasion plans that they knew would wash up on a beach where German sympathisers were present. Both ploys in themselves were made to look like the Germans had managed to find something that the allies wanted to keep hidden. Taking that to the modern world we could somehow prepare a squadron of these new planes in such a way that they would 'accidently' be picked up by Russian satellite surveillance. Having detected the base, the next step would be to have an agent on the ground go in to investigate further. If we prepare the base close to Aberdeen, we can be pretty sure that the nearest agent would be Tanya. It would be likely that she would be contacted by Rostov to try and find out more about the base. If past actions are anything to go by Tanya would then contact SIS to pass on the request and then we can pass on false information.'

'Wouldn't that put her life at risk when Russia finds out she has fed them false information?' This from Joan Stapleford.

'We would have to ensure Russia did not find out the information was false. At the same time as we are laying the decoy, we would be secretly preparing for actual production of the planes and training the pilots such that in a years' time when hopefully Richard's budgetary constraints are not as tight, we can go into full production. In two years' time we should have the real squadron in place.'

'I still think it would be very risky for Tanya.' Stapleford looked worried.

'She is in a risky business and has to take her chances. I would rather a Russian agent was put at risk than the whole of Europe.'

Green made no secret of his frustration with Stapleford but then directed his attention to Jason Bhatia.

'Jason, please work with Duncan and the general to put together a deception plan as outlined.'

'Then its settled. The defence budget will not have a massive increase in the next budget but we work on the agreement to provide gas to Germany in exchange for them increasing their defence spending and putting all theirs and

France's armed forces back under the indirect control of NATO,; we wait and see what happens in Turkey, although I have a sneaking suspicion that Duncan is not telling us everything that is happening there, and we prepare a decoy plan to convince Russia that we have more resources than we actually have. Is that about right or have I missed something?'

When no one answered Green closed the meeting and left the room. There was a lot to do over the next few weeks.

Chapter 41
August 2027

Shetland Island

'I hereby declare the Caratacus Field in full production.'

The king of the United Kingdom pushed down on a large red button and the clear section of pipe that ran in front of the royal enclosure showed a black liquid starting to pass along the pipe and into the onshore production facilities. Of course, the Caratacus field had been in full production for a week before the official opening but with a royal launch it was prudent to ensure all was working well before the big red button was pushed.

Standing on the specially built platform slightly behind the King and his wife were very many dignitaries including the prime minister and most of his cabinet as well as the senior management of Oceanic Energy Company Plc. As the royal couple moved towards the waiting hospitality building which after today's ceremony would become the leisure centre for the people that would be based in this remote production facility, Jim Simpson and Richard Green walked side by side. The previous twelve months had been a real struggle for both men but today was a day to celebrate as the oil flowed.

For Green the biggest challenge had been to bring the United Kingdom back from the brink of bankruptcy whilst trying to work with Europe to improve relationships marred as a result of the UK leaving the European Union. At the same time there was the threat of Russia to contend with.

For Simpson just managing the final stages of the development whilst being acutely aware that security of all the facilities had to be a serious consideration, had taken all of his time. After the offshore facilities had been installed on location the connection of the accommodation module and the pipeline to the production facilities had gone smoothly. The onshore facilities had been targeted by terrorists about four months ago but this had been foiled by the security forces.

Simpson would never know that Jean Robertson, who was standing only a few yards away, had given the information that allowed the security forces to be prepared for the attack.

'Congratulations, Jim. You must be a very proud man today.' Green opened the conversation.

Over the course of the last year the two men had met many times and had become close friends.

'There were times when I wondered if we would ever get to this point but here we are and I still have some of my hair that hasn't gone prematurely grey.' Simpson smiled before becoming serious again. 'As we were standing listening to the speeches, just then I couldn't help thinking about those people that contributed to the project but paid with their lives. Apart from a single serious injury in the fabrication yard the project was on target to be the safest ever in the history of the development of the North Sea. But that all changed with the loss of the Triton drill rig and the Kalevala installation vessel. The Triton was a reminder that we work in a hostile environment that is just waiting to catch out the unwary but the Kalevala was just an act of evil.'

'I recall with vivid clarity both of those incidents.' Green also looked serious. 'it was the explosion on the drill rig which first bought the potential of Caratacus to my attention. It is all too easy in such circumstances to forget the human cost. What was the outcome of the final report?'

'Final death toll was 19 people but another three individuals had such severe injuries that they will eventually die of those injuries. The cause of the explosion was as suspected a shallow gas pocket and a failure of the emergency shut down valve. The source of ignition has been put down as a result of a spark from a faulty electrical connection but I suspect that can never be proven. David Grant has been prosecuted for breach of safety regulations but the trial has not yet taken place. Saebo Drilling in the meanwhile has gone into administration so whether he is found guilty or not he's finished. I feel sorry for him. He put everything into that company and to lose it all in this way is cruel.'

'I agree. I recall he was with you when we first met in Downing Street and he came over as someone that genuinely cared for his people. But whilst he could not be held to be responsible for the accident, as CEO of the company he has to carry the can for its consequences. Unfortunately, it goes with the job. What about that other incident? The sinking of the installation vessel. I understand that was sabotage. Did you ever find out who was responsible?'

'No, we didn't, but weren't you convinced it was the Russian?'

'Ah, perhaps I forgot to mention that we subsequently received information that let the Russians off the hook at least for the sabotage of Kalevala. Interpol tracked down the perpetrator and he is now serving a life sentence in a French jail but he was only ever a paid assassin. He still refuses to tell who paid him. Investigations have rather bogged down. It does however appear that the order to sink the ship came from someone in Naples.'

'Interesting. As you are aware, we were very fortunate in that an Italian installation company were able at short notice to step into the breach. It cost OEC a fortune but at least the project was saved. They were based in Naples. You don't think that they could have had anything to do with the sinking? Quite soon after the Caratacus facilities were installed the owner of the Italian company, a rather unpleasant chap called Marco Paglia was arrested for corruption. Something to do with his previous employment. Anyway, he was murdered whilst awaiting trial so if he was responsible, he has subsequently paid for it.'

Green knew the story from briefings he had had with Duncan Smith. He was aware that Interpol was convinced that Paglia was the instigator of the sinking but that he had used the Camorra to carry out the work. The trail from Paris had resulted in evidence that Paglia had paid a known thug called Constance Luigiano to organise the sabotage. When confronted with the evidence Paglia had owned up to giving instructions to sabotage Kalevala but had made a specific point that no one was to be hurt. The sinking of the ship in open water had been an accident as the charge was meant to explode before the vessel sailed but the saboteur had been interrupted before he could set the timer correctly. Paglia had agreed to testify against Luigiano and had been arrested for his own safety but in Italy the mob was everywhere and despite all precautions someone had managed to murder the unfortunate Paglia whilst in jail.

Green wasn't about to share this information with Simpson who continued to talk about the sinking.

'The installation vessel that sank was owned by Saunders Marine. The health and safety executive did carry out an investigation. I don't recall the final death toll but it was over twenty. As the cause of the sinking was clearly sabotage no charges were bought against anyone at Saunders Marine or the Korean fabricators.'

'I rather lost contact with David Saunders after the sinking of the Kalevala but understand that despite all the odds his company survived. The vessel insurers paid out and Saunders has started to build a second Kalevala. He even went back to the same Korean yard. I think between you, me and the gate post that he got a very good deal. David did tell me at one of our last meetings that the Koreans felt so guilty that they had not stopped the sabotage that they had offered to fabricate the second Kalevala for a price that was 15% less than the original price. The vessel should be available for service in two and a half years, just in time to be used to help with the development of the two other pre-salt discoveries.'

'Talking of which you must be very pleased with the way that has developed. The amount of tax you are extracting from my pocket from Caratacus will now be tripled unless of course you decide to reduce the tax take from all three as a consequence.' Simpson looked across at Green with a broad grin on his face.

The amount of tax that OEC was paying from Caratacus was enormous but then so were the profits. Many hours of discussions between the OEC and government legal teams had been held and both men knew that nothing would now be changed.

Green smiled back and continued walking. The discovery of even larger oil and gas fields in the North Sea had been the icing on the cake which had allowed him to think that they would get away without declaring the country bankrupt. Already the bond market had stabilised and the interest rates for the rollover of the bonds due for payment in a few months' time had come down considerably. At the same time the unwinding of the worst of the socialist's policies, including re-privatisation of certain industries, the removal of artificial price caps and exchange controls and the reduction in corporation and higher tax rates, had started to pay dividends. The deficit was beginning to stabilise. It still hadn't gone down but it was not going up as fast. With the North Sea windfall, Green was hopeful that within two years there should be a surplus to start reducing the overall debt. It had been a close-run thing but it looked like the United Kingdom would avoid the fate of Venezuela, a country that had descended into anarchy and civil war in 2019 as a direct result of similar socialist policies.

Green had to admit if only to himself that he had been lucky. Without Caratacus he could not have seen how he could have prevented a default but he had also been lucky that Russia had been contained despite the dire state of the NATO European forces. Duncan Smith had been proven correct in that there was a coup d'état in Turkey which had resulted in a pro-western leadership taking over. Turkey had remained in NATO and that had prevented the Americans from having an excuse to bail out. Within weeks of the change of leadership satellite images had shown Russian troops beginning to mass on the borders of Lithuania and all indications were that Russia was about to throw caution to the wind and invade the small Baltic state. Turkey and Germany had at the same time suddenly found themselves short of gas as the Russians turned off supplies with the excuse that terrorists had sabotaged critical equipment. As Turkey supplied gas to southern Europe, Bulgaria, Greece and Romania also found themselves short of energy. However, having been pre-warned they were able to fall back on reserves and the importation of liquified natural gas. Norway, the Netherlands and other gas producers also increased production. That in itself would only have been a temporary solution as Europe was so dependent on Russian gas. Had Russia invaded The Baltic States the temporary measures would not have lasted long. But Russia did not go ahead with the invasion and within a few days the build-up of troops on the border was reversed. The plan proposed by Duncan Smith seemed to have worked.

As soon as the troop build-up became evident the new fighters' abilities were made evident by allowing a Russian spy plane to see the plane visually whilst not having a radar image. As expected, this raised quite some concern in Moscow. Whether Jean Robertson had been asked to provide any verification was unknown to British Intelligence. She had only been in contact one more time since supplying the information about the sinking of Kalevala and that had been to warn about the attack on the onshore production facilities. Having passed on this information the British had been ready to thwart the attack which had left Robertson feeling very exposed so when the call had come to investigate the new aircraft, she had decided to keep the information to herself. Instead she had made her way to a remote air field in the North of Scotland, as directed by Dmitri Rostov, and from a suitable vantage point had taken sufficient high-resolution photographs to demonstrate the existence of a squadron of the new stealth fighter/bomber. These she had passed back to Rostov. Neither she or Rostov would ever know that the squadron actually consisted of F 35 planes superficially modified to look like the image of the new fighter.

Robertson wasn't yet ready, if she ever would be, to totally walk away from her past life but she knew the time would come very soon when she would have to choose. As she walked back to the first oil reception alongside Jim Simpson's wife, she wondered how long it would be before she would be directed to leave OEC and start a new career in politics.

Meanwhile in a small room in an old house in the outskirts of Moscow two old friends sat naked side by side on a wooden bench. Alexander Khurin and Igor Antipov both knew that they had lost. The plot to recover the old territories of the Soviet Union had been thwarted.

Even after the coup d'état in Turkey and the subsequent stabilisation of Turkey both Khurin and Antipov were convinced that the planned annexation of the Baltic states could go ahead. Even the surprise appearance of the British fighter hadn't been enough to stop their optimism particularly after the photographs taken by Rostov's agent in Scotland had indicated that the British were playing a bluff. Whilst they could not be sure, the experts that had analysed the photographs had reported back that it was highly likely that the planes shown in the photographs were not the same as the one recorded on the reconnaissance planes camera. The conclusion was that although Britain had a new aircraft it had not yet been put into full production and that this posed no danger to the invasion plans.

The mistake that the two old friends made was the oldest one in the Russian rule book of power. Trust no one. Unbeknown to Khurin and Antipov, Boris Romanov had his eye on the top job and saw the plan to expand the borders of Russia as his opportunity. Having worked behind the scenes to ensure the coup d'état in Turkey took place, at the same time he was fermenting internal unrest to the rule of Khurin. As Defence Minister he had command of the armed forces and had already laid the ground work by subtly raising doubts in the minds of his senior officers to the invasion plan of Khurin. When the new British aircraft was identified he made sure that the report of the experts doubting the number of available planes was not passed on to his commanders leaving them to consider they were a real threat. The final nail in the coffin of Khurin and Antipov was when Romanov was able to convince Vitali Nikolaev, the Russian Foreign Minister, that the invasion plan would lead to the destruction of Russia.

In reality Nikolaev was already doubtful about the plan. He had been receiving feedback from Russian embassies around Europe that the west was rearming rapidly and that within some of the targeted countries, the opposition parties that had expected to be pro-Russian were more concerned about losing their EU subsidies than any gain they could perceive from being back within the Russian sphere of influence. When he had been approached by Romanov to effectively support him in removing Khurin from office in order to protect Mother Russia, he had at first been suspicious but Romanov had prepared well.

He already had his generals on side and by a combination of promises, bribes and misinformation he had persuaded the majority of the Russian Dumas to support him. By offering Nikolaev the position of Prime Minister and showing him the strength of his support in the Dumas, Romanov got his full backing. All that was required was for the right moment to oust Khurin. That had come when he gave to command to begin the invasion. Romanov had immediately called an emergency meeting of the Russian Parliament and had put down a motion that Khurin and Antipov be removed from office as enemies of the Russian state. The motion had been seconded by Nikolaev. Despite much bluster and the call on members of the GRU to support his presidency, Khurin had been well and truly out manoeuvred and the motion had been passed. Within a week Russia had a new leadership and the armed forces had stood down.

In exchange for going quietly, Khurin and Antipov were allowed to remain at large provided they retired from politics and did not leave the confines of Moscow.

The threat to Europe was over, at least for the time being.